Advance Praise

"Jessica Gabriel is lovable and quirky, and her sex life is titillating and laugh out loud. Describing one encounter like a Reuben sandwich had me hoping she'd call me next time to share dating stories over Moscato and Yodels."

— Lauree Ostrofsky, author *Simply Leap*

"With humous and witty short chapters, *A Place Like This* highlights the evolution of family and reminds us that as long as we're alive, there is time for love, joy, and plenty of sex!"

— Leah Omar, author *Between Sunsets*.

"This book is the perfect blend of humor and heartfelt moments. From the comical characters Jess meet driving Uber to her feelings of abandonment when she is an empty nester, Cari has written another fun, sexy read."

— Michelle Paris, author *New Normal*

A PLACE LIKE THIS

A
PLACE
LIKE
THIS

Cari Scribner

Apprentice
House Press
Loyola University Maryland

First Edition

Paperback ISBN: 978-1-62720-414-9
Ebook ISBN: 978-1-62720-415-6

Cover by Brittney E. Duquette
Edited by Barbara Lombardo
Internal Design by Sienna Whalen
Editorial Development by Claire Marino

Published by Apprentice House Press

Apprentice
House Press
Loyola University Maryland

Loyola University Maryland
4501 N. Charles Street, Baltimore, MD 21210
410.617.5265
www.ApprenticeHouse.com
info@ApprenticeHouse.com

Also by Cari Scribner

A Girl Like You

For Miloh, my Bubbles

I ALMOST TOSSED THE WEDDING INVITATION IN THE RECYCLE bin along with the coupon for an oil change and a handful of other junk mail.

Then I took a second look.

It was just a postcard, nothing fancy, probably just right for a beach wedding between my ex-husband Bryan and his fabulous fiancé Sarah.

It was almost dinner time, but the air was still heavy with humidity. We call these days in late August the dog days of summer with their unrelenting 90-degree temps refusing to let go. Welcome to Upstate New York. The only way to make it through the summer heat was to look forward to glorious autumn, with its chill in the air, crunchy red leaves on the sidewalks, and our favorite holiday, Halloween.

I fanned my face with the postcard for a minute before going into my house.

I pulled up a chair at the kitchen table, the place where all news, good and bad, seemed to make itself known.

My 22 year-old son Ian wasn't home, and my 24 year-old daughter, Madison, who was known to make regular visits to my house, was at work. If they were around, we would come up with something funny about the unexpected invitation, like, what was the proper attire for a beach wedding—bikinis? Not for me. My 57-year-old body wasn't a good candidate for anything skimpy. I was still trying to regain my fitness at the gym.

Bryan had texted me the wedding date a month before, but still, when I held the postcard invitation in my hands, it felt real for the first time.

I could already picture the shells on the shore, frothy waves, and turquoise water. There would be a trellis with flowers and Sarah would wear a white sundress and look like an angel. Bryan would be tan and glowing.

It was the kind of informal invite that didn't include a card to send back indicating your "plus one" and whether you wanted sirloin or salmon. But those were the details of an elaborate first wedding, not a pared-down second ceremony. Instead, there was a casual note to respond on Facebook or by text.

The invitation caught me off guard. I hadn't been expecting one. Did Bryan really want me there, or was he just being polite? Did Sarah—who, no lie, looked like a bathing suit model—know he'd sent one to me? Of course, she must. Inviting your ex wasn't exactly something you hide.

I was happy for Bryan, right? I was happy for him.

We had been married only three years before our divorce and his move to Wilmington, North Carolina to be near his family. In the many photos he posted on Facebook, where I regularly stalked him, he looked bronzed and was always smiling in a place of seemingly perpetual sunlight.

My first marriage, to Adam, the father of my kids, ended with him taking off in an RV to see America one tourist stop after another. He'd invited me to take up the nomadic sightseeing life, but Ian and Madd had been teenagers, and I couldn't even consider uprooting them to become a roving family on wheels. Adam came to town whenever he could to go camping with Ian, who had been trying his best to magically make his father and me friends. Not gonna happen.

My marriage to Bryan, an artist with an affinity for all things Halloween (one of our biggest commonalities) petered out for the usual reasons: blame, lack of communication, one person not taking out the garbage.

But the straw that broke our marriage's back was his immense distaste for New York winters. I loved all the winter things that brought me back to childhood: snowmen, tongue-burning cocoa, flakes that glittered as they fell on eyelashes, snuggling up in red fleece blankets. In the end, Bryan headed South to be with his kids and grandson, whose pre-school teacher turned out to be perfect for him. Bryan hadn't even been looking, but "The One" came into his path nonetheless. Clearly, they were meant for each other.

My Maltese puppy Lucy padded into the kitchen, still stretching from a late afternoon nap on the back of the couch. She always had one ear turned inside out. I leaned down and scooped her up with one arm, breathing in the baby powder scent of her neck.

I wanted to get up and pull out the chocolate-covered pretzels I'd bought in a moment of weakness, or even a glass of Moscato, but Lucy settled herself on my lap and I couldn't bear to move her.

So I did the next best thing. I pulled out my cell to call my best friend Eddie. To hell with texting. This was a five-alarm emergency that required actual conversation.

"What's up chickie? Eddie answered after one ring. "Can't be good if you're making a phone call."

"Yeah, I got the invitation. To the wedding. Bryan's

wedding."

I remembered there was still leftover Bucket of Spaghetti in the fridge, maybe even a meatball or two, and the thought made me feel better for a moment.

"Ahh, so he actually invited you? The invite was addressed to you?"

"No Eddie," I said crossly. "It was addressed to Lucy. He wants her to be his guest at the beach wedding."

"OK, don't get cranky. So what do you think? Grab some sunscreen and head down?"

I grunted in reply.

"I'll be your plus one," Eddie said cheerfully.

I groaned again.

"I'm not actually planning on going, silly. Just called for some sympathy."

"Well here it is," Eddie said more seriously. "I know it must be hard—painful even—to get a wedding invitation from your ex, but you've made a whole new life for yourself. Nothing can keep you down. Come on, you know that."

Truth be told, I had been down for some time after Bryan left. I had taken to my bed wearing my old college sweatpants until Madison dragged me out and forced me to shower and have a bowl of cereal.

"Thanks Eddie."

Eddie had been my best friend since high school, through thick and thin. He had always liked Bryan, and was disappointed when we'd gone our separate ways just a year before. I had spent the year getting a new job at the Meredia Town Hall, enjoying the company of my kids, and jumping into the tidal waves of online dating with its wicked undertow. Yes, there had been a lot of laughs, but also lots of heartache when promising relationships fizzled out.

Lucy stirred on my lap, and I knew it was time to make a mad dash to the fridge to search for spaghetti.

"We still going out for margaritas this weekend?" I asked Eddie.

"Wouldn't miss it for the world. And the wedding invitation?"

"A definite no thank you."

"Well it's good you're keeping an open mind."

"Bye Eddie."

I ate the spaghetti cold from the container, sharing the last meatball with Lucy.

2

Two weeks later it was September, the much-loved fall season in Upstate New York, with the brilliant blue skies and slanted sun bringing cool nights so we slept with the windows cracked open. When the tips of the maple tree in the front of my house showed the slightest tint of orange and the summer crickets went silent, it was time to start decorating for Halloween.

Ian helped me haul the dozen or so plastic bins from the basement, then disappeared back inside the house before I could ask him to help decorate. Lucy nosed the bins that always smelled like cinnamon.

But I was waiting for 11-year-old Lily, my little friend from down the street, to scooter up the sidewalk and start the festivities.

"I'm here," she announced, rolling up the sleeves of her pink hoodie. "Wow, that's like, a mountain of boxes, where do you wanna start?"

"With the big ones. There's a giant cauldron somewhere with a fog machine in the bottom. Looks like some kind of evil potion boiling over."

"Probably made with frog's legs and toadstools," Lily said solemnly. "Gross."

"Pretty much."

Lily opened a bin full of rubber rats with yellow teeth,

swooping bats, a black cat with green eyes like my daughter Madison's, and an array of loose body parts.

"Cool," Lily said, holding up a plastic severed finger.

"Yikes, you might not want to go through that box, honey."

"I'm old enough," she squared her shoulders. "Besides, it's good for kids to be a little scared. Builds character. That's what grandpa says."

Sawyer, Lily's grandfather, and I had met early in the summer and had been together ever since, doing our best to make each other happy. Sawyer was easygoing, attentive, and witty. So far, so good, I often thought.

"Ooh, what's this?" Lily pulled out a life-sized green witch's head with warts on her pointy nose.

We rooted around until we found her body, cloaked in a long black cape with a purple liner, then the metal stand to set her up. Once assembled, she was taller than me. Then again, I'm not exactly statuesque. Lily patted down the witch's matted black hair while I put the "crystal" ball in her hands, then flipped the switch so the ball glowed with LED blue lights.

"What's she holding?"

"Crystal ball. She's a fortune teller. She can see the future." I adjusted the witch's crooked fingers.

Lily shrugged. "Who wants to know that? That's no fun."

Not for the first time, Lily was right. Who wanted to know what the future would bring? I'd had a tumultuous year since my divorce from Bryan and his move south. I'd started a job as a clerk in the Town Hall, where I was overwhelmed by the magnitude of the paperwork and also by the constant chatter of three cronies and one dog who took up residence at the office every day.

And I'd lost my sweet girl, Penny, a six-year-old Yorkie, without warning in April, which had brought me to my knees. If it hadn't been for my kids and Eddie, I think I would still have been in bed. Then I found Lucy at the shelter where I went for grief group therapy, just waiting for me to find her and bring her home.

Sawyer lived near my hometown, in a brownstone where his wife had died from cancer five years earlier. He was very close to his son, Lily's father, and since I lived up the street, this was Sawyer's neighborhood too.

My daughter Madison had said I'd never meet anyone sitting on my front porch, so I'd exhausted myself with online dating, going out for wine spritzers by myself Friday nights, even speed dating, which had been a train wreck. I'd learned a lot about myself along the way, until the universe knocked me upside the head and showed me it was OK to be alone. And then, when I stopped looking, I met Sawyer on my front porch.

Go figure.

After enduring her own hysterical and heartbreaking series of first date nightmares, Madison settled happily into a steady relationship with Billy. They took a whitewater rafting excursion to celebrate their one-year anniversary. I liked Billy. It warmed my heart to see the way he looked at Madd from across the room.

The thought of the wedding invitation, still in the caddy where I stored my mail, came to mind, but I brushed it away. My answer was still "no thank you."

"Looks good," Sawyer said from the sidewalk. "But isn't it a little early? It's only September."

"It's never too early to decorate for Halloween," I said, trying to untangle a string of purple and orange lights.

"Well, I'm a little scared already."

"You haven't seen anything yet," I said, securing a metal sign that said "Bates Motel" to a porch beam. "Wait until we get out Mummy Man, who creeps up the side of the house reaching for the window. I put a black spotlight on him so he's all shadowy at night."

"Oh, that's awesome," Lily announced, chasing her grandfather around with a small plastic Frankenstein.

Lucy ran down the porch steps to join the game, yipping and trying to catch up with Lily.

"What's this?" Sawyer asked, pointing to a folded-up square of black material with a zipper down the front.

"Coroner's bag. You stuff it with dry leaves so it looks like a body's in there. Think it's over the top?"

"Everything with you is over the top," Sawyer said. "Think you're overdoing it?"

I sighed. How could anyone possibly overdo Halloween?

I opened another bin. "Can you help me with this?"

Sawyer held one side as I stretched an orange spider-web across the bushes, then scattered it with small plastic spiders.

"Done?" he asked.

"Are you kidding? Not even close."

"Yeah," Lily said, already gathering leaves for the coroner's bag. "And it's only the beginning of September."

3

"It's that time of year!" Madison texted. "Get out your overalls and straw hat and let's go pick apples Saturday."

"Sounds great," I texted back. "Which orchard? The one with the bigger trees or the one with hot cider donuts?"

"Cider donuts, of course. Did you even have to ask?"

Ian and I were out on the sidewalk when Madd and Billy pulled up in their Subaru.

"Hey broski, haven't seen you in a while," Madison said as we climbed into the back seat.

"Yeah, school," Ian said glumly.

Ian was in his second year at the community college.

He had never been a big fan of school, and I'd hoped the independence of college would change his mind. In his first year, he seemed to enjoy the freedom of coming and going but had recently started complaining again about the professors being indifferent, going off on tangents during lectures and the fact that there were very few women in his classes studying electrical construction. He didn't want to be single forever.

The orchard was a 20-minute drive from town, out a winding country road flanked by wide fields of corn stalks just starting to turn brown.

For as long as I could remember, every October at one of the fields, the owners cut a huge maze in the shape of something Halloween-y, like a spider web or grinning Jack O'Lantern.

The kids and I would suit up in warm hoodies and hiking boots because the corn fields always seemed to be muddy. It was a haunted maze, so actors dressed like Jason, Freddie Krueger, and an evil chainsaw-wielding clown were hiding around every corner to jump out and startle us.

Adam had never gone. He hadn't seen the fun in being scared and running through a corn maze shrieking and getting hopelessly lost.

We always relied on Ian's innate sense of direction to guide us through, but one year he deserted Maddy and me and we were left in the middle of a ghoulish ghost maze. Worse, there were no other groups of people wandering through that we might have been able to follow.

We turned several corners to find ourselves at dead ends. Suddenly, the white-masked killer from "Scream" came running at us, and we shrieked and went in the other direction, crashing off the path into the stalks, knocking them down as we went.

The hooded figure followed us, and we found ourselves cornered.

Madison had been around 11-years-old, so I got in front of her to protect her as if the actor was real.

"We're actually completely lost," Madison had said, peering around me. "Can you show us the way?"

The guy took off his mask and we saw it was only a teen-aged boy, quite sweaty from the chase.

"Take two lefts, then straight, then a right," he said. "There's a werewolf right near the exit so don't be worried if he jumps out to block your way."

We followed Scream's directions and made it out, where we found Ian drinking cider sitting on a haybale.

"Geez, what took you so long? I think you set a family record for the most time in a maze."

The kids went to the haunted mazes with their friends in the years that followed, but always came home with muddy boots and stories to tell.

We were lucky to find a parking spot at the apple orchard. It was a brisk day with blue skies and a chill in the air. The aroma of donuts wafted from the country store, where kids were picking up the largest pumpkins by the stems, certain to break off. In the apple barn were baskets of a dozen varieties, but nothing compared to picking them off the trees.

"Remember the year the cider witch pelted Madison in the eye with a Snicker's bar?" Ian said, his mood apparently lightened.

At the end of September, a witch stood on the lower slanted roof and tossed candy to kids, usually harmlessly, but one year she'd aimed too high at Maddy's outstretched hands and a Snicker's bar smacked her cheekbone. It hadn't fazed her enough to not eat the candy, and Ian had laughed all the way home.

"Thanks for the memory," Maddy said.

"Is that why you don't like Snickers?" Billy laughed.

"I do, but I'd rather have a Mounds bar."

We walked down the dirt path to the orchard of trees and headed to the Cortlands, our favorite apple because they stayed tart even a week after being picked.

When the kids were younger, the grove owners used to put short, worn-out wooden ladders against the trees so they could climb and reach the highest apples in the tree.

They didn't have the ladders anymore, probably because of the risk of falling. But I had plenty of pics of young Madd and Ian at the top of the ladders, triumphantly holding up enormous apples that would take them more than an hour to eat.

Ian had a habit of looking for tart apples by sampling one from every tree, then tossing them on the ground to turn mushy and attract hornets.

"If you're going to try one, eat the whole thing," I reminded them.

The kids had also competed to see who could find the smallest apple. One year, Madison found one the size and shape of an egg. I had a photo of that, too.

Billy and Ian wandered off to look for the random chickens that strayed from the farm into the orchard.

"I still love fresh Cortlands," Madison said, biting into one.

We began filling the paper bag we'd brought from home.

"Remember the year a hornet flew up your shirt and stung you on the belly?" she asked.

"God, I do remember now that you say that. It itched for at least a week!"

"Good times," Madison said. "We were so lucky to have a fun Mom."

The kids had been the center of my life when they were young—still were, although they didn't need me that much anymore. They had been my little best friends.

Things changed after Adam took off. I became a single parent overnight, and the many details of managing our lives—homework, trips to the dentist, grocery shopping, getting a desk job—had taken its toll on the three of us. The good times seemed fewer and far between. It was a loss of time that I would always regret, but there was nothing that I could have done to change it.

The kids and I were still exceptionally close, and I was grateful for that. Madison had lived with me until she was 23 and got an apartment with a high school friend. But it was close by, and she remained a regular fixture at our house, dropping by for food or just to visit.

I didn't even want to think about Ian moving out, although it was inevitable. He wasn't home all the time and stayed upstairs a lot when he was, but I always knew he was around if I needed him.

We filled the bag with so many apples it was overflowing, then carried it over to the scale to be weighed and paid for.

Ian and Billy reappeared after we stowed our bag of fruit in the car and headed into the country store, where we spent an inordinate amount of time wandering through the aisles of what was once called penny candy, fresh produce, salad dressings and maple syrup. But what we really wanted were cider donuts dredged in cinnamon and sugar. By the dozens.

We munched happily all the way home. The inside of my car was littered with sugar and we all had cinnamon on our chins. An ideal autumn day.

When I got home, I took the invitation back out and held it in my hands like something fragile.

Was "no thank you" really the answer? I had no idea what to do.

Later that night, I realized there was only one thing I could do: Consult an expert.

4

GIGI DID PRIVATE READINGS FROM HER HOME OUTSIDE MY town. I had to use Google Maps to get there. I bribed Nadine with a promise of cocktails after the psychic session to get her to go with me.

"Maybe we need a Mojito or two before we go, not after," she said.

I'd met Nadine in a night class at the Meredia High School led by Gigi, an impossibly petite, incredibly intuitive wonder woman. The class was about interpreting auras, and Gigi had pretty much left Nadine and me to figure it out ourselves while she flirted with Eddie, who's happily married to Don. His being gay and married hadn't deterred Gigi from making it clear she wanted to bump auras with him. She had decreed Eddie's gold aura to be intensely erotic.

Gigi's daughter Brenda, a morose teenager dressed all in black who had a habit of rolling her eyes at her mother, answered the door to their house.

The front room was overly decorated with fringed, jewel-toned scarves displayed on a mannequin, a silver bowl of glittering stones, a row of antique chairs, lamps that looked like chandeliers. In one corner, incense was burning. It looked like a gift shop. In fact, I thought I saw a price tag on the ear of a marble elephant with its trunk triumphantly raised.

"This is amazing," Nadine said, touching a peacock-feathered masquerade mask.

"Hands to yourselves!" Gigi yelled, appearing out of nowhere.

I hadn't forgotten Gigi's brusque manner, giving orders that made us feel like we were still students in high school. She had chastised Nadine and me for sitting in the wrong chairs and was horrified when Nadine checked her lipstick in a mirror we were supposed to use to see our inner child.

But Gigi was the closest person I knew to be psychic. I'd done a Google search for psychics and found a long list of people ready to connect others with lost loved ones or predict the future. None of them came with resumes, so it was impossible to tell their accuracy rate. In the end, I called Gigi, bracing myself to be scolded along the way.

"Come to the inner chambers."

Gigi parted a curtain of amber glass beads and ushered us into a smaller room.

Around the room were at least eight antique dressers with oversized mirrors, some of them smoky with age. A few of the drawers were open and more gauzy scarves were draped over them.

There was a vintage dark violet couch I guess you would call a settee, and for a moment I was afraid she was going to tell me to take off my sneakers and lie down awkwardly as if I was in therapy.

"Sit," Gigi pointed to a pink padded Victorian chair.

Nadine and I looked at each other. Who was she talking to?

"You, over there," she waved her hand to a row of unmatched chairs with peeling red paint and seats in need of wicker repair.

"Me?" Nadine asked.

"Who do you think?" Gigi said impatiently. "Your aura is turning gray with confusion. Sit down and do some deep breathing to connect with your higher self."

I settled into the pink armchair and Gigi sat on the sofa, plumping up velvet pillows to put behind her back.

"The waning moon affects me," Gigi said, holding the back of her hand to her forehead. "Usually it's my teeth. This time it's my knees."

Nadine and I nodded as if this made perfect sense.

"Me too," I said, wanting to align myself with Gigi.

"I don't hear any deep breaths!"

Dutifully, Nadine began inhaling loudly, exhaling like a lion. I was reminded of my Lamaze breathing when Madison and Ian were born. Not for the first time, I felt a sharp pain in my stomach remembering those days with Adam when we welcomed our babies into the world. Now we barely spoke. And I'd found on most of my dates, the men weren't interested in hearing birthing stories.

Gigi closed her eyes and pursed her coral lip-sticked mouth.

"Like I said, your aura is grey, a sign of indecision. You're not feeling very strong. You are facing a conflict?"

"I am," I cleared my voice.

"Shush! No talking. Just nod your head yes or no."

I quickly nodded yes.

"This is about a man?"

I nodded again.

"Ah, always confusing, these matters of the heart."

Gigi reached down to massage her knee, making her

silver bracelets jangle. I tried hard not to giggle.

"No fidgeting!" Gigi said.

"Sorry," I said out loud. "Whoops."

Gigi looked over her red eyeglasses sternly at me before continuing.

"So, this man, he was close to you?"

I waited to see if the question was rhetorical.

"Yes? Close?"

I nodded yes.

"Ah, I see the trouble. You are wondering if you should attend the wedding, and if he is the one for you."

I blinked my eyes in astonishment. Gigi was actually psychic. She had read my mind.

Gigi spun her crystal in silence.

"Well, I can't say if he is for you, but I can see he is a soulmate."

I breathed in sharply. Soulmate? That must mean Bryan is the one—

"But be clear on this, we can have more than one soulmate in this lifetime," Gigi said.

Crap. That did not help me at all.

"They can be people, or animals, or any living thing," Gigi said.

Tears formed in my eyes thinking of Penny. Without question, my little dog had been my soulmate, my spirit, my heart.

From somewhere out in the hallway, I heard the chime of a grandfather clock echoing hollowly off the walls. I looked around and swore I saw a stuffed owl on one of the dressers. I tried to catch Nadine's attention, but she also had her eyes closed as if meditating. It reminded me of one of the old guys at the office, Wes, whose narcolepsy struck at any moment during the day.

Well, there I was, in the company of two sleeping women.

"I see this man as happy," Gigi said quietly. "But he wants your approval to feel joyful and celebrate."

I wanted to think of Bryan as joyful. Really. I did.

"Should I go to the wedding?" I blurted out, unable to contain myself.

Gigi opened her eyes. "That, I cannot tell you. Your aura has dimmed. You are indecisive. Let the moon show you the answer."

I nodded, again, as if this made perfect sense. Ask the moon? And how exactly, would it answer? Morse code?

I heard Nadine give a short laugh and was glad she'd been awake to hear Gigi's advice.

I paid Gigi $80 and got up to leave.

"Would you like a cup of turmeric tea?" Gigi asked, suddenly polite. "I'll get Brenda to make it. Brenda!!"

"Oh no thanks," I said quickly. "We need to be somewhere else, ah, soon."

Gigi put her hand on my back as we left, and I swear I felt a tingling, like tiny sparks. Was she doing Reiki on me? On my back? Maybe she thought it might need healing from being sore during the waning moon.

"Good night. Come again," Gigi said as if we were all new best friends.

Nadine and I left her porch and walked to my car parked at the sidewalk.

"Did ya really think she would give you a thumbs up or down for going to the wedding?" Nadine asked.

I nodded.

"I was hoping for a little more clarification."

"Well, we will just have to wait and see what the moon says."

"Oh shush," I said.

We settled in the car, and I started it up. Nadine fiddled with the radio station.

"I suppose I could have asked her about me and Hunter," Nadine said, the laughter gone from her voice.

Nadine and her husband, Hunter, had been married 17 years before separating six months before. Their son, 15-year-old Tristan, went back and forth to her house and his father's new apartment.

"You could have," I said gently.

"Yeah, I don't know."

"You can make an appointment," I urged her. "I'll go with you."

Nadine shrugged.

"Maybe. But then again, I don't want to hear any bad news."

"It might not be bad news!"

I knew it was still raw, and Nadine always looked forlorn when she talked about Hunter, and I suspected there were things unspoken between them. She had described the last several years of her marriage as a battle zone with constant arguments over everything from what kind of veggies to buy to how high to set the thermostat. They'd been sleeping in separate bedrooms for more than a year, and she had fallen into a pattern of having dinner with her son instead of waiting until Hunter got home from work. He was a day trader, and his stress level was always very high, Nadine had told me. I hadn't met Hunter, but I could see the way her face changed when she talked about him, from hopeful to very sad. I wanted to help but didn't know how. Talking to Gigi was a stretch, but who knew what could happen?

"Let's get that drink," Nadine said. "And talk about that terrifying stuffed owl. What the hell was that? Taxidermy?"

5

"I'd like to once again voice my strong opposition to this plan," Eddie said, stirring his coffee at my kitchen table.

"Duly noted," I replied.

"I think you should leave well enough alone," Eddie continued, ignoring me completely. "It might be hard for you, and him, and for that matter, the fiancé."

"Sarah."

"Yeah, Sarah," he said. "The whole thing could become a hot, awkward mess."

I picked Lucy up and walked around the kitchen jiggling her like a baby. She was a puppy and needed constant movement. As did I. Sitting all day at work was starting to take its toll on my middle-aged ass.

"Point taken."

"And stop sounding like a court clerk," Eddie said. "This is Bryan's life, and you should leave well enough alone."

Eddie had always liked Bryan. In the three years we were married, the two of them had gotten together several times a month for bowling, to watch a game at a sports bar, or the indoor golf they both loved that I never quite understood. Virtual golf? Wasn't half the fun walking the green and talking about par, whatever that was? Or what to drink at the club later, gin and tonic or bourbon?

Madison came in the back door carrying a delivery box.

"Surprise, surprise. Another order from Amazon," she said, setting it by my feet. "Let me guess. More Halloween leggings?"

"Nope. I have enough of those," I said, sliding the box into a corner with my foot.

I would open the burgundy satin pillowcases later. Not that I was looking to sex up my bed. OK, I was looking to do that, but there was another perk to the pillowcases. Silk was supposed to keep your hair from getting tangled when you tossed and turned in your sleep. I was still trying to grow back my long hair that I rashly had chopped off the day after Penny died.

"How many pairs of those do you have? Like, fifty?" she asked, opening the fridge to grab a tangerine.

"I don't know. I've never counted," I lied. I had thirty-two pairs.

"So, what are we debating now?" Madd asked, peeling the fruit.

"Glad you're here," Eddie said, holding out his hand for a wedge of orange. "I'm trying to show your mom the many flaws in her apparent decision to run down to Wilmington and crash Bryan's beach wedding."

"First of all, I can't run—"

"He's kidding right?" Madd interrupted.

"I was thinking about it, and then Gigi said we're soulmates –"

"Oh God," Madison said, holding out her arms to take Lucy on her lap. "That crazy woman who put the moves on Eddie?"

"She gave up when we explained he was gay and married," I said patiently.

"OK, the next obvious question is, what does Sawyer think about it?"

The kitchen felt overly warm, and I wasn't even cooking. Which wasn't unusual, considering my specialty was ordering the takeout bucket of spaghetti with extra meatballs.

"I haven't said anything to him, actually."

"What?" Madison threw a piece of orange peel at me. "This is a very bad sign Mombo. You can't make decisions like this without him even knowing."

I went over to the sink and turned on the water, pretending to scrub the basin. Of course I hadn't talked to Sawyer about Bryan's beach wedding. I half-hoped I could make it look like a casual girl's getaway weekend with Nadine; just toss a (one piece) swimsuit and some sunglasses and maybe a bottle of Tequila in the car and head south.

But there was something else. I was a free, single woman. I'd fought hard for my independence. I didn't need Sawyer's permission to go. It would be my choice.

Yes, we were committed to seeing each other exclusively, and believe me, I was hugely relieved to be out of the dating scene. We had only been dating a few months, but that didn't really matter. I wanted to always make my own decisions from now on.

I turned off the water and dried my hands on a towel with a pink paw print.

Maybe I shouldn't have asked my daughter and my best friend for their opinions about the trip, because really, all I needed was Nadine's support as my co-traveler.

I had some vacation time from my lackluster clerk's job at the Meredia Town Hall. Even though I did all the work, my co-worker, grouchy Joe, could get off his butt and actually over some of the tasks, like answering the phone that rang constantly, paying bills, or reconciling bank statements for the town. Instead, he kept himself busy grousing with his three cronies who the spent days there. One always brought his dog, who had his own seat by the window so he could bark at pigeons hiding in the eaves of the historic downtown buildings.

"I haven't made a final decision," I said, brushing a few stray puppy hairs off my Frankenstein leggings. "Who wants to walk Lu with me and get out of this stuffy house?"

They both stood up, and Lucy did a happy little dance by the door to the porch.

"You and Lily outdid yourselves," Madison said, ducking her head under the motion-sensor flying bat.

"We did, didn't we?"

"Which way should we go, Miss Lulu?" Eddie asked the puppy.

Lucy bounded to the left down the sidewalk and we followed, crunching orange leaves as we went, kicking fallen acorns, and thankfully, not talking anymore about the damn wedding.

6

It was Friday, date night, but Sawyer and I were usually too tired to go out for dinner and a movie, so we settled on Netflix and cheddar popcorn.

In other words, we were officially old.

At least I can say with certainty neither of us dozed off on the couch, which was fortunate, because Friday night was also sex night.

It's not like we didn't have sex any other night of the week. My sex drive was on higher speed than Sawyer's, who seemed just as content to cuddle. For me, cuddling was foreplay.

I actually counted myself lucky, because I had dated a man named Hudson with, ahem, erectile problems. Major ones. Like going soft in the middle of sex. Eddie had joked I should have mentioned the Viagra option, but the relationship had ended (badly) and the subject never came up. I've gotta say, it now was very satisfying to think of Hudson struggling with thwarted sexual encounters.

Sawyer got up and stretched his back after the movie, which was so unremarkable I couldn't even tell you the title.

We turned out the lights and went to my room.

Sawyer spent more nights at my house than I did at his because Lucy preferred to be home. So did I.

In the bathroom, I scrubbed at my waterproof mascara

with a make-up remover cloth that was supposed to clean off make-up and simultaneously moisturize my skin. In the end, I just looked like a ring-eyed raccoon, and my skin still felt dry. I sighed and turned out the bathroom light.

I sat on the edge of my side of the bed and pulled on fuzzy socks. It wasn't time yet to use the heated blanket, but autumn had settled in, bringing chilly, cozy nights that I adored.

"You can leave those off," Sawyer said, reaching over to stroke my chin-length hair.

I tossed the socks to the floor and got under the covers.

"Come over to my side," he said. "I've got it all warmed up for you."

Sawyer was the ultimate human radiator, always just the right temperature, never sweaty or clammy. A former college football player, he still had broad shoulders and a solid chest that I loved to fall asleep on. But in the middle of the night, I would turn away to my side and curl up with Lucy, the way I slept with my dog Penny the year after Bryan left. Back when I was single. Old habits die hard, I guess.

"Turn over," Sawyer said as I slid towards him. "Let me rub your back."

He pulled off my sleeping shirt in one smooth move, then stretched out next to me to work out the knots that formed while sitting in one place all day. Knots weren't the only things that had become permanent parts on my body. I was still trying to work off the ten or so pounds I'd put on after menopause, leaving me with what was once affectionately called "love handles," now known simply as a "muffin top." Thank God I wore leggings year-round and elastic waist bands didn't dig in like jeans. I had become a regular at the Y, but I was still trying to regain my fitness, and nowhere near brave enough to get on the locker room scale. Yikes.

Sawyer kneaded my shoulders and traced my spine with his fingertips. I let out a sigh and stretched out on the bed. He smoothed my hair to one side and ran a trail of warm kisses around the back of my neck, and with that, I was ready for him. It had never taken much foreplay to turn me on.

In my mind, I pictured him pulling me up onto my hands and knees, pushing my hips slightly forward to get a good look at me from behind. He would lean his face in and take a deep breath as if my feminine scent was elixir, then use one finger to open me up and test my wetness. Without asking, Sawyer would plunge into me urgently, almost roughly, but I'd be ready and take it eagerly. He would pump powerfully, pulling my hips towards him in rhythm that always led to simultaneous, sputtering, crashing orgasms.

That was the fantasy.

"Wanna fool around?" he asked in real life.

Really, he never had to ask, because I pretty much always wanted to after the love life I'd had after Bryan left. But the encounters I'd had while online dating went wildly beyond my fantasies, into a kind of submission that made me lose myself almost entirely.

"Sure," I said, still face down.

"Well then, why don't you roll over so we can start."

Ah, the sweet words of romance and desire. Sawyer was a man who believed in being specific, and sometimes I secretly wanted the thrill of mystery, of giving myself up to him and his urgent desires. Did he have urgent desires, or was I alone in this?

He reached over and switched off the lights.

I turned on my back and he pulled me gently into his arms, kissing me and breathing into my ear. I imagined him holding my arms over my head, pinning me down, and telling me I was naughty. Bringing himself up to my face and using his erection to open my mouth to take him. It wasn't like I hadn't given him a proper blow job. It was just out of our ordinary sexual routine.

This was our routine; we would kiss, and I would rub his chest and he would touch my hard nipples too gently, then he would ask me the same words every time:

"Are you ready?"

I always was, but when he asked permission, it kind of killed the mood for me. I didn't want to give permission. I wanted to be taken.

Sawyer would ease himself into me, and start a slow motion with his hips, really more rocking than anything. It was perfectly fine sex. He was very capable.

It always lasted a few minutes. He showed no diminished abilities due to age, I had to give him that. He was silent when he climaxed, then immediately rolled off as if he was afraid he would crush me.

Then came the words:

"Did you get off?"

Sometimes I had accomplished an orgasm. But it was rare just from the friction of sex. Most times I needed direct stimulation, and if I told him that, he would gamely rub me until I figured he was wondering how long it would take. Many times, I would just take over myself, because I knew how to do it right, although nothing matched the magic of my vibrator. But it seemed rude to pull it out and use it after actual sex.

So I rubbed myself, and it would be a perfectly nice orgasm.

Sawyer kept a washcloth on the nightstand for me to wipe myself so that there wouldn't be a wet spot.

Then came the cuddling until we fell asleep. Sometime during the night I would roll away from him.

The falling asleep part actually happened within minutes after the sex, although I had to give him credit, Sawyer did pull me into his arms. Once he was breathing deeply, I would carefully extricate myself and roll over to my side of the bed. After sleeping alone for a year, I'd grown accustomed to it, and really, Sawyer was so warm it made me sweat, and not in a good way.

It was a perfectly fine activity, having sex with Sawyer. Kind of like a pretty good Reuben at a sandwich spot. Fine, but nothing fancy or overly satisfying.

7

THE NEXT DAY WHEN I GOT INTO WORK, THE THREE STOOGES were already at their table in the clerk's office, studying the Brew Coffee pastry menu. It was yellowed and coffee-stained but none of them ever thought to pick up a new one.

"Elephant ears? Have we tried those yet? What are they, anyway?" Sal said, tilting his head to the side thoughtfully.

"Flaky pastries shaped in swirls," Paulie said dreamily, almost drooling. "Only problem is, they don't have any filling, not even some jam in the center."

Wes appeared to be nodding thoughtfully at the confection conversation, but after a minute his friends realized he had dozed off again. He sometimes forgot to take his medicine for narcolepsy.

"How 'bout you Missy?" Sal called over the counter to me. "Biscotti? Scone? They've got your favorite chocolate chip."

The guys knew me too well. Elephant ears, I could easily pass on. But a good short-bready scone? No way.

I pulled out a $5 bill.

"Nope, my turn to treat," Paulie said, waving a hand. "Wes? WES?"

"It's his sleep apenya again," Sal said.

None of the men had learned to pronounce sleep apnea in the years they had been talking about Wes's condition.

Sadly, his sleep apnea seemed to have worsened again.

He sputtered and opened his eyes. "Coffee break time?"

The question was absurd of course, since technically for the men, it was always break time.

"Cheese Danish please," Wes said.

As the door shut behind Paulie, Jerky went over to his favorite chair by the window to jump up, but it took him three tries.

"Dog ain't as spry as he used to be," Sal said.

"How old's he?" Wes asked.

"Geez, on about 11 now," Sal said. "Trying not to think about it. Been my best friend all these years."

"They figure out what all that panting was about?"

"High blood pressure, can you believe it?" Sal answered. "Strapped a tiny little cuff on him to check it. Giving him blood pressure medicine every morning now with his breakfast."

"He's got a lotta life in him," Wes said.

I looked at my picture of Lucy on my desk, thanking God she was just a puppy.

Joe came out of the bathroom whistling.

"You missed the coffee break order," Wes said mildly.

"Well, why didn't ya let me know?"

"What were we supposed to do, knock on the door?"

"I gotta catch up with Paulie then," Joe said, practically jogging out the front door.

Well, there you had it. Twenty minutes and counting for the men to organize the morning coffee run.

I was working on the minutes from the zoning board meeting the night before. A very nervous woman had applied to build a two-story garage. The board chairman, who was known to be abrasive, had quizzed her relentlessly about how she intended to use the building.

As a garage, I had thought. But the chairman believed she was planning to turn the second floor into an apartment and rent it out, which was prohibited under zoning codes. In the end, the board voted down her request, and she left in tears.

Good thing I didn't have the money to make any renovations on my house, I had thought.

"How'd that zoning meeting go? That young lady given the green light for her garage?" Sal asked.

I shook my head.

"Rumor was, she was gonna add running water and make an apartment up there,"

Sal continued. "I say, who cares, let her do it if she needs a little extra money in her pocket."

I smiled at Sal. He was always there to cheer on the underdog.

Paulie came back with an enormous bakery bag and handed out the pastries.

"Jesus, Paulie, you buy out the whole place?"

"They're mostly his," Paulie said, pointing to Joe.

"Couple jelly donuts to take home for the missus," Joe said, turning faintly pink.

Joe and his wife had a falling out the year before, when she left to visit family in Florida and didn't return. Joe had been miserable for weeks before confiding in us he didn't think she was coming back after winter ended. When he asked for advice, the guys and I told him to go down there and beg her to come home and bring flowers and/or candy. They had returned together a few days later, and Joe had smiled for a week after that, for reasons I didn't care to picture in my head.

I finished my scone and pulled a stack of paperwork out of my inbox, which Joe had filled to the point of overflowing, again.

"Don't forget, I'm off the end of next week," I reminded him.

"Oh yeah, how many days?"

"Just three."

"You headed anywhere nice?" Sal asked from the table.

"To a beach, actually."

"Which beach?" Wes asked, always ready for a new discussion.

"Ah, in Wilmington."

"You taking Route 146 south?" Paulie asked.

"That's not the best way to get there," Wes said. "She should take the thruway then get on the turnpike, there's practically no lights."

"The turnpike's always backed up, seems like they're always doing some kind of construction," Paulie said.

Paulie and Wes spent the next ten minutes debating the fastest way to get to Wilmington. I didn't bother to tell them I was just going to follow Google Maps.

"Well enjoy it missy," Sal said. "Just make sure to drive safe."

8

"You did what?" Nadine sputtered, spitting out a bit of mint from her Mojito. "Why is this the first time I've heard about this?"

"It's not exactly casual conversation," I said. "I don't come right out and say, 'I'm Jess. I was with a dom.'"

Nadine had quickly agreed to join me on the road trip to Bryan's wedding. We'd been giddy with excitement when we left home, but after six hours on the road, we were grimy and exhausted. Why was riding in a car so tiring?

We had made a quick run for pizza at a tourist stop, but now what we really needed were some adult beverages and a decent night's sleep.

Nadine had found us an amazing Airbnb apartment in Ashland, Virginia, with a jacuzzi and a great view of the city skyline. We'd dropped our overnight bags and almost stayed in for the night, but after a long, incredibly dull drive, we were antsy.

We found a bar in town that was built like a warehouse, with steel beams on the ceiling and an edgy vibe. It was the kind of sleek, sophisticated bar I wished they had back home in Meredia.

We were well into our second round. We'd snagged a silver high top table with surprisingly comfortable metal chairs and a waiter was ready to bring us more drinks every time we glanced his way. The best we could do in Meredia was Nick's, and that was a tavern. Although it had a certain charm.

At 7 p.m., it was still early for the bar scene on a Saturday night, and the place was half empty. Even so, Nadine leaned closer over the table as if she expected me to whisper all the details.

Only Eddie knew the whole story, but I had no problem talking about it with Nadine. The weeks with Daniel were like nothing I'd ever experienced, scarily addicting, exhilarating followed by exhausting, but never by shame. I had been a willing partner and only quit after Daniel asked to bring another woman that he knew to bed with us. The idea of a previous lover familiar with Daniel's body was not a turn-on for me. He'd pushed hard to get me to change my mind, and in the end, I had to walk away entirely.

"So, you met him online?" Nadine said, whispering like me..

"Yeah, and he seemed perfect at first. Smart, funny, attentive, a great listener," I said, feeling a tiny twinge of regret that it was over. "He gradually worked into the conversations that he liked women with a submissive edge."

"OK," Nadine whispered. "Go on."

"Then he had what he called 'tasks' for me, like sending him private photos."

"Are we talking above or below the waist?"

"Both," I said, signaling the waiter for more drinks.

It had been unexpectedly exciting to expose myself to Daniel with the intimate pictures. In return, he sent photos of his erections, which he said were meant for me. I felt like the sexiest woman in the world sharing intimate pics. Then the clothespins arrived.

"OK, so these tasks, did they escalate?"

"They did," I said, as the waiter set down my Margarita.

Nadine blinked, studying me closely and hanging on every word.

I stirred my drink and took a long sip from the salty rim.

"Yeah, so then Daniel mailed me this gorgeous fancy box, and inside were a dozen clothespins, you know, the wooden ones you'd use to hang sheets outside. At first I thought he wanted me to do his laundry!"

Nadine laughed again, then blotted her burgundy lips with the cocktail napkin.

"As it turned out, he wanted to see me clamp each of my nipples with one..."

Nadine nodded as if it made perfect sense.

"Kinky," she said.

It had been exactly that, but Daniel didn't want me to feel pain. It was more for the visual effect of hardware on soft skin. I had kicked the box under the bed, but around 3 a.m. become so intrigued I locked my bedroom door and eased one on. The left side hurt like a pair of pliers, but the right one barely pinched, so I took a bunch of selfies and sent them to Daniel before I changed my mind. The photos were an art form to me, something inexplicably beautiful.

Two drinks later, I told Nadine every last detail.

"Well, basically, when we finally had sex, one of the clothespins ended up—south."

"South? You mean your—"

"Sweet spot, yes."

"Wow," Nadine sat back and considered this for a moment. "Did it hurt?"

"I mean, it wasn't something I'd do ever again. It definitely pinched. But it was only on for a few seconds."

I don't think Daniel had ever wanted me to be hurt, but his boundaries had seemed limitless. There were sexual encounters I just never saw myself doing, but the clothespins were wildly erotic for me. But when he had pushed the suggestion of a threesome with a former girlfriend, I had bolted.

Daniel had an active case of Lyme disease, and I frequently wondered how he was feeling these days.

When we were dating, he had hidden his episodes from me, even when he had to be hospitalized for his symptoms. It was clear to me that he saw the Lyme was a sign of weakness. I just wanted to be part of his life—his whole life, including his illness. But he was cold to me about it and shut me out when he was feeling out of control of his body and his emotions.

I missed the thrill of being with Daniel and sending photos to him. But I was relieved to not be pursuing him anymore. The more I chased him, the faster he had run.

"Wow," Nadine said again, finishing off her drink and wiping her mouth with a bar napkin. "That's quite a story, sister. The best I've got is having sex in the front seat at the drive-in with Hunter because we were too worked up to climb in back."

I laughed.

Nadine had a lot of stories to tell about her marriage to Hunter and raising their son Tristan. She talked about the bad times too, but I still had hope for them.

"Don't look now, but someone is staring you down," Nadine said, motioning with her chin behind my right shoulder.

I cleared my throat and turned slightly.

"I said don't look!"

"OK. Gheesh. Well, who is it?"

"Businessman, blonde hair, blue suit, polka dot tie," she said. "The tie is loosened. Martini."

"Wedding ring?"

"Not that I can see."

"He's probably looking at you," I said, draining my drink.

"Take a look. But for god's sake don't be obvious," she said.

I reached behind my chair for my purse, pretending to be searching for something, and glanced up at businessman.

He held my gaze and smiled.

I felt my face flush. Maybe it was just the cocktails.

"Jesus, sit up straight," Nadine whispered. "He's coming over."

I pivoted in my seat, wishing I could check my hair, which felt like it was glued flat on my forehead. A breath mint wouldn't hurt either.

"Hey," businessman said, standing by our table. "I hate to drink alone. Mind if I join you?"

It was a generic pick-up line, but it worked.

I suppressed a giggle. Nadine kicked my leg under the table.

"Why not? Have a seat," I said. Hell, what happens on a road trip stays on a road trip. I wasn't going to do anything more than have a drink with Nadine and our new cute friend.

"I'm Gideon," he said.

Gideon. With his perfectly straight white teeth and

squared shoulders, he did the masculine name justice.

We introduced ourselves. I was glad we didn't shake hands because mine were cold from the ice in my drink.

"You ladies live around here?" he asked lazily, signaling for more drinks without asking us, which I liked.

"Nope, on the road. For a wedding. My ex's actually," I answered in short sentences with too much information.

"Ah, the ex's wedding. That sounds interesting," Gideon said, settling back in his seat. "Tell me more."

"There's not much to tell. He's getting married in North Carolina. Beach wedding. Sunset, you know, the whole nine yards."

"And how are we feeling about the ex getting remarried?" Gideon passed out the drinks on the high-top.

"She's fine," Nadine jumped in before I could share my mixed emotions. Which was for the best because no one wants a sappy drinking partner.

"Yeah, she looks fine," Gideon said, staring me down.

I gulped my drink, then wiped my palms on my ghost leggings.

"And you're the best friend along for the ride to make sure Jess doesn't embarrass herself?"

"Pretty much," said Nadine.

"So, why are you in town? Do you live here?" my voice sounded a bit like a squeaky mouse in cartoons. Why was I so jittery? Wasn't alcohol supposed to make people less inhibited?

"Nope, on business," he said, running his fingers over the rim of his martini glass. "Corporate trainer for Verizon; on the road several days a month."

"That sounds interesting," Nadine said.

"It's not," Gideon laughed.

"I have Sprint," I chimed in, although no one asked me for that bit of information.

"We need to make a bathroom run," Nadine said, kicking my foot under the table.

"I'll be here when you get back," he smiled.

She pulled at my arm, and I followed her to the back of the bar.

The lights in the ladies' room were blessedly dim. I didn't want to see my smudged black eyeliner.

"What do you think?" Nadine asked.

"What do I think? I think it's great to have a cute guy chat us up in a new town. I also think I'm more than a little tipsy," I said, trying without success to fluff my defeated hair.

"I think he's into you," Nadine said. "And he's pretty damn adorable."

"I have a boyfriend, remember? And I think he likes you."

Nadine held up her hands to stop my words.

"Not interested. Nope. I've only been separated six months. Give me like another year, or two, before I even consider looking at another man."

"I'm sorry, am I being bossy?"

"It's fine," Nadine said.

"Gideon is a someone to have a drink with, nothing more. My life is complicated enough right now. I'm on my way to my ex's wedding, who I think I may still be in love with."

"Yes. You're right. Let's go get some sleep."

Gideon's teeth seemed to have become even more white and sparkly when we got back to the table.

"We're going to call it a night," I announced.

Gideon frowned. "Really? Ok. I'll walk out with you."

We filed out of the bar in a single line.

It was too highly lit in the parking lot, and I hoped my mascara hadn't flaked off.

"Where's your car?" Gideon asked.

"We left it at the Airbnb," I said.

"Oh, is that around here?"

"It's just a few blocks down," I said.

"Mind if I walk you there?"

"We don't mind," Nadine piped up.

We walked in an awkward threesome on the sidewalk with Gideon in between us.

"This is nice," he said when we reached the building. "You have a room here?"

"A whole apartment," I answered.

"I'd love to see it," he said, smiling dangerously.

I was certain that's not all he wanted to see, and my mind was already made up.

"Actually, we have to get back on the road early," I said. "But thank you for walking with us."

Gideon gave a deep bow, which I thought was kind of cheesy, and for a moment I thought he might try to kiss our hands.

Nadine and I turned at the exact same time and bumped into each other in our hurry to get inside.

"Is it too late for cookies?" Nadine asked once we got into our Airbnb apartment.

"It's never too late for Oreos."

"Where were all these men when I was single and attempting to online date?" I asked, prying open a cookie to lick the middle.

"Hiding, apparently," Nadine said, holding up an Oreo.

We clinked cookies together and said "Cheers."

Then we conked out with crumbs in our bed and smiles on our faces.

9

WE ROLLED INTO WILMINGTON SATURDAY MORNING, BOTH of us disheveled, my car littered with empty Chips Ahoy and Pirate's Booty packages. The cherry Slurpees had seemed like a good idea, but three hours later we both were carsick from all the sugar and had red stains on our teeth and lips.

"My legs feel like Jell-O," Nadine groaned as she got out of the car.

"Yeah, my ass has gone numb," I complained.

We headed immediately to our next Airbnb to clean up.

Fresh from the shower, I put on a sundress with pink flamingos and slid my feet into sandals.

"What do you think?" I asked Nadine. "Does this look about right for the ex-wife?"

"You look great."

"Do you think I should've let him know I was coming?"

"I don't think you knew if you were coming until the last minute," Nadine said, reaching out to squeeze my hand.

We drove to the beach a few blocks away as the sun went down in a postcard perfect orange and blue sky. I dug out my sunglasses, wishing I'd bought something fancy instead of functional. Tortoise cat eyes maybe. Or something over-sized that made my face look slimmer. Oh well.

I sat in the car stalling after Nadine pulled into a parking spot. She got out and started feeding coins into the meter.

"Coming?" she asked, leaning in my window.

I fiddled with the hem of my dress nervously.

"Nervous?"

"Not really," I lied. "I'm just rethinking the sundress. Maybe capris would have been better."

"All your capris are Halloween patterns," Nadine reminded me. "And I don't think ghosts are wedding apparel."

"You're probably right."

We started walking down the wooden path leading to the beach. I stopped and grabbed Nadine's arm.

"Wait. I don't think I can do this."

I felt short of breath.

"We came all this way," she said reasonably. "Now you don't want to go to the wedding?"

"Can we just walk up to the pier?"

The last time I had been on a pier on the ocean was during our family trips to Maine when the kids were little. It was a 10-hour drive from what had been our family home back then. As soon as we got there, we consulted the chart with the schedule for high and low tides. Low tide was nirvana for all of us.

We didn't visit the Maritime Museum or the aquarium or daytrip to see the lighthouses and eat chowder. We spent every day at the beach as the tide rolled out. Ian and Madd bravely waded out past the small spitting waves, but I always worried about sudden dips in the sand hidden underfoot and watched them like a hawk. They inched forward like snails, feeling with their toes for the place where the sand sank down.

We staked our claim with our blanket on a square of

sand, held down at the corners with pails and shovels and our flip-flops. Adam dug a hole for our striped umbrella, then another hole for the purple pinwheel Madd loved to watch spin in the ocean breeze.

Adam and I had the same discussion every year about how often to re-apply sunscreen. I would quote new research about how dangerous sunburns were for kids, and slather them with SPF100.

When Ian was little, we carted along a portable playpen, jars of baby food, tiny sunglasses and baseball caps, diapers and wipes. We chased him the next year when he began to toddle down toward the water. As a little boy, he would take off down the beach so fast that only Madison, with her gazelle-like legs, could catch him. Both of them, at different times, got knocked over by waves, coming up gasping and scraped all over by sand before I got there to save them. But they went right back in to take on the tide once again.

Ian made a tradition out of taste-testing the ocean water and declaring it salty as pretzels.

Seagulls would squawk over our heads, diving down towards the nearby sand looking for food remnants. The children used to toss bits of crackers to them until a huge commotion of birds arrived and scared Madison.

Once the kids were big enough to safely navigate the vast Maine beach, we would walk at low tide to a cluster of black rocks covered with sharp barnacles. Madd and Ian would dig in the puddles and look for spidery crabs, tiny and quick. If they found any, they would put them into beach pails of sea water and watch the crabs around until it was time to return them to the ocean.

We would walk in the other direction to a deep inlet

of water that was home to all kinds of sea life, fast fish, clumps of foamy seaweed. Madd swore one year she saw an eel brush by my leg, but I never felt it go by or I would have shrieked and jumped out of the water. Every single year in Maine, one of us found a perfect sand dollar, the star still clear, fragile sides unbroken. We said the person who discovered it was going to have good luck all year.

A small engine plane always flew over the beach with a banner advertising free pizza delivery. A tired, hot teenager would push an ice truck along the beach, and I always got the kids grape popsicles. At dusk, people came out with kites that dipped and swooped into the horizon.

They were days and weeks and months and years I thought would never end, but they had slipped away and now they were just memories. Not for the first time, I wondered if Adam ever thought about our many joyful trips as a family now that he had separated his life from ours.

Nadine's voice shook me out of my reverie. She pointed to a spot far down the beach where there appeared to be people milling around out of the water.

"OK, let's go," she said.

"No," I said desperately. "We can't walk on the beach; they might see us."

"We can't even see them! I don't even see a tent. There's gonna be a tent right?"

"I assume so," I said, still pulling on her arm. "Let's take the sidewalk up to the pier."

We left the beach and walked past a row of shops displaying boogie boards, beach chairs, umbrellas, and energy drinks. There was an open-air eatery with fried clams that smelled out of this world.

"Stop walking so slowly," Nadine scolded me.

"You stop walking so fast," I cranked back.

We reached the entrance to the pier.

"Wanta go get some food? Those clams looked good," I said.

"Stop stalling," she said. "Although maybe get the clams on the way back."

I sighed. I had no choice but to walk out the pier leading into the ocean. The wooden slats were weather-worn and waves foamed at the enormous gray boulders buffering the pier. Barnacles clung to the posts holding the pier, which seemed to shift in the water with the tide.

"I see the tent!" Nadine said, pointing down the beach. "It's white. Well, of course it's white."

I took off my sunglasses and squinted. There was a large tent and rows of chairs and lots of people, none of whom I could clearly see.

"What I wouldn't give for binoculars right now," I said.

"What? I thought we came to see the wedding, not spy on it."

Spying seemed like a much better option.

"We're too far away to see anything," Nadine said, brushing sand off the back of her leg. "What exactly is the plan?"

Madison said I always had a plan. And I did.

"See that sand dune down there? We can go and hide behind it. From there we'll at least be able to hear what's going on."

Nadine sighed.

"Come on then," she said, moving back down the pier.

We walked back past the souvenir shop with seashell ankle bracelets, bikinis, and sunglasses that looked far trendier than mine.

When we got to the dune, I was relieved to see we could hide behind it without even having to crouch.

And then I heard Bryan's voice. I couldn't make out his words, but he sounded jubilant.

"Is that him?" Nadine asked.

"Shush," I whispered. "They'll hear you."

"I think this six-foot pile of sand between us and them will muffle our voices."

I moved to the edge of the dune and peeked carefully around it.

There he was, wearing a white button-down shirt, jeans, and flip flops. I recognized Sarah beside him from the photos he had texted me. In a fitted white sheath dress, she looked incredible. More like a swimsuit model than a pre-school teacher.

She was carrying a loose bundle of daisies. It wasn't my first choice for bridal flowers, but that was just about the only flaw I could find at the stunningly perfect beach wedding.

A young boy wearing a bowtie and a t-shirt was running around in the sand. It was Ben, Bryan's grandson. I couldn't believe how big he had gotten. He was no longer a toddler. He was a bonafide little kid.

Music started, "Ode to Joy," and the cluster of people stood up from the folding chairs. I leaned out a little further to see Bryan, who had the widest smile I swear I'd ever seen on his face.

I loved him. I would probably always love him. But seeing him this happy melted my heart. He deserved this beautiful beach life. He wasn't meant to live in frigid, unforgiving winters in upstate New York. The stormy springs. The already too-chilly autumn.

Most of all, he wasn't meant to live with me.

I looked over at Nadine, who had made herself a little seat of sand. She nodded and smiled at me.

I had a good life. I knew that. But that didn't stop me from feeling a pang of envy watching Bryan and Sarah read their vows.

It was over in what felt like seconds, and everyone applauded as the newlyweds kissed. Then Sarah held her hands triumphantly over her head and yelled, "We're married!"

More music played as the guests crowded around the couple. Their voices and laughter rose over the sound of the tide, seeming to reach the now pink sky.

"Well, that was really nice," Nadine said, standing up and brushing off her skirt. "Now what shall we do?"

"Go in and congratulate them," I said, half-surprising myself.

"Really? Good for you. You go girl."

I trudged into the sand, wishing I'd worn flip-flops I could have slipped off so I wasn't walking like a duck towards Bryan, who stopped talking and looked directly at me.

He smiled and waved, his face equal parts surprise and joy.

I waved back and he signaled for us to go over to the group.

"Jess!" Bryan said, meeting us halfway. "I'm so happy to see you!"

We hugged immediately, but he was the first one to let go first.

"This is my friend Nadine," I said, pointing to her.

"I've heard a lot about you, Bryan."

"All good I hope."

"Of course," she said.

I thought again about Ian and Madd as children on the beach. I had only been away three days, but I missed my kids, and Lucy, tremendously.

"Sar, this is Jessica," Bryan said.

Sarah beamed at me.

"It's nice to finally meet you," she said, holding out her small, manicured hand. Her nail polish shimmered like seashells.

"You too."

The four of us stood in what quickly became awkward silence.

"Ben looks so grown-up in that tie," I said at last.

"He's a piece of work," Bryan said, his face glowing. "My best buddy."

The guests were gathering up their belongings from the backs of the chairs and the guitarist was putting away his instrument.

"We have to go eat clams," I blurted out.

"She's right," Nadine chimed in, saving me. "We haven't had any food since breakfast, and that was leftover Oreos."

"We're all getting together at the Shrimp Shanty," Bry said. "You two are more than welcome to come."

"Thank you, but we're really worn out, long trip, you know," I said. "You guys go and have fun."

"We will," Sarah said, and for the first time I noticed her perfectly placed dimples.

Nadine and I turned and slogged in the sand back

towards the dune. I not only felt worn out; I felt twisted up and hung out to dry.

"Jessie!"

It was Bryan, jogging to catch up with us.

Nadine kept walking to the boardwalk.

"Yeah?"

"Listen," he said, breathing easily as if he hadn't just done a sprint. "Listen. It means so much to me that you came down here."

"Of course," I said, swatting away a sand fly.

"No, I really mean it. I'll always remember this."

"That's nice to say."

"I'm not just saying it."

He pulled me back into his arms, this time holding tight.

His neck smelled like coconut sunscreen and that unmistakable salty sweetness of the sea.

"You go on," I said, releasing him. "Go celebrate with your bride."

I watched Bryan run back to the wedding party, then turned to Nadine, who was heading away from the dunes toward the ocean.

"Where are you going?" I called out to her.

"Race you back to the boardwalk!"

She started to jog.

I kicked off my sandals and carried them as I ran down to the edge of the waves, where I broke into a trot to catch up with her.

The sand was firm beneath my feet from high tide, and I ran past white seashells like the ones Maddy collected as a child.

Nadine was pretty far ahead of me when she stopped,

which was good because I was breathless.

So much for building endurance at the gym!

When I caught up, I leaned over to catch my breath, sweaty, and suddenly Nadine turned back towards me and kicked saltwater on my legs.

"Oh, you're asking for it now," I said, scooping up sea water to splash her back.

Then we were in the ocean up to our ankles, splashing until my carefully chosen flamingo sundress was wet, laughing like children.

10

"So, how'd it go?" Eddie asked, putting down his fork. "Details, I want details."

"Don't pester her so much," Eddie's husband, Donny, said mildly. "More wine?"

"Good plan, ply her with wine, then we can get her to talk."

I held out my glass for more Moscato.

"It went fine," I said, savoring the sweet wine.

"Fine? That's all I get, 'Fine'?"

I got up to help myself to more Caesar salad with strips of grilled chicken.

What could I say? That the wedding was picture-perfect, Bryan was glowing, and the sun bounced off Sarah's curls? I could say it took most of the ride home to even begin to accept the fact that Bryan now belonged to someone else— that Sarah was his "one." Or tell them about the gnawing doubt in my stomach about ever letting Bryan go? So he hadn't been a fan of winter, we could have compromised maybe, moved to a warmer state that still let me be close to my kids. We hadn't even talked about a compromise—we'd jumped straight to separating.

I wasn't ready, or maybe even able, to talk about my mixed emotions, so instead I said, "Honestly Donny, what's your secret to this amazing chicken?"

"I marinate it," Donny said, looking pleased.

"Can we forget about the damn chicken and get back to wedding?" Eddie said.

He wiped his chin with a napkin.

"Sorry, honey," he said to Donny. "The chicken really was fantastic."

I crunched a crouton, trying to ignore the fact they were both staring at me.

"I can't hold him off any longer," Donny sighed. "You better talk."

"Well, for starters, I finally told Nadine about the clothespins."

"Holy shit!" Eddie began laughing. "That was a revelation."

"She was cool about it."

"Yeah, she would be," he agreed. "Now, fill me in about Bryan."

"He was happy," I said. "They both looked really happy."

"So, what, did you stand up to interrupt the ceremony? Throw some sand around? Storm down the beach in a huff?"

"None of the above," I said, brushing crouton crumbs off my tarantula leggings.

"And here I was looking forward to some big hoopla. So how did it feel to see him?"

I stood up to clear my salad plate, turning my back to them.

"It felt, I don't know, kind of awkward, like he was someone I had been married to but at the same time, didn't recognize."

A fairly large part of me wanted him back, I thought, but didn't say out loud.

Eddie and Donny nodded in unison.

I straightened my shoulders.

"It was very…. nice. Friendly, you could say. Bryan looked better than I remembered him."

"Suntan?" Donny asked.

"Happiness," I said, wiping off my hands on a dish towel. "It suits him."

Eddie nodded gravely at me.

"Good for you taking the high road. Proud of you."

It was time to change the subject.

"So what's it gonna be tonight? Scrabble or Monopoly?"

"Neither," Donny said, pulling out a bag. "I got us a 1,000-piece puzzle of Kellogg's cereal boxes."

"Ohhh, Apple Jacks, my favorite," Eddie said, rubbing his hands together.

"Please. It's Coco-Puffs all the way," I said.

"Well neither of those are Kellogg's, so you both lose," Donny laughed at us.

"Fruit Loops? How about Fruit Loops?" Eddie said.

Donny studied the picture on the puzzle box. "Actually, you're right about that one."

"Remember how Lucky Charms used to turn the milk green and taste like pure sugar?" I said, getting hungry all over again.

"Well, they are magically delicious," Donny said.

He opened the box and dumped the pieces on the table, and the three of us began sorting.

Eddie was humming "Here Comes the Bride" under his breath, but I ignored him completely. The Bryan's wedding story had been told. It was time to move on, and I planned to do exactly that.

11

"THOUGHT I'D STOP OVER," SAWYER TEXTED THE WEEKEND after we got home from Bryan's wedding. "You busy?"

"Swiffering the kitchen floor, so I'd love a distraction. Want me to make grilled cheese for lunch?"

"No thanks. I'll be over soon."

Less than ten minutes later, Sawyer came in, taking his shoes off at the door because my floor was still wet.

"Want some coffee? Tea? Diet Coke?"

"No thanks," he said again.

I frowned. It wasn't like Sawyer to refuse an offer for a drink.

We sat at the kitchen table. I looked around for Lucy, but she seemed to be off napping somewhere.

"Well, how was it?" Sawyer said.

"The trip? It was exhausting."

"I meant the wedding. How was the wedding?"

Sawyer was tapping his fingers on the table. It made me nervous.

"It was nice."

I wished he would stop the tapping.

"Just   nice?"

He was just repeating my words; the worst kind of conversation.

I smiled and put my hand on his, in part to stop the tapping.

"Just nice sweetie," I said. "Are you sure you don't want a Diet Coke? Or lunch?"

Sawyer cleared his throat and didn't answer my offer.

"What's going on here?"

Sawyer crossed and uncrossed his legs. His socks were navy with flamingos. They were from his funky wardrobe reserved for the weekend.

Yes, he had a weekday and a weekend wardrobe. Weekdays were pressed khakis and a button-down shirt. Weekends, which I liked best, were broken-in jeans and a flannel. And the funny socks.

I realized I was letting my mind wander to avoid focusing on Sawyer's tone of voice.

"Listen," he said.

Listen? Oh boy, this did sound bad, I thought.

"I thought I would be OK with you going. Thought I was OK. But while you were gone, I had second thoughts."

Second thoughts? I had explained it was something I needed to do. For closure. I'd told him it was important for me to go. What I hadn't done is ask his permission. It had taken me almost a year to find my resilience and realize I was whole, with or without a partner. Yes, Sawyer was important to me, a great friend and lover, but I didn't belong to him in any sense of the word. That implied a sense of ownership, and my independence wasn't something I planned to relinquish ever again.

I sat up straighter in my kitchen chair.

"If you had a problem with it, we could have talked about it. But you know it was my choice."

"Of course," Sawyer said, finally looking up. "You make your own decisions. That's one of the things I love about you."

"So, then what is it?" I felt suddenly impatient.

"I just don't think you went there for closure. I feel like you went there to find out—"

"Find out what?"

"If you're still in love with him."

For a moment, the words hung in the air between us. Then they fell down onto the tiles of the kitchen floor like dead weights, only soundless. The silence was deafening.

Clearly, he expected me to give him an answer, and I wasn't prepared to give him one, because I didn't really know myself. I still adored Bryan, wanted the best for him, even missed him. But I wasn't about to get into a discussion about it with Sawyer; it shouldn't be necessary.

I had gone because it felt like the right thing. It still did. I wasn't going to sift through the many emotions with Sawyer that led me to making the trip to Bryan's wedding. This was one kitchen table discussion that wasn't going to happen. My heart. My choice.

I realized Sawyer was watching me intently, but I just stared at the spot on the floor I had missed with the Swiffer.

"I think we need some time apart," he said, clearing his throat. "I think it's for the best, Jessica."

Jessica. He was using my full name like he didn't even know me well.

"I'm sorry–" he started to say.

I pushed back my chair and stood up quickly.

"Don't apologize. Of all things, do not apologize."

"All right."

We stood still for a moment. I could hear the whoosh of cars going by my front porch. They drove too fast for a neighborhood with young kids. Damn people.

"So let me get this straight," I said shakily. "You're saying it's over between us? Or are you saying we need to take a break?"

Sawyer cleared his throat.

"Not a break, no. My feelings aren't going to change. And I don't think yours will either, whether you admit it or not. I think you're still in love with Bryan."

I didn't want to discuss how I felt about Bryan with Sawyer in my kitchen with my knees shaking. I didn't even know how I felt, so how could I put it into words?

What I did feel was anger that Sawyer was trying to tell me how I felt. Was it any of his business? And in that moment, I realized how much distance there had been with Sawyer and me right from the start.

"OK, well that's it then," I said.

A pulse was starting at my temples and my mouth felt dry. But I realized I wasn't going to cry. I'd come too far to cry over a man. Even a good one.

Sawyer sat down on the radiator to put his shoes back on. They were brown leather loafers. I'd always thought he looked cute in them. He had size 11.5 feet. I knew that because I'd gotten him running sneaks for his birthday. With neon stripes. He had loved them.

"Goodbye," Sawyer said, shutting the door quietly behind him as he left.

Eddie was at my door fifteen minutes after my text.

He immediately put his arms around me and pulled me in for a hug.

"Drink?" he said.

"Please."

Eddie got out the bottle of Fireball and poured us both a shot. We downed them quickly. It burned going the back of my throat, but I didn't care.

"I'm with you honey-bun, you don't have to explain everything to Sawyer. You're a strong, smart woman. You know what you need to do."

"True," I said, sniffling into a dinner napkin. "But he wasn't entirely wrong. He just wanted to hear that I didn't love Bryan anymore."

"And you couldn't say that," Eddie finished my thought for me.

"But it's a different kind of love," I held out my shot glass for more cinnamon whiskey.

"Of course it is, I understand."

"Why does everything terrible always happen in my kitchen?" I said.

Eddie sighed. "I don't know, chickie, it's just where all the action is."

12

"HERE YOU GO TOOTS," JOE SAID, BALANCING A PILE OF CHECKS on my already overcrowded in-box. "Time for you to take over sorting out payroll."

I sighed. This was another in the string of new tasks Joe had passed down to me in recent months. I was already doing accounts payable and receivable, answering the phone, and dealing with people walking in with questions or, more often, complaints.

Meanwhile, even after a year, it remained a total mystery to me what Joe's job entailed, besides chatting with his cronies and shopping the Duluth catalog online for overalls and denim vests.

I hadn't formulated a clear plan yet for confronting Joe about his lack of productivity, so I bit my lip and took the payroll checks to process.

Most of the employees had direct deposit but a good number still wanted paper checks. I pulled out the DPW staff's checks and the one underneath was Joe's. It didn't surprise me because Joe didn't trust electronic banking. He never used an ATM and still waited in line for tellers.

What did surprise me was the amount of his paycheck. Math was not my strongpoint, but even I could calculate that he was making 25% more than I was. I had never seen the paystubs before, so this was a shock to me. My mouth went dry and I wished I kept mints in my purse, because this was one of those panicky moments when I needed one.

OK, take a breath, I told myself. *Take two.*

I rubbed my eyes and wondered if it was time to get glasses. Maybe I wasn't seeing the numbers clearly. Then I tried squinting, but it was right there in black and white: Joe was making more money for doing way less work, basically eating donuts with powdered sugar all over his chin.

I was angry and resentful for the rest of the day and worked myself up into a tizzy by the time I got home. Sure, Joe had been there longer, but the disparity in our pay was outrageous.

Even the thought of chocolate or wine failed to comfort me.

Sleeping was impossible. I tossed and turned all night.

By morning, I had a plan. I would make my case for a raise to Linda, the trustee who hired me and stopped by to check in at the office from time to time. But I would have to meet her some place other than the office, away from Joe's prying eyes and ears.

I texted and asked if she could see me at the bakery up the hill from the office, because going to see her at Brew Coffee was too risky. Joe's friends would waste no time alerting him to the meeting if they saw us.

Linda agreed to meet me at 7:30 before the office opened. She was already there when I arrived.

Linda was a slender, elegant woman with peach nail polish and coral lipstick. She was wearing a yellow skirt and matching jacket as if she was going to a dinner party.

Had I known she would dress up, I wouldn't have worn slacks and a plain cardigan.

"Good morning Linda," I said, sliding into a seat.

She was dunking a tea bag in a cup of hot water. I hadn't stopped to order a drink at the counter because I was already quite nervous and didn't want to risk sloshing it on the glass-topped table. And I was just one jolt of caffeine away from giddy, nervous giggling.

"Jessica," she said formally.

I realized she must have thought something was terribly wrong for me to ask for a meeting away from the office.

"Thanks for coming," I said.

My throat was feeling very dry, and I already regretted foregoing a drink.

"So how is everything going at the office?" Linda asked, blowing daintily on her tea.

"It's... well... I have a concern."

Linda tapped her peachy nails on the table as if she was impatient for me to get to the point.

"Joe makes way more than me," I blurted out.

Linda furrowed her brow. I could see her gray eyeliner was a little smudged at the corners. Or maybe she did that on purpose for a smoky look.

What was I thinking? It was time to state my case.

"Well, I recently started doing payroll, something I barely have time for because of all my other job duties. I realize he's been there longer than me, but honestly, I do a good share of the paperwork plus answer the phones and deal with walk-ins."

I left out the part about Joe doing little more than chat with his friends, give Jerky treats he kept at his desk and visit the bathroom. Oh yes, but there was the time he made a chain out of paper clips and taped his eyebrows together to see if it looked like a unibrow. There were the endless conversations about town gossip, the county fair, a country music festival rumored to be coming to Meredia and which restaurant had the best New England clam chowder.

Linda clicked her tongue.

"Yes, he has been there almost 15 years, Jessica. You're only in your first year, correct?"

"I finished my first year in March."

"Hmm. As I remember, there are annual increases in the budget."

"Yes. Two percent."

Linda sipped her tea, leaving behind a coral ring of lipstick.

"I suppose I should take a look at this year's budget and figure out the difference."

"It's 25 percent," I said firmly, trying not to interrupt her.

"Oh my, that is something worth looking into. Tell you what, I'll crunch the numbers and then talk to the board members."

"Thank you," I said, extremely relieved.

"How are things going in there?" Linda asked, blotting her lips with a napkin, then taking out lipstick to reapply.

"To tell you the truth, it sucks." That's what I wished I could say.

Instead, I said, "Just fine, thank you."

"You're welcome," Linda said, smiling, and I remembered how she had made me feel at ease during my interview for the job.

"And you?" I asked vaguely, since I had no idea about her life outside being on the board. She looked like the type of women who had a large collection of pearl necklaces and silk scarves and maybe a singing parakeet for a pet.

"Good, dear. Now I need to run."

"Of course, thank you," I said again.

I stayed in my seat to avoid the awkward exit from the bakery and parting of ways on the sidewalk.

"What's gotten into you?" Joe growled when I walked into the office a few minutes later. "You look like the cat that spilled the cream."

As usual, his metaphors were all mixed up.

But I kept smiling, because even he wasn't going to bring me down.

Linda texted me the following week that the board had approved a 15% hike in pay for me, with another 5 percent in the new budget to come.

Best of all, because he had pawned off processing payroll onto me, Joe would never know.

I gave myself an actual pat on the back that night for sticking up for myself and demanding—well, asking for—what I was worth. It was becoming second nature to be assertive. I had come a long way from the frightful world of online dating. So I hadn't met "the one" yet. He was out there somewhere.

13

THERE HADN'T EVEN BEEN ICE ON THE FOUR STEPS LEADING to my porch when it happened in early November. All I had to blame was my own clumsiness.

I was carrying two bags of groceries from the car, anxious to get inside and open the package of mint Oreos that usually were sold off the shelves before I got there.

And I was also trying to balance the weight of the bag holding the 12-pack of clementine seltzer, my other favorite thing in the world.

I was busy planning the perfect snack in my head—Oreos and orange seltzer—when, out of nowhere, in a nano-second, I missed a stair and felt myself falling, as if in slow motion. I went down hard, dropping the paper bags into the shrubs lining the porch.

I was in serious danger of a face-plant, so at the last second, I put down my hand to stop my fall, then landed on both of my knees.

My first thought was to see if anyone had witnessed the fall, as if no one had ever tripped on stairs before in their life and falling was some kind of disgrace. My second thought was wondering if the eggs in the grocery bag had smashed.

I did a mental scan of my body to see if there was any damage, but the only thing that hurt was my right wrist, a dull throb. I wiggled my hand and winced. There was some kind of injury, probably a sprain or a strain or something minor that would likely only require ice, Oreos, and seltzer.

Thankfully, Ian was home from class. I abandoned the groceries in the bushes and went carefully to the front door, using my left hand to open it.

"Ian?" I called up the stairs. "Do you know where the Tylenol is?"

"Kitchen cabinet over the stove," he called back. "Headache?"

"No, I took a little fall, just stumbled really."

Ian came immediately downstairs.

I held out my wrist.

"What happened," he said, examining it. "That looks bad."

"It's nothing, really," I said, sitting down and placing my hand on the table, trying not to wince.

"You need to ice it," Ian said.

He opened the freezer and took out a bag of frozen peas, laying it gently on the back of my wrist. Then he got me the Tylenol and a glass of water.

We sat at the table for several minutes.

"Was there ice out there?" he asked, concern written all over his face.

"A little," I lied, not wanting to admit I had been rushing inside for junk food.

"I'll put out some rock salt later. How's it feel?"

"Fine," I said. "Can't feel a thing."

"That's because it's half frozen from the peas. Wiggle your fingers."

My fingers felt OK, but when I moved my thumb, a twinge shot up to my elbow.

"Don't tell me you're fine, I can tell by your face you're not. I'm taking you to the walk-in clinic," Ian said decidedly. "Don't try to argue about it."

"Can I at least pack some cookies for the road?"

"Mom, we have more important things to do right now. Here. Let me zip up your jacket."

Ian grabbed his ski jacket, then took my elbow to help me out the door, down the damn steps, past the Oreos, and into his car.

The waiting room at the clinic was full of people who were coughing and blowing their noses, and all I could think was that Ian and I were going to catch something: this year's flu strain or strep throat.

We sat in the orange plastic chairs for almost an hour. Ian leafed through a two-month-old copy of Sports Illustrated.

As my wrist began to thaw, I had to admit, I wished I'd brought the peas. And the cookies, because I was starving.

"Jessica Gabriel?" called out a kindly nurse with blue hearts on her scrub suit.

We waited another 20 minutes in the exam room until a good-looking (but too young) physician's assistant came in.

"Take a fall?" he asked.

"Ice," I lied, again.

He sent me down for an X-ray and for the first time it occurred to me I might have broken the wrist. How would I drive? Get to the office? And for that matter, get any work done? God forbid I didn't do any work like Joe; the office would come to a standstill.

"You were lucky," the PA said another half hour later when he came back into the exam room. "No break. But from the pain and swelling, it's definitely a sprain."

"Oh, that's good," I said, hugely relieved.

"Does she need a cast?" Ian asked, still looking worried.

"No, I'll wrap it, but don't plan on using it for the next few weeks."

"Using it?" I had an immediate image of eating Bucket of Spaghetti with my left hand, opening mail with my teeth, and driving one-handed.

"Needs to stay immobilized as much as possible," the PA said, signing paperwork and handing it to my left hand.

"You have to be careful on steps," he added, making me feel both elderly and foolish.

"Can she get it wet?" Ian asked, still focused on practical questions.

"Try not to. Cover it in the shower."

Then I pictured rolling Saran Wrap over my bandaged wrist and trying to hold it outside the shower curtain to keep it dry.

Really?

"Can she drive?"

Thank God Ian was there. I still hadn't processed the fact the wrist was sprained.

"I wouldn't recommend it."

We went back out to the reception desk and Ian dug out my debit card to pay for the visit.

Back out at his car, he opened the door and carefully helped me get in, strapping my seatbelt.

"I think I'll be able to drive," I said, looking down at my hand. The ace bandage felt tight, and my fingers already looked purple-ish.

"Not a chance," Ian said emphatically. "I don't have any morning classes this term. I'll get you in, then maybe one of the guys at work can drive you home. Do you think they would?"

"I can ask Sal," I answered. Sal was the most grandfatherly of the three men in the office.

When we got back home, I realized I couldn't bend down and pick up Lucy. But when I sat down and patted my lap, she sprang up easily like an Olympic gymnast. I petted her awkwardly with my left hand.

I couldn't text one-handed, so I had to resort to using my cell to make an actual phone call.

Eddie sounded alarmed when he answered.

"What's wrong? You hardly ever call!"

I told him about the day's events.

"Are you all right?"

"I'm fine. Of course, the wrist already itches badly under the sweaty bandage, and I can't get to it."

"You need to be more careful. You've always been a little, shall we say, ungraceful. If you feel yourself slipping, fall backwards so you land on your ass next time."

"Yup, because I do have plenty of padding there."

"I didn't say that, chickie."

"You didn't have to!"

I slept with the hand propped up on a pillow next to me. Lucy lay by my other side, sensing something was wrong.

The next morning, I struggled into a pullover sweater to avoid the need to button a blouse.

Ian, who had never in his whole life been a morning person, was already in the kitchen ready to go.

"Thanks honey," I said when we got to the office.

Ian opened the heavy office front door, and I went in. Shock immediately registered on the men's faces from where they sat at the conference table.

Sal dropped his raspberry Danish on the napkin and jumped to his feet.

"What in high heaven?"

Sal was at the door in record time, considering he was pushing 75. He took my left arm and led me inside.

"It's just a sprain," I said.

With that, the men resumed their pastry eating.

"Does it hurt much?" Sal asked worriedly.

"Nah," I reassured him. "Just when I put pressure on it."

I struggled to input invoices with my left hand on the keyboard, and when the phone rang, Joe pretended not to even hear it, leaving me to balance the phone under my chin. But I didn't care because I was still riding the high of the salary victory.

Sal met Ian and me at the office door every morning after that, always looking concerned.

At quitting time, Sal would help me into my winter coat and escort me in a gentlemanly way down to his Chevy.

I never mastered doing any semblance of writing with my left hand or buttoning up my coat, and I skipped blow drying and resorted to a ponytail most of the time.

After three weeks of eating only microwaveable dinners, washing my face with one hand, and going to work without eyeliner or mascara, I'd had enough.

At my follow-up appointment, Ian and I faced the same room full of hacking people. The same PA came into the exam room.

"Well, how'd we do?"

"I couldn't scramble eggs or tie my shoes," I replied, not caring if I was whining.

"Yeah, it's no fun being one-handed," he said, carefully unwrapping the bandage. "But I must say, you did a good job keeping it dry."

"We put a grocery bag over it for her to shower," Ian offered.

Neither of them knew how much trouble it had been to work up a decent lather with my left hand.

"How's it feel?"

The skin where the bandage had covered was ghostly white and shriveled and the base of my thumb still had the shadow of a bruise. But I could wiggle all my fingers.

"The wrist is going to be stiff, so you'll need to do some strengthening exercises," the PA said, handing me a brochure with a man on the cover lifting a jug of cranberry juice.

"I've got a squeeze ball she can use," Ian said.

For the hundredth time that month, I thought about how much he had helped and that I would have been lost without him.

"Here's the name of a good physical therapist," the PA said, scribbling a note I hoped I could decipher on a script paper. "I really suggest you go; otherwise, you could lose some of the hand's mobility."

I sighed. Working physical therapy into my work schedule wouldn't be easy.

"You gotta make the therapy appointment, Mom," Ian the mind-reader said.

"Sure do," the PA said before leaving the exam room.

I decided he was much too cheerful delivering news about a possible immobilized hand. And also too young.

As Ian drove us home, I felt a little sorry for the weak,

pasty wrist I really didn't recognize.

But most importantly, I had my freedom back to pour a glass of wine when we got home. Then, I went immediately to the bathroom to take a shower, reveling in the joy of being able to wash my hair two-handed.

14

WITH THE WRIST EPISODE OVER, ONE NIGHT IN DECEMBER I scrolled online through my checking account, realizing I needed to face facts: despite the raise in my paycheck, my budget was far from balanced.

I got up and switched on the electric kettle for tea. New Age cold remedy, because thinking about my financial future made my throat ache. And for that matter, my stomach turn over.

I texted Eddie, kneading the squeeze ball with my right hand. I had regained full strength in the hand, but it still felt good to use the stress ball.

"You around?"

"Yup. Whatcha doin'?"

"Well, my life is in financial ruin," I texted.

"Welcome to the club, chickie."

"I'm serious. I'm just barely covering the bills," I sipped the too-hot tea.

"Didn't you get a raise?"

"Yes," I smiled, still proud of myself. "But I'm stretching my budget pretty thin."

Lucy padded into the kitchen and put her front paws on my leg to be picked up. I scooped her up and kissed the back of her ear, feeling better despite myself.

"Well, I guess it's time to find a side hustle."

"Like start making beaded jewelry on Etsy? Or potholders?"

"Ah, well, how do I put this? You're not exactly the crafty type."

"Thank you for pointing that out," I said, bouncing Lucy on my lap like a baby. "I guess I don't really have a specific talent I can capitalize on."

"Give it some thought, Jess. I'm sure something will jump out at you."

I looked at lists of side gigs on YouTube that night, but sadly, cleaning pools, power washing houses, being a virtual assistant or doing interior painting weren't in my skill set.

I briefly considered starting a juicing business, selling fresh fruit and veggie smoothies at the local farmers market, but it would be months before that opened up again, I didn't have a good blender, and I needed money now.

"So, what's your plan?" Madison asked, peeling an apple at the sink a few days later.

"I don't have one," I sighed. I was still feeling discouraged, verging on desperate.

Madd got out the cutting board to slice the apple, then scooped peanut butter into a bowl.

"You always have a plan Mombo."

She sat down and put the bowl in the middle of the table. I took an apple wedge and dredged it in peanut butter, shaking my head.

"Nope. I got nothing."

I heard Ian whistling before he came in the back door, dropping his gym bag in the laundry room.

"Starving," he said, wrinkling his nose as he looked at the apples. "Why are you two always eating girl food?"

"Maybe because we're girls, and we can't eat the whole world like you can and still stay thin?"

"Huh," Ian said to his sister. He opened the fridge and rummaged around, finally coming up with leftover chicken.

"We have any fajita wraps, Mom?"

"Second shelf behind the yogurt," I said. "Shredded cheese is in the cooler drawer with the tomatoes."

Ian piled chicken and cheese on the flour wrap and put the plate in the microwave.

"So, what problem are we trying to solve tonight? You both look overly serious. Like, even more than usual."

"Mom is broke," Madd filled him in. "She needs a side gig. Something other than walking Lucy or online dating, obviously."

"Hey," I said defensively. But she was right. It appeared my list of marketable skills was quite limited. And making things wasn't my strong suit, unless you counted Margaritas.

The microwave dinged and Ian got his chicken fajita out, which smelled amazing.

I sighed and picked up another apple slice.

"Let's think outside the box," Madison said. "What do you hate most about your job now?"

"Off the top of my head, I'd say the monotony, the math, the unfair workload, the interruptions. Pretty much everything but the pastries the guys get, and my waistline isn't thanking me for those."

Lucy came into the kitchen and stood patiently near Ian, waiting for a bit of chicken. All she had to do was look at him. None of us could resist her little puppy dog face.

"So, something where you don't have someone breathing down your back all the time?" Madison said.

"That would be great, yeah."

We munched our apples and watched Ian inhale his mouth-watering fajita. Life just wasn't fair.

"I know what," Ian said, wiping his mouth with a napkin. "Have you ever thought about driving for Uber?"

"Uber?"

"Yeah, you know, where you drive people around and they pay you, like a taxi using your own car."

"I know what Uber is, silly."

"Think about it, it could be the perfect job for you. You'd be your own boss, set your own hours, and you have the personality for it."

"Mom's not really that great of a driver," Madd piped in.

"Hey," I said, defensive again.

"She will have to keep her lead foot off the gas pedal," Ian said. "I'm gonna see what Uber drivers make."

He pulled out his cell.

"Do you need some kind of advanced license, like Class B or something?"

"I think that's for truckers," Madison said. "You're definitely not doing that."

"Look at that, $27 an hour is the average for Uber driving," Ian said excitedly. "I think this could be it."

"Don't you have to drive a newish car?" I asked.

"Yours is new enough I think," Ian replied.

I didn't really know or care how old my car was, as long as it held together and took me where I needed to go safely.

"Yeah, drivers can use cars up to ten years old, so you're good."

"What do you think Madd?" I got up to clear the apple and Ian's fajita plate.

"You think you could handle it with your bad wrist?" her green eyes clouded over with concern.

"Sure," I said confidently. "It doesn't bother me at all. And I'd probably only drive a few hours at a time."

"Well then, I say give it a try. Just don't do the bar circuit after midnight, because you run the risk of someone drunk puking in your back seat."

"She could leave out barf bags," Ian suggested.

"No thanks."

"Geesh, I might sign up too, now that I see how much money they rake in," Ian said, standing up and pushing in his chair.

15

THE NEXT DAY, I SIGNED UP ONLINE TO DRIVE FOR UBER. I scanned and sent in photos of my driver's license, registration, and car insurance. It took a couple days for them to run a background check.

A text came through the next day, sending me a link to the app.

"Welcome to Uber."

It was simple to use the driver app. All I had to do was click it on to activate and it would begin to scan for riders in my immediate area. It was a little nerve-wracking because once it found a rider, their location would flash on my phone, and I had ten seconds to accept it or turn it down.

It was an exciting adventure, kind of what online dating had been in the very beginning before it became pathetic and nightmarish.

My first Uber trip was on a Friday after work. I was hoping to catch the dinner crowd.

When the app flashed the pick-up spot, it was in fact a restaurant. Jackpot! But it was a woman leaving after a drink or two. She had big hair piled up on her head held in place by hairspray that gleamed like shellac.

"The last time I Ubered, the driver had a parrot in the passenger seat," she said matter-of-factly after she climbed in settled herself.

It was only my first Uber drive and already I was entertained. I had to hear about this.

"Like, right on the seat?"

"Nope," she said, examining her pointy acrylic nails. "It was on a perch that looked like a tree branch."

I tried to picture it. "Wow."

"Yup, and it kept turning its head in that strange way birds do and staring at me. I thought, if it got off its perch and flew at me, I'd punch it in the face."

I tried not to laugh, but it was hysterical, bringing a bird to work. The Uber site clearly stated drivers couldn't have their pets in the car, but I wondered if I could put in a little doggie seatbelt and take Lucy to Uber with me.

That night I checked the Uber site, and it definitively stated the only animals allowed in the car were service dogs.

The next day, a woman carrying an enormous square handbag climbed into the back seat and stretched out her legs.

"What a day I've had," she said, putting the bag beside her.

"What do you do?"

Her face lit up and she opened the bag, which turned out to be a display case with necklaces and earrings inside, most of them beaded.

"Very nice," I said, glancing briefly in the rearview mirror.

"You a jewelry gal?"

"Not really," I said, anticipating a hard sell.

I wasn't even making enough driving Uber to splurge on earrings.

"My stuff is different," she said, rummaging around the

case and holding up a necklace with gleaming off-white beads that looked like broken seashells. "This one is custom. I'm dropping it off tonight."

"Um hmm," I said, not wanting to take my eyes off the road or offer her any encouragement.

"You have kids? Did you save their baby teeth after the Tooth Fairy left money under their pillow?"

I had absolutely no idea what I'd done with the teeth. Nor did I care, for that matter.

"This mom put all her children's lost teeth in a shoebox because she could not part with them."

Wow. And I thought I was sentimental. I had Maddy's toddler dresses and Ian's Halloween costumes, but teeth seemed overdoing it.

"So, I bleached them and made this necklace. Glued them in like Swarovski crystals. Ta da!" she held it up proudly.

I took a quick look in the rearview mirror again at the gaudy necklace, studded with what were clearly now incisors and molars.

Yikes.

I was glad it was a short ride for the tooth jeweler.

Nick's Tavern quickly became a regular stop for me to pick up riders, usually around midnight when people were smart enough to know they'd had one too many beers.

It was always hard to find a spot, so one Thursday night around 10 p.m. I had to park across the street to wait.

A woman in a red raincoat came out of Nick's. She had perfectly highlighted cinnamon brown hair and pointy-toed black stilettos.

I gave a little honk, and she crossed the street, picking

her way around wide cracks in the road so she wouldn't catch her heel and lose her balance.

She got in the back seat carefully, as if I had something breakable back there.

Her destination was a neighborhood I knew, where all the trees had been left to grow wild. It was lovely and woodsy.

"How are you tonight?" I asked politely. The Uber instruction video said making pleasant conversation could lead to better tips, and I was all for that.

She looked out the window without answering. I wondered if she had even heard me. Well, it looked like it was time to turn on the radio.

"My husband is leaving me," she said a few minutes later.

I wondered if he had taken off in a camper like Adam.

I turned down the volume on the radio.

"I'm sorry."

"Not as sorry as me," she said, sweeping her fingers through her perfect hair, creating frizzy waves.

I didn't know what to say, so I said nothing.

"There's no one else. It would almost be easier if there was," she gave a short laugh.

I stayed silent.

"He said he just doesn't love me anymore. Fourteen years of marriage. Down the tubes."

She pulled Kleenex out of her purse and dabbed her eyes.

"I'm sorry," I said again, unable to come up with anything helpful.

"You married?"

"I was. Twice. Didn't work out. Marriage just isn't for

me."

"So, you're single?" she asked.

"Yes, I am."

"I have never lived alone. No idea how to even begin to do it."

I was once in her shoes. I had relied on Adam during the marriage to balance the checkbook, fix broken things, paint the deck, snow blow the driveway, take out the garbage. Before he'd immersed himself in the RV life, he had been good company. He had always asked about my day and seemed to really be interested. We shared grocery shopping and went out for a dinner date together a couple times a month.

When he left to travel the country, I had felt the ground roll out beneath my feet. I could actually lean in and feel the wall of grief.

He had given up the life we had built for our children. I knew he had been withdrawn and distant, but I never would have guessed he wanted to get the hell out for good.

I dropped off the sad woman, wishing I could make her feel better.

"One thing's for sure, I could never be an Uber driver," Nadine said on a Saturday when I picked her up for a late breakfast.

"Oh, but it's so glamorous. The long hours. Lousy tips. People that smell like mozzarella."

"What? Like cheese?"

"It's like half my riders just ate pizza. Makes me famished, and the smell lingers in the car after they've gotten out."

"I used to have a recipe for a good pizza sauce," Nadine

said. "Wonder where it went..."

"I just stick with takeout spaghetti in a bucket. The kids love it too."

"Anyway, I couldn't be a driver because you have to keep your car so damn clean all the time."

"That's true," I said sadly. "I can't eat chocolate chip muffins in here anymore; they leave crumbs everywhere. But I can manage egg sandwiches!"

16

It wasn't by any means easy adding Uber to my work life, but I managed to juggle it. Mostly, I slept less and tried to get accustomed to working seven days a week.

Besides the extra money, there was a sense of adventure that came with driving people around.

And then it happened. On my first call of the day the weekend before Christmas, I picked up Mr. Wonderful. Just like Madd had said.

He was exactly my type. Dark hair with a hint of gray at his temples, black eyeglasses that made him look very serious and so tall he had to duck his way into my back seat.

He was the first passenger I'd had in my car that was wearing a business suit and a dotted necktie.

I picked him up outside a bank, and his destination was a brick office building in a business district outside Meredia.

"How's your day going?" Mr. Wonderful asked as I pulled away from the curb.

So, he was friendly to boot!

"Good, you?"

"Not too bad."

"You heading to work on a weekend?" I asked even though it was clear he was, being that he was in a business suit heading to an office complex.

"Yup. Someone's gotta do it."

"True."

"And car's in the shop; waiting for the mechanic to call and tell me the damage," he smiled ruefully.

I had to remind myself to keep my eyes on the road and not get the dreaded red light on my cell from the Uber app, indicating I was over the speed limit. Rumor had it if you got three lights in a row, your Uber driving license was suspended.

"That sucks," I said, immediately wishing I'd used more sophisticated language.

"Yeah but it's nice to kick back and let someone else do the driving."

"Oh, certainly."

"So, you like Uber driving?'

"It's OK," I said, inhaling the scent of his cologne. "The driving is kind of a pain but it's nice meeting the people. I met a woman that made jewelry from children's baby teeth.

"Was she the actual Tooth Fairy?"

So he had a sense of humor! I liked him even more.

"I'm Wyatt," he said. "I'd shake your hand but then you would take it off the wheel and risk death for both of us."

"Jessica."

"Good to meet you, Jess."

I was secretly thrilled when people immediately calling me Jess. I always took it as a good sign.

His drop-off was the new office complex in Merida. Obviously, it was work.

"What do you do?" I asked.

"I'm a talent recruiter," he said, looking at me in the rearview mirror.

"Nice. Like a head-hunter?"

Did they call it that? It sounded like a primitive tribal act of war.

"Yep. I match people with jobs, high-end techie stuff usually," Wyatt said, sounding very confident.

High-end. So he wasn't, for instance, recruiting people for desk jobs like mine.

We arrived at the office complex too soon.

"It was great talking with you Jess," he said, handing me a tip.

"Have a good one!" I said, sounding a little too chipper.

I looked at the folded dollars as soon as Wyatt disappeared through the revolving door at the entrance to the brick building.

There were two twenties and a ten; the highest tip I'd ever earned. And tucked inside was his business card. It had a work phone number and a cell.

17

I FORCED MYSELF TO WAIT SEVERAL DAYS BEFORE TEXTING Wyatt.

I caved on Thursday night after my dinner of Special K cereal with almond slivers.

"Hey Wyatt, it's Jess, Uber driver extraordinaire."

I cursed myself after I sent the message. Extraordinaire? What was I, a circus MC announcing the high wire act? Who talked like that? Apparently, me.

Two hours and 36 minutes later, I got a reply.

"Hi Jess, good hearing from you."

"Sorry if I'm bothering you. Are you busy?" Now I sounded nervous.

"I'm making some calls; can I get back to you in a bit?"

"Absolutely," I said, sounding overly eager.

At 11 p.m., I gave up and went to bed.

"Well, that's that," I told Lucy as she settled by my feet.

Just after midnight, my cell buzzed an incoming message.

"You awake?"

I pushed off the blanket and sat up quickly. Lucy rolled over and sighed in her sleep.

"Yes. Awake," I suppressed a yawn.

"A night owl. Just like me."

I wasn't exactly a night owl. But I was not a morning

person either. I usually hit my peak around noon.

"Wasn't sure you'd text," he wrote.

"Well, you did leave a good tip."

Crap! Now it sounded like I was for sale.

I straightened my shoulders.

"Do you want to get coffee sometime?" I texted.

"I'll do you one better. Let's have lunch."

I was thrilled. Lunch was a much bigger commitment than coffee. When you went for coffee, you could beg off in under an hour. Lunch meant at least sixty minutes.

"When?"

"You free this weekend? Wanta meet at Ginger's downtown?"

"Sounds good."

I was relieved he hadn't suggested Brew Coffee. Although they did have excellent paninis.

"Noon?"

"That works for me."

"Sweet," Wyatt texted. "See you soon."

It was too late to text Nadine. The big news would have to wait for first thing in the morning.

18

GINGER'S WAS A BRIGHT BISTRO WITH HUGE WINDOWS THAT let in the late morning light.

It was one of those New York winter days when the air was crisp and cold, the sky a dazzling blue, sunshine everywhere.

Wyatt was already there. I've always liked a punctual guy.

He was standing inside, and his face lit up when he saw me. Such a positive sign.

"Is this good?" Wyatt asked, pointing to a cafe table in a cozy corner far from the door.

"It's great."

A server came out of nowhere. He was wearing his jeans too low and had a blue bandana wrapped around his hair.

He took our drink orders—hot tea for both of us—and asked if we were ready to order.

Eddie and I had been there many times and I knew the caprese salad to be out of this world. It was a plateful of thick rounds of fresh mozzarella sandwiched between slices of ripe tomatoes, drizzled with balsamic.

"What wrap do you recommend?" Wyatt asked the server.

"The chicken Caesar, by far."

"I'll take that then."

I ordered my caprese and the server disappeared. I was glad I wasn't facing the sun because I didn't want to be squinting at Wyatt and showing the fine lines between my eyes. What do you call them? Crow's feet? Whatever.

"How's it going today? You working?"

"No, I'm off on weekends," I answered automatically about my town job. "Oh, you mean Uber. I might head out later tonight. I should. It's been a slow week. You know, everyone hibernating."

"You'd better bundle up. Supposed to be a cold one."

Wyatt had crinkle lines around his eyes when he smiled that were adorably boyish. Why do wrinkles age a woman but look so cute on men?

"So how is it driving Uber? Guess you have to keep your car pretty clean," Wyatt said, squeezing his lemon wedge into his drink.

"Well, the back seat anyway."

He laughed. "No stray muffin crumbs allowed?"

How did he know I was a carb fanatic? Did I look like I ate too many baked goods? Darn those Three Stooges for their pastry run almost every morning, preying on my lack of self-control.

"No pizza boxes." Crap, why was I so focused on food? I had never had an old pizza box in my car, at least not in recent memory.

"You must have had some strange passengers. I couldn't do it. I don't think I like people enough," he said laughing.

"Yeah, it's been interesting. I've had people doing just about everything in the back seat. Shaving. Changing their t-shirt. Eating takeout Chinese food."

"Yikes. Does the smell of General Tso's linger?"

"That's where Febreze comes in. Always have it in the car. There have been riders who actually smell worse than lo mein."

Wyatt laughed again and our glorious food arrived. It was going great, and I was having a great lunch too!

"So, you have kids?" Wyatt asked, chewing politely with his mouth closed.

"Two. Madison and Ian. Both in their 20s. But Ian still lives with me, thank goodness."

"No empty nest yet?"

"Nope. Not ready to deal with that! How about you?"

"One daughter, Ella. She's in school out west where her mother lives."

School? As in high school? Could she be as young as 16? How old was he anyway?

"University at Berkeley, studying fashion design."

Phew. That was a close one.

We talked about our latest Netflix binges and how he wished he could have a dog—an excellent sign—but traveled too much. He asked the server for a refill which thrilled me because it meant we might linger.

"I know you're going to drive later, but what are your plans for the afternoon?"

Fantasize about you, I thought.

"Um, probably Swiffer my kitchen floor."

Could I be any more boring?

"Sounds like fun, but if you can wait to do house cleaning until another time, wanta help me pick out a Christmas tree?"

Wow! A fan of the holidays. Sure, it wasn't Halloween, but it was a definite second place winner.

"I'd love that," I said, trying not to gush.

Wyatt waved away my hand as I reached to take out my wallet to pitch in.

"You can treat next time."

Next time! I was practically giddy as we stood up and put on coats, scarves, and hats.

I followed Wyatt in my car a few miles out of town.

The Christmas tree farm was the one where we always took the kids because there was a tractor-pulled hay wagon that shuttled us bumpily up the hill to the acre of trees. Madd always wanted an enormous tree that would graze our living room ceiling and Ian would pick out a straggly Charlie Brown tree.

I remembered the first year we took Ian to cut down a tree. He was barely a year old, and Adam had him in one of those backpack child carriers. Ian wasn't yet walking but managed to stand up in the backpack quite well, reaching out to grab at branches, losing a mitten, trying to escape the carrier.

My heart lurched the way it did whenever a memory hit. Did the kids remember the happy family times? Did Adam? I believed I was the only one that kept the memories, simultaneously sweet and wrenching. It made me feel the deep fracture in our lives when Adam had left and our family life abruptly halted.

Wyatt was holding out a hand to help hoist me onto the hay wagon. There were even plaid wool blankets to drape over our legs. The driver/tree farmer asked if anyone needed a saw.

"Guess I didn't come prepared," Wyatt said, taking one.

I tried to climb down gracefully when the wagon

dropped us off but caught my snow boot on the edge and fell into Wyatt. Which wasn't exactly a bad thing.

We trudged around the rows of trees until we lost sensation in our fingertips.

"This one's pretty damn near perfect," he said, pointing out a slender Balsam fir.

"Sure is."

Wyatt bent down to reach the base of the tree and started sawing.

"Well, I guess I don't have a career in forestry," he said ruefully.

"It's the saw," I said. "It looks about a hundred years old."

"Thanks for saying that."

Finally, the tree started to tip and fell over. Wyatt grabbed it by the trunk and dragged it back to the pick-up area for the wagon ride back down.

A teenager helped us unload the tree, wrapped it expertly in plastic netting and carried it to Wyatt's car to tie onto the roof.

We walked over to an outdoor firepit to thaw our hands. There was a startlingly authentic-looking Santa nearby handing out candy canes to children. Even his beard looked real.

"Want to help me bring it home, or do you want me to take you right back to your car?"

Honestly, I wasn't ready for the date to end. It was going so perfectly.

19

His neighborhood was an upscale street of tall narrow brownstones in Ashton. He had a beautiful brick home with a front door the exact shade of cream.

I hesitated at the door.

"You're not an ax murderer, right?"

"Nah, I don't even own anything sharp. And I left the saw at the tree farm."

"Come on in," he said, holding the door open for me.

It was clear Wyatt's house belonged to an unattached guy; there were no feminine touches anywhere. The living room had a wraparound leather sofa with one of those lounge seats on the end, and the coffee table looked like reclaimed wood buffed to a sheen. The throw blanket—it looked like cashmere—was draped so casually it was clear Wyatt had placed it on the couch carefully. There was a huge, framed photo of a row of leafless tree silhouettes on the mantle but other than that, the room was bare and sparse.

I loved it. My house was a jumble of magazines, candles in various colors and fragrances, and dog toys. In fact, I had a general dog-décor theme going on, from a wall canvas that said "If I can't bring my dog, I'm not going," to our key holder in the shape of a dog bone.

We pulled in the tree. Wyatt didn't even complain about

the trail of pine needles the tree left on the cream-colored carpet.

"I'm not prepared to set it up," he said with a laugh. "Gotta dig out the tree stand from god knows where. Want some coffee? Tea?"

"Tea would be great."

"Make yourself at home."

I sat down on the plush couch that looked like it had never been used. Where did he sit to watch Netflix? Lie in bed?

Wyatt brought in two mugs and settled down next to me. Right next to me. On the same cushion.

We sipped silently. Mr. Wonderful indeed!

"I haven't given you a proper tour," he said, standing up. "Come on."

We walked through a beautiful formal dining room and a bathroom so clean it looked like it was never used. His kitchen was all stainless steel with a large wood block island and four silver swivel stools. I didn't see a fridge or dishwasher then realized they had cabinetry on the front and blended in seamlessly.

A straight row of tall glass jars with cork tops was filled with every kind of pasta I could imagine. All full, as if he had never opened them.

Wyatt led me upstairs. There was a long hallway with three closed doors that must be guest rooms. I was mightily impressed.

No wonder he was so confident. He must be killing it in talent recruitment.

The door to the master bedroom was open and he didn't hesitate to sail through.

Nor did I.

The room was bigger than my entire kitchen. There was an actual seating area with a leather sofa and side chairs. But the centerpiece was a magnificent mahogany bed right out of a luxury furniture showroom. The head and footboards were seamlessly curled, as if cut from a single massive piece of wood.

"Wow."

"Thanks."

I hadn't realized I had said it out loud.

"We can sit and talk, or I can show you what you've done to me."

I was curious.

He reached out and touched the back of my neck, then pulled me into his arms without hesitation.

"Like it?"

"The room? It's amazing."

Wyatt brought my hand down to his erection, so hard it was a visible bulge under his jeans.

"Oh, I like it," I said, beginning to rub.

"Take it out," he said, breathing into my neck.

He didn't have to ask twice. I quickly unzipped and pulled his jeans to his knees. He climbed out of them and pulled off his t-shirt. Of course, he was well built in that muscular way that wasn't overdoing it.

Wyatt stayed standing so I got on my knees.

He was so hard I could only get the tip inside my lips to suck. There was no conceivable way he was going down my throat without me choking and gagging on the spot, which would be a real mood-killer.

He was groaning, which was very encouraging. It was

a signal I was hitting all the right places. It made me feel womanly and proud.

Wyatt moved back to sit on the edge of the bed. I took off my t-shirt, knowing he was watching closely.

I leaned down to climb in bed on him, or with him, but he pushed my head down to his lap. Not with any force, but a push nonetheless. Mr. Wonderful lost a few points right then.

I trailed kisses down his sternum to his flat stomach, but when I moved down to his erection, I found it was no longer there. It was more of a deflated balloon.

Holy crap. Not again. I'd experienced thwarted sex with men when it was over before it had even started.

"Pull on it," he said.

Dutifully, I took Mr. Limp in my hand and tried to stroke. It was impossible to work up a rhythm. He just kept slipping out of my hand.

It was also very dry, and it didn't seem polite to ask if he had any lube. I considered spitting on my hand, but things had gotten very strange, and I wasn't sure how much effort I wanted to put into it.

"Let me do it," he said.

I thought I had heard him wrong, but he actually moved me out of the way and started jerking himself. He was hard again in a minute. I know it was one minute because I was watching the digital clock on his nightstand as I waited for him to stop and let us go about the business of having mutual sex.

And waited. And waited.

His eyes were closed as he jerked faster, pumping vigorously.

Was I supposed to get off by watching?

I was shocked when he grabbed the edge of the sheet on his bed and spread it over his lap. Within seconds, he had what looked like a mind-blowing orgasm. All over the side of the sheet.

He kept his eyes closed as he caught his breath.

"Sorry," he said. "Looks like I gotta do some laundry today."

In 9th grade I had what I thought to be a serious boyfriend, the love of my teenager life. We were together a few months, during which he bought me a silver ring with a heart on it, which I believed cemented our love and commitment.

We spent most of our time making out on the plaid orange couch in the basement at his house. Once in a while he made careful attempts to cup my boobs, but we never went any further.

One night we went and parked at the viewing spot at the airport (another plus: he had a car and driver's license). We drank a couple cans of Miller Lite his older brother had bought for him.

The passionate kissing went on for an hour. Finally, I reached for his erection and rubbed it from outside his jeans. He moaned and orgasmed without me even touching his actual penis.

It was then that I had realized how horny 16-year-old boys could be.

"I really needed that," he said, not overly concerned about his wet jeans.

We broke up a few weeks later when I thought I saw him checking out Maureen Voss in the cafeteria. I swore I saw him watch her ass as she sashayed by with her blue plastic tray of chicken and gravy on a bun.

We argued and, like everything else in teenage land, hadn't given it another try and just parted ways.

The episode in the car had been flattering. This jerk session with Wyatt was just plain appalling.

"Well, that was—" I didn't bother finishing my sentence.

"Sorry," he said again, pulling the sheets off the bed. "It's been a long time."

Since he jerked? Or had a spectator? Or what?

"I think I should get going," I said, looking around for my t-shirt, the only item I'd removed.

I put my shirt on as I walked out of the bedroom and then went down the stairs.

The Christmas tree was still propped up in the corner, but I could see it was sparse on one side, far from perfect. Kind of like Mr. Wonderful.

"Let's try again, maybe Friday?" Wyatt called from upstairs.

I didn't wait to answer. I shut the front door behind me and jogged to my car. Well, it was more of a run.

I had never imagined something like that in high school, let alone in adulthood. Never.

20

"SOME MEN JERK FOR SO LONG, THEY GET USED TO IT AND can't get it up with anyone else's hand–or whatever," Eddie explained to me the next day at my kitchen table.

"It was insane," I said, chewing a honey wheat pretzel. "It was a show I didn't want to see."

"When was the last time he'd had sex? Just out of curiosity."

"He said it had been a long time. Whatever that meant."

"You know, he may just be used to sex with someone— or something—else."

"Like?"

"Sex doll?" Eddie said.

I sighed.

"What shall we order for dinner? I've had enough Bucket of Spaghetti for a while."

"Hot dogs?" Eddie said, laughing at his own joke.

"That was lame. Just like Wyatt."

We got pesto chicken pizza and settled down to watch Netflix.

"I'm done dating for a while."

"Good thing you have your Uber career to focus on."

I swatted him with a pillow, then leaned my head on his shoulder, glad for human comfort.

21

It was January, the one month of the year when even I couldn't find much love for upstate New York. The winds howled, ice built up on driveways like hockey rinks, Christmas trees were tossed to the curb.

I wore wool Fair Isle sweaters with cotton turtlenecks underneath and corduroy skirts with lined black tights to work. It was way too cold for Halloween leggings, so I had to resort to jeans. But even layered up, I had to run to my car and curse at the heater and the inordinate amount of time it took to warm up.

I tried driving the bar scene one Friday night, turning on the Uber app and heading to a downtown outside Meredia. I had napped after my workday in town hall, so I was ready for a midnight shift.

I'd driven a few carloads of semi-drunk, silly college kids back their dorms, then picked up a couple who both looked like super models.

He was wearing an untucked Polo shirt over black stonewashed jeans. His partner was wearing a very short sequined blue dress beneath a fake fur coat.

They were beautiful. They were also quite tipsy.

Their destination was almost a 30-minute drive; it would be a good fare. Maybe after that I could call it a night.

"How are you guys?" I asked.

"Great," sequined woman hiccupped. "Just danced our asses off."

"Do you know the club?" Polo man asked.

I did know the club, I'd just never been inside. And certainly never danced my butt off. I wished I could. It would sure beat cardio at the gym.

Polo man pulled out a silver flask and took a long drink.

I frowned. I had a rule about not eating in my car but hadn't set one for drinking. Kids frequently got in with Slurpees or Starbucks. I decided to let it go, at least for a little while.

He handed it to the woman, and she took a delicate sip.

"Want some?" he said after taking the flask back from her.

It took me some time to realize he was offering it to me. The driver.

"No, thanks though, I need to stay sober," I said, explaining something he should already know.

Maybe they were more drunk than I'd originally thought.

The man put his hand on the woman's very toned thigh, but she slapped it away.

"Wait till we get home, baby," she cooed.

"You know you're gonna conk out," he said.

I immediately hoped she would win, and he would wait until they got home to have whatever incredible sex beautiful people had.

Still, she tipped her graceful neck and let him plant it with kisses, moving gently towards her ear.

It was the first time I'd ever worried about sex in the back seat of my car while I drove.

"You two OK back there?" I said, thinking it was time

to remind them someone else was in the car. That would be me.

Their lips were locked, so it was impossible for them to answer.

I sighed and flipped the rearview mirror so I couldn't see them. We were almost to their home.

"Wait, honey, hold on," the woman said, sounding scarily like she was gagging.

A second later, she was doing more than gagging. She leaned into his chest and wretched all over his Polo shirt.

"Oh crap," I said, opening my window even though it was a cold night.

"She's OK," he said. "She does this from time to time."

"Maybe don't drink so much?" I suggested.

I pulled into their driveway and mercifully, they immediately got out.

"Here, and sorry," the man said, handing me a bunch of twenties.

"Be careful," I yelled as she weaved towards the house.

I got out to inspect my back seat. Turned out, all her puke had landed on her boyfriend's shirt. That would be quite the laundry job.

Not a bad night after all, I thought, tucking the $100 into my purse. Not bad at all.

22

I WAS HOME ON A THURSDAY NIGHT IN MID-JANUARY HAVING leftovers from Bucket of Spaghetti, wishing I'd saved at least one meatball, when a text came through.

"Hey sexy."

I didn't recognize the number.

"Who's this?"

"Jeremy. Don't tell me you've forgotten."

How could I possibly have forgotten him? I'd met Jeremy the year before in a bar when I was on my kick to go out every weekend, which was definitely getting out of my comfort zone. I'd been at Nick's Tavern for a few hours, been hit on by a drunk 34-year-old, and had a cute guy ask if the seat next to me was taken. When I said it wasn't, he brought over his girlfriend to plunk her adorable ass into the bar stool.

I was just gathering up my winter coat to leave Nick's when an older (and ruder) man and a quieter bearded man came over to me. I knew at first glance that even with the beard, Jeremy was younger than me, but he didn't seem to notice—or care.

He'd friended me on Facebook, then invited me to his rented house on Campbell Lake to meet his adopted grey-hounds, beautiful creatures with incredibly thin, agile legs and alert eyes. Then he'd invited me up to his white birch

Adirondack-style bed and proceeded to take me on a sexual journey I would not forget in this lifetime. But the next day, after I'd sent him a flirty text, he sent a message to me by accident that made it clear I wasn't the only recent visitor to his bed. After that, I deleted his cell in my contact list.

"Hey Jeremy," I chose a neutral answer.

"How've you been?"

"Good, great. You?"

I leaned down to give Lucy a string of spaghetti and watched her play with it like a toy until it was stuck on her nose. She slurped it up.

"Awesome," Jeremy texted. "What's it been, a year since we got together?"

"Eight months." I cursed myself for being so specific. "I can't recall" would have been so much more casual.

"I was wondering if you wanted to visit me."

Did I want to visit him? I wanted to do more than visit. But I had a few questions for him before we made any plans.

"Are you seeing anyone?"

"Nah, I've been too busy with the calendar."

Jeremy was a photographer shooting a landscape calendar while pursuing a career in film. I'd seen his lovely black and white shots of storm clouds and rolling fields.

"You seeing anyone?" he texted.

Ha. I was free and clear and in dire need of physical contact—preferably with a human male.

"No, I was seeing someone for a while, but he didn't give me enough room to make my own decisions."

I cursed myself for over-sharing. Why would Jeremy care?

"That's too bad. So, when can you come see me?"

Was twenty minutes too soon? I ran through my mind the steps I'd need to take, shower, just leave my hair to air dry, throw on leggings and a sweater, drive to the lake and try not to get lost this time.

Wait. I wasn't going to jump. This time I was going to be less available. Or give that appearance anyway.

"I don't know, my schedule is kind of full."

"How about tomorrow night?"

True, spending Friday night alone wasn't my idea of a great time. I thought about Jeremy's adorable smile, as if it was meant just for me.

"Can I text you tomorrow and let you know?" I hoped my reply would make it sound like I actually had other options.

"Sure babe. Talk soon. XO."

Oh God, he texted kisses. Be still my heart.

The next day went by agonizingly slowly at the office. When 4:00 came, I grabbed my coat and darted before the peanut gallery could catch me in another senseless conversation.

"Looks like I'm free tonight," I texted Jeremy when I got in my car.

I drove home and scooped up Lucy for a walk.

"Come anytime Jess," he texted half an hour later. "I can't wait to see that pretty face and sexy ass."

See, already he was starting with the sweet talk. Sexy ass. Ha. Although not as droopy as before I'd joined the gym, it still resembled, well, a 57-year-old woman's butt. Jeremy's body, which I clearly remembered because I had fantasized about it for months, was firm and tan like a lifeguard. And it had been winter when I last saw him, so that was his natural golden skin tone.

I decided 7:30 was the right time to go see him. Any earlier and it might look like I couldn't wait to see him. Which I couldn't. But I would force myself to show a little self-control.

In the shower, I shaved every inch of my body, hoping not to leave behind any razor burn. Lucy was lying by the bathroom door when I opened it, sound asleep, my little guard dog.

Under the circumstances, vampire leggings seemed about right. I scrunched up my hair, then patted it down, then turned my head upside down to fluff it up. Either way it wasn't exactly how I wanted it, so I gave up. I kissed the top of Lucy's head and hurried to my car, trying not to freeze to death.

Last time, it had taken me more than an hour to find Jeremy's house on the twisted road running around the lake. I'd made the embarrassing mistake of parking in his neighbor's driveway, then dropped and almost lost my keys in the dark. This time I was determined to be more graceful.

Google Maps got me to his house ten minutes early, and as I was debating giving it some time before ringing his bell, Jeremy came out on the porch.

"Hey, beautiful."

Clearly, he couldn't see my messed up black eyeliner and flat hair in the dark. He, on the other hand, looked amazing, better than I even remembered. Sweet Jesus. He was beautiful himself.

The greyhounds bounded to the door, then ran away when I tried to pet them.

"They're skittish," he said. Then he pulled me inside and bent his head down to kiss me. So, apparently, we were going to pick up right where we left off.

I peeled off my winter layers: the pom-pom hat, scarf, lined gloves, jacket, and fleece vest underneath it. Jeremy waited patiently.

"I have a bottle of wine upstairs. Is red OK?"

OK? It was fabulous. Last time, he had handed me a Miller Lite tall boy, and I'd spilled it on myself trying to climb into the impossibly oversized living room chair.

Maybe I should have been mildly offended he assumed I would go straight to his bedroom, but why pretend? I wanted to be there as much as he did.

Without a word, I followed him upstairs. The white birch Adirondack-style bed was made up with a new comforter instead of a thin blanket like last time, and thankfully, the Greys stayed downstairs. Last year, the dogs were passed out in the bed and instead of moving them, Jeremy pulled the blanket down on the floor for us to have our way with each other. Worse still, the dogs had woken up and watched us, though at a certain point, I didn't care.

Jeremy poured wine into stemless glasses which thankfully would make it less likely I would spill all over the bed.

"Come here, Jess," he said, sitting on the edge of the bed.

OK. He didn't have to ask twice.

I went to him, and he put his arms around my waist, then leaned down and pulled my leggings down in one smooth move. They balled up by my ankles and I had to balance one hand on his shoulder so he could tug them off. Note to self: next time wear a skirt. He smiled at my navy ankle socks and slid those off next.

Wanting to help, I pulled off my black t-shirt, tangling up my hair in the process.

He traced the lace on my push-up bra, then reached behind me and deftly unhooked it with one hand, tossing it to the floor. Clearly, he'd had a lot of practice with that.

"Pretty lady," he said, stroking the outside of my breasts, purposefully avoiding my hard nipples.

My knees felt wobbly, and I didn't want to stand any longer, so I crawled onto his bed in a way I hoped was catwalk-sexy. Or at least not ungainly.

Jeremy took off his shirt and pulled down his jeans, his erection already showing clearly through his biking briefs. I sat up immediately to look more closely.

"You want some of this?" he asked, running his hand across his hard on.

I did. I just couldn't decide how I wanted it first. Or second. Or third.

"Take it out," he instructed.

I pulled off his briefs in one impatient movement, dropping them to the floor. His penis had a glistening drop at the end, and when I leaned my face forward, Jeremy touched my chin for me to open my mouth and lick it off. Then he gently slid himself into my waiting mouth while I swirled my tongue, making us both moan with pleasure.

I had been with guys who would have taken over at that point, holding my head and thrusting into my mouth, but Jeremy stood completely motionless in front of me, letting me take him at my own pace.

I remembered some instances of marital sex with Adam when I was sucking on him and all I could think of was, when in hell was he going to finish? Towards the end as we distanced ourselves from each other, I just wanted to go to sleep.

Jeremy pulled out of my mouth and pushed me down on the bed firmly. I'd never told him about my submission fantasies; it hadn't really come up in casual conversation last time, but he was clearly in charge, and I loved it.

"You look amazing. Did you wax?"

"No, just shaved. In the shower," I said, as if he might think I shaved on the sidewalk in front of my house.

"I want to see how you taste," he said. "If I remember right, it's like honey."

Oh God, his sweet talk was killing me.

"Someone's wet and ready," he said, pulling my legs apart to look at me.

He lowered his face and used the tip of his tongue to flick my erect clit, flick, flick.

"Yup, honey," he said. "I was right."

He bent his head back down and I squirmed all over the bed as he licked me with the full length of his tongue, using his fingers to hold me open.

I arched my back frantically, pushing against his fingers.

"That's good, put it right into my hand," he said, cupping my pelvis while keeping his fingers moving rhythmically inside me.

I could hear sloppy wet noises and could have been embarrassed at how much I was turned on, but all I cared about was bucking my hips to keep my clit right underneath his tongue.

I nearly went over the edge but wasn't ready for it to end.

"Relax. I'll get you off more than once," he said, reading my mind.

With that, I took a deep breath and threw myself over

the edge, floating as if I had wings, feeling it, holding onto it, not wanting it to ever end. My orgasm came over me in waves and just at its peak, Jeremy leaned down and kissed me.

I shuddered and felt my clit start to retract, but he kept stroking it firmly with the pad of one finger, coaxing it back into life.

"Ready for more?" Jeremy smiled, and not for the first time, I wondered where he'd been when I was in my 40s. But back then, I'd been married with two kids and not feeling exactly sexually adventurous.

Oh, yeah was I ready.

Jeremy stretched out on his back and pulled me over.

"Hop on."

I didn't need a second invitation. Swinging one leg over his hips, I held his erection with one hand and slid down, taking him in all at once, my own moans filling the quiet room.

"That's it, take it," he whispered.

I started by rotating my hips to feel him touch my walls inside, rolling, rolling, then began rocking up and down until he began making noise. He reached up and pulled my hard nipples and I leaned over his face frantically for him to suck. When he began to nibble, I felt myself start going over the edge. Again.

"Hold on, flip over," he said.

Reluctantly releasing his penis, I lay flat on my stomach on the bed. Jeremy pulled at my waist until I was on my hands and knees.

"You want it?" he asked, gently stroking me with the very tip of his erection.

I bucked back against him, trying to take it in, but he backed out of reach.

"Say you want it."

"Umph," was all I could mumble in my immense frustration.

"What was that?"

"Yes. I want it. Please."

"Very nice," he said, slowly pushing inside me.

Lots of women talk about the perfect fit, just the right length and width, but I'm telling you, when Jeremy slid into me, it was so snug I could barely move. Good thing I didn't have to. He was going to do all the work.

"You feel so good clamped around me," he said. "Can you feel it?"

Oh God could I feel it.

Then he bent his body over mine to reach around and play with my nipples as he pumped and nipped gently at my neck.

"Are you ready?" he asked, face still buried in my neck.

"Oh yes."

I can't say it was a simultaneous orgasm, if that even existed, but within seconds we went crashing over the edge, and I felt myself soaring, lost in the momentum, not knowing or caring where his body ended or mine began.

I flopped down on the bed face first, not caring if I had a sweaty forehead.

Jeremy got up and went into the bathroom to bring out a washcloth for the dribble down my thighs.

"You're amazing," he said, lying down next to me.

"No, you are."

"Do you want to spend the night?" he asked lazily, not

bothering to pull the sheet up over his legs. "I'll give you some more sex when we wake up."

Holy shit that was tempting, and I knew I'd be ready in a few hours for more of his body, but I had a little dog waiting for me at home, and besides, it would look more casual if I didn't stay.

Casual was all we would ever be. I knew that this time around.

"I gotta hit the gym early," I lied. I would never be a morning gym person. I could barely drag myself there in the afternoon.

"OK, next time," he said.

Would there be a next time? I had no answer, but in the lightness of my afterglow, I didn't care, because it had been a long time since I'd taken advantage of being a single woman, making my own choices and doing whatever the hell I pleased.

23

It was mid-January and winter was holding upstate New York in its icy grip.

My 10-year-old winter jacket, an old style down-filled thing, had seen better days. The down had lost its puffiness. In fact, the whole thing was deflated. I thought I heard it hissing as it lost air.

"You need DownTech, Mombo," Madd texted me after listening to me complain about the possibility of getting frostbite.

The following Saturday, I put on my useless old jacket and headed to the sporting goods store to find something warm that wouldn't cost me a week's pay, because I had gone overboard at Christmas (as usual).

I got sidetracked by cute fleece-lined navy blue knit hats with huge pom-poms on the top. There were even matching mittens. Then I wondered, when, exactly, could adults actually wear mittens? Not for driving. Maybe a spontaneous snowball fight? Would that even be fun? Somehow snow always ended up down someone's neck and there was possibly nothing worse in the world.

I remembered my "waterproof" mittens getting soaked in January snow as my sister and I played outside. Sometimes our mother would line them with plastic bread bags to try to keep our hands dry, but one way or another, our fingers would tingle, then go completely numb. Especially the thumb, poor thing, stuck out on its own away from the rest of the fingers.

We had small red shovels that we used to dig holes in the enormous snowbanks left by the plows at the end of the driveway. We dug tunnels with only one way in and out, then huddled in them to spy on the boys that lived across the street. That would be, I would say, the start of my claustrophobia.

If Madison and Ian had ever, in a million years, sat in a tunnel with heavy wet snow on the top, much less with the plow still making rounds and dumping more snow on the banks, I would have run to them screaming while dialing 911.

Things were different today. Clearly, children weren't so valued in the '70s.

I knew I didn't need another hat and I had no use for mittens, cute as they were, so I went to the ski section of the store. There were dozens of types of jackets, all so flimsy I found it incredible they could keep me warm. But the colors! Brilliant yellow, lime green, hot pink. I took a violet jacket off its hanger and put it on, then went looking for a mirror. It felt kind of snug.

"Excuse me, Miss, is this your purse?"

Holy crap, I had done it again. I had hooked my bag on the display rack then started walking away.

Embarrassed, I turned around and saw a man holding my purse, concern written all over his handsome face. He had sandy colored hair, looked about my age, and the kind of skin that looked tan all year through, and was wearing, of course, a DownTech jacket.

I was suddenly hot from wearing the jacket indoors and also from facing the purse-finder.

"Thank you," I said, taking my purse. "And thank you for calling me Miss."

"What do people usually call you? Sir?" The man's eyes crinkled adorably when he smiled. He had that little cleft in his chin like George Clooney. His teeth were so white they seemed to sparkle under the fluorescent lights in the store.

"Jess, actually," I said, struggling to get out of the damn too-small jacket I was trying on.

"Hi Jess, I'm Eric," he said, helping me take the jacket off. "I like it."

"Excuse me?"

"The jacket. It suits you. Will keep you warm on the slopes."

The slopes? Oh, slopes. Well of course he thought I skied. I was, after all, in the ski section.

I glanced at his left hand. No wedding ring!

"Which mountains do you ski?"

My mouth went dry, and I tried desperately to think of a local ski resort, but all I could come up with was Space Mountain, the ride in Disney World, and I certainly couldn't say that.

"I don't ski, actually," I said reluctantly.

"Too bad," Eric said, looking like he meant it. "What do you like to do during winter?"

Make microwave s'mores? Snuggle Lucy? Cry over the kids' old school pictures in photo albums? I realized I had absolutely nothing to contribute to the conversation about winter sports.

I looked quickly around and saw a display of

cross-country skis and snowshoes. I chose the lesser of the two evils.

"Snowshoe!" I said triumphantly. "I snowshoe!"

OK, so I hadn't ever actually clamped wide, netted snowshoes on my feet to walk on top of snow, but how hard could it be? It was walking.

"Awesome," Eric said. "Me too. I'm new to the area, but I hear there are some great trails in Ashton Park. Ever go there?"

"Sure, all the time. I mean, not every weekend, but frequently," I said. Technically, I did drive through the park on the way to Nadine's house.

"I've been looking for someone that snowshoes. Do you wanna go sometime?"

"To the park?"

"Yes. To snowshoe," Eric said patiently. "The weather has been perfect this month."

Perfect? I'd been freezing my ass off. Despite that fact, I couldn't bear to turn down an offer from cute Eric.

"Of course!"

I knew I sounded giddy. It was a combination of attraction to Eric and utter panic at the idea of snowshoeing, being that I was not exactly naturally graceful.

"Great," he said, pulling his phone out of his delightfully fitted jeans. "What's your number?"

I looked over at the snowshoes on display while giving him my cell number. How hard could it be?

24

"WELL, FOR STARTERS, YOU WILL NEED SNOWSHOES," EDDIE said patiently.

I had gone straight to Eddie's house after leaving the store to tell him my web of lies.

"And a jacket," I lamented.

"You didn't even get the jacket?" Eddie asked incredulously.

"No—I was too upset about the fact that I had to learn how to snowshoe like, immediately. I forgot all about the jacket!"

Eddie rubbed his eyes.

"OK, when is this snow play date?"

"I don't even know! I just need to be ready! He could call anytime."

"Don't start to panic. Maybe you'll get lucky, and the snow will start to melt."

I wasn't lucky. Snow fell steadily that night, leaving everything looking pretty and fresh by morning.

It was without a doubt perfect snowshoe weather.

So, I dragged Eddie back to the store and grabbed the purple jacket off the rack and tried it on again.

Eddie browsed the snowshoe display.

"Here," he said, bringing over a pretty light blue pair that still looked ominously large. "These support up to 200 pounds."

"Thank you for that. I don't think I'm quite that heavy. Not yet at least."

"Well, you might be carrying a backpack," he said.

"Backpack? Where are I am going to go that would require a backpack? The forest?" I was starting to sweat in the DownTech jacket.

Then I sat glumly down on a small bench to try them on.

"How do you tell the right one from the left? They look identical!" I said, trying to control my growing panic. "And how the hell do you walk in them? They're ginormous!"

"You don't really walk, you sort of—stomp," Eddie said, kneeling down to strap them onto my feet.

"Stomp? Like Bigfoot?"

"Well, try to be lighter on your feet," he said. "The snow-shoes keep you from sinking in too deep. They distribute your weight evenly."

He thought about it for a minute.

"Actually, you need to glide on the top layer of powder snow."

"Oh sure, glide. That sounds easy."

Eddie held out his hand to help me stand up. No, it was more like he hauled me up.

They didn't seem that bad. They were so oversized, I felt steady in them, and for a moment thought I wasn't in danger of keeling over.

Then I took my first step. It was more of a waddle.

"No, don't shuffle," Eddie said. "You need to put one foot ahead of the other. Just walk normally."

I had two-foot-long metal frames clamped onto my

winter boots. Just walk normally?

"How do you know so much about this?" I asked Eddie with obvious irritation in my voice.

"Don and I snowshoed at Acadia National Park that one winter in Maine," he said, smiling at the memory.

"Oh yeah I remember. The poles might help," I said, looking around. "Where are the poles?"

"Yeah, let's get you some poles," he said, looking more enthused. "They should make it easier to balance."

Eddie went over to the rows of 8-foot poles.

A store clerk with a worried look on his face approached me.

"I'm sorry, but you can't use the snowshoes inside," he said. "You have to sit down to try them on. They dig up the carpet."

Well, apparently, I would not be learning to snowshoe in the sporting goods store.

$238 later, I realized I would have to plod around in the snow every weekend until the end of winter to justify the purchase. It was the equivalent of at least four days of Uber driving.

25

"I'm in a creative slump," Nadine texted me that Wednesday as I was leaving work.

"Nonsense. You're creative as hell."

Nadine was a freelance graphic designer and had an incredible portfolio. There was the ant carrying a tiny suitcase for a pest control company. The cartoon hot dog with absolutely no phallic connotations for the local burger and hot dog stand. A cute guy wielding a wrench for Stan the Man's Plumbing.

"Can I come over and bounce some non-ideas off you?"

"Wine or tea?"

"Tea, sadly."

Nadine came with her laptop and settled in at the kitchen table. I carried over flowered mugs of our favorite green tea.

"So, what are we working on?" I asked.

"A vacuum sales store. They do repairs too," Nadine sighed. "Got anything chocolate?"

"Ice cream, Yodels, or Mallo-Puffs?"

"Let's do the Yodels."

I got up and pulled out the box of chocolate-covered cakes rolled up with cream filling and set four on plates. Hey, it was probably going to be a long night.

We sat in silence and chewed.

"God I love these," she said.

"I know, right? These and Ring-Dings were the highlight of my childhood." "They take the cake," Nadine said, smiling.

"See? You're already being creative!"

Nadine booted up her Mac.

"The place has the most boring name in the world: Meredia Town Vacuum Sales."

"Oh, I know that place. They're supposed to have good prices on repairs. You can get your filters cleaned for like twelve bucks."

"Well, cheap filter cleaning isn't exactly a snazzy selling point. I need a logo and tagline."

"I suppose 'suck it up' isn't appropriate?"

"Not appropriate, no, but points for humor on that one."

We sat in silence to mull it over.

Lucy suddenly rushed the front door, barking in the way that signaled an Amazon package had been delivered to the front porch.

I got up and brought in the small box.

"OK, what'd you buy this time? Rice steamer? Monogrammed hand towels? Gym socks? Magnetic eyelashes?"

"You're close," I answered, opening the box. "Gleaming highlighter. It's supposed to contour the face, and, you know, diffuse light to take attention off wrinkles or enlarged pores. Make you gleam, basically."

"You don't have any wrinkles, babe."

"Thank you. But you haven't seen how I look with a magnifying mirror."

Nadine took the highlighter and looked at the back at

the package.

"Hmm. I don't see instructions how to use it."

"Great. I have no idea what part of my face to highlight. Not my nose or chin, obviously."

"Let's give it a try. Come on," Nadine got up and went into the bathroom.

I was certain under the room's lighting she could see my dry lines and large pores.

She took out the tiny round brush, dredged it in the powder and patted it under my cheekbones—if I had them—and across my jawline. Then she stood back to admire her work.

"Well, you are gleaming."

I looked in the mirror. The highlighter was so shiny it nearly glittered, and although it looked OK on my cheeks, my jaw was shimmering, not in a flattering way.

"What? All you need is some eyeliner and maybe lipstick to top it off."

"Yes, because I want to be all dolled-up for a night at home."

I took a Kleenex and smudged the highlighter on my cheeks. It looked better when it was transparent, but I guess invisibility wasn't the idea behind it.

"Back to work?"

"So much for the procrastination," she said, examining her eyebrows in the mirror. "Man, why didn't you tell me I needed threading?"

"Because your brows look fine."

"Are we overly concerned with our appearances?"

I turned out the light and went back to the kitchen.

"That's what it means to be over fifty."

"Agreed."

We stepped over a dozing dog and settled back down at the table, returning to our original task.

"So sucking isn't a good reference. What comes to mind about vacuums? They go zoom? Vroom?" Nadine said.

"That's it! Vroom Vacuum Repairs!"

"It does have a ring to it."

"How about this? 'You don't need a broom. You just need vroom.'"

"Bam!" she said, holding up her hand for a high-five. "And we didn't need wine to come up with that!"

"Well, the Yodel sugar rush did help."

Nadine typed into her Mac enthusiastically.

"Done. I'll do the graphics tomorrow."

She closed her laptop.

"So, tell me about this snowshoe guy, he must be in great shape."

"Oh God," I said, twisting the end of my ponytail. "He looks like a seasoned member of the U.S. winter Olympic team."

"Well, if you ask me, sounds like a fun date."

"If you call tripping over your feet fun. Have you ever seen the size of snowshoes?"

"They have to be big to distribute your weight in the snow," she said reasonably.

"Basically, I am hoping for the snow to all melt overnight, making it impossible to go out."

"But you already bought the gear, silly."

"I kept the receipt," I said, proud of being so practical.

I changed the subject. "How's Tristan?"

Nadine smiled the way she always did when she talked about her son.

"He's great. Just made the golf team."

"He's a nice kid," I said. "You and Hunter did an awesome job raising him."

"Thanks," she said, sounding a bit sad. "At least we did one thing right."

"Have you seen Hunter lately?"

"Yeah, from the living room window. He drops Tristan off on the driveway."

"Maybe go out and meet them at the car sometime."

Nadine sighed. "We'd just start up again, and I don't want to argue with him anymore. We bickered constantly. If I said the sky was blue, he'd say it was green. We even fought over whose turn it was to grocery shop. I didn't want Tristan to think that's how a marriage should be."

I understood completely. When Adam had withdrawn, I tried my hardest to fill in the gap and be super parent to the kids. After he left, the three of us formed a new family unit. I worried constantly I wasn't doing enough as a single parent, even though I tried my hardest. We hadn't been a happy couple with two kids as I had always pictured it would be with Adam. That was a loss I would always mourn.

Ian had stayed in touch with Adam (and tried unsuccessfully to do the same with Madison, who remained angry at his departure) and went to meet him when Adam camped anywhere across New York State. I knew that was the best thing for Ian, to still have his father involved in his life. I knew it, but someplace deep down, I hadn't cleared out my anger at Adam for leaving us.

"Come on," Nadine said, standing up. "Let's see those honking big snowshoes."

26

IT WAS A GOOD THING I WAS PREPARED WITH SNOW GEAR, because Eric texted the following Saturday asking me to meet at Ashton Park. The sun was out, and it looked like a perfect snowshoeing day. Whatever that meant.

I drove to the park, found a good spot, parked, and opened my hatch to take out the snowshoes. The cleats on the bottom of one had gotten jammed into the other somehow on the ride over. As I struggled to separate them, Eric appeared out of nowhere.

"Jess! Glad you could make it."

I yanked the snowshoes apart and turned around to see Eric, who was cuter than I remembered. He was dressed in layers: turtleneck, fleece jacket and a navy ski vest over the top. I began to sweat in my new jacket again. Layers, why hadn't I thought of dressing in layers?

Eric put his snowshoes on the ground and stepped into them without any apparent effort, snapping them on and flexing his feet.

I sat in the hatch of my car and attempted to do the same. But my heavy winter boots didn't slide into the base. They didn't seem to fit.

Goddamn Eddie, had he picked out a pair that was too small for me? Did they even come in foot sizes?

"Here, let me loosen the clamps," Eric said, bending

down to adjust them. "You've got the straps too tight."

"Oh yeah, I was wearing different boots last time I used them," I said, as if I even had another pair of sturdy winter boots.

And then it was time to stand up. I took my poles out and used them for balance, sliding my butt out of the car in what I hoped was one smooth move.

"OK, let's head this way," Eric said cheerfully, using his ski pole to point to a path marker nearby.

"Great! Let's go," I said, trying to sound equally cheerful.

With that, Eric strode off in a way I could only classify as effortless.

I clomped behind him, somehow making it to the path.

Eddie had said keep my steps light to stay on top of the powdered layer of snow. Only problem was, the snow was packed down on the trial and instead of powder, there were patches of ice on the surface.

"Careful on the ice," Eric called back to me.

He was skimming along, already hitting his stride.

I dug my poles into the surface of the snow and moved ahead, barely taking my feet off the ground.

There was no stride for me. It was a shuffle.

"You OK?" Eric said from a good twenty feet down the path.

"I'm good! You go on ahead and I'll catch up."

"You sure?"

"Yeah, sure," I said, trying to sound casual and not let the desperation show on my face.

With that, he went around a curve in the path and was out of sight.

I considered unsnapping the snowshoes and walking

the rest of the way, at least until I was back in Eric's line of sight.

Instead, I continued my slow shuffle along the path. The trees in the park had snowy branches, the sun was out, and the sky was bright blue, but I kept my head down to be on the lookout for ice.

The poles were a godsend. More than a few times, I felt myself start to fall sideways, which I felt certain would result in a broken ankle, but managed to prop myself back up.

"Coming through," a woman said from behind me.

I didn't want to get off the path into the snowbank, so I just leaned myself to one side with my feet planted in the same spot. Fortunately, she was light on her feet and skipped by without coming into contact with me. She had silver-gray hair and had wisely dressed in layers.

A good half-hour later, I shuffled to the end of the trail, where Eric was sitting on a wooden bench waiting for me, looking a bit worried. His snowshoes were leaning on the edge of the bench, and I realized with utter joy he wasn't going to suggest we try out another path.

"You OK?"

"Yeah," I said, more than a little out of breath. "Sorry."

"No problem," he said. "Helluva lot of ice out there today, and the snow was really packed down."

"Sure was!" I said, squeezing in next to him on the bench.

I immediately bent down and unstrapped my boots from the snowshoes. All my toes felt cramped, as if they'd been holding on for dear life inside my boots.

"Walk you back to your car?"

"Thanks," I said, struggling to get my poles tucked under my arm.

When we got to my car, Eric pulled me into a big hug. An official friendly but not romantic goodbye.

I didn't hear from Eric again, but whenever there was a fresh snowfall, I got out the snowshoes and clomped around my backyard, finally finding my stride.

27

THE TIME HAD COME TO FIND SOMETHING TO DO FOR FITNESS other than the stationary bike and treadmill where I sweated my ass off but never seemed to lose an ounce.

The next day at the Y, I stopped at the front desk to pick up a flyer of the free classes they offered at the gym.

Spinning. Nope. Step. Pass. Salsa dancing. Really?

I wanted something that didn't involve a lot of sweating in a room full of younger people or anything you needed a dance partner for.

Then I saw it: water aerobics!

It was Saturdays and Sundays at 10 a.m., so it had the extra benefit of not having to get up early on weekends.

Then, with a sinking heart, I realized it would require getting into a swimsuit. I could not remember the last time I'd worn one. Maybe at the town pool when Adam was still around and the kids were young?

That night, I dug through the chest of drawers where I crammed my "thin" clothes. I couldn't bear to get rid of them, on the off chance I'd ever be a size 10 again. Near the bottom of a pile of shorts, I found the swimsuit that I had, in fact, worn to the town pool more than a decade before.

It was a one-piece with black on the bottom and horizontal red stripes on the top. The idea was to draw the eye upwards to the cleavage and disguise your stomach by some kind of illusion, magic really.

Reluctantly, I got undressed and pulled on the suit, then sucked in my gut and looked in the full-length mirror.

It was ridiculous, really, that the suit was supposed to have a slimming front panel and the eye would be drawn away from the lower half of your body. Neither were true.

But the real problem was my thighs. The suit was tight around the openings for the legs, causing serious bulging.

Goddamn stationary bike! How could my legs still be so chunky?

Then I thought about the late-night nachos with the kids, the cocktails with Nadine, the pancakes-for-supper with Eddie. I tried to forget about the many buckets of spaghetti.

Clearly, I wasn't going to shrink before the water aerobics class, but wasn't that the goal anyway? To tone up?

Maybe I could get a cute cover-up and wait until I was at the very edge of the pool to take it off. I could slide into the water before anyone saw my thighs. Or better yet, bring a towel to tie casually around my waist as if I had nothing to hide! Then toss it on the side of the pool as I jumped in. Maybe the splash would distract people.

I sighed, stripped off the suit and put on pajamas. Then I went on Amazon to look for an old lady swim skirt, the ruffled kind that went partway down your thighs and looked somewhat jaunty. Thankfully, there would be no breeze in the indoor pool to lift the skirt from behind and flash my untoned ass.

I found a black one that didn't scream "old lady," ordered a size 12, then added a size 14, in case they ran small. Or in case I ran large, which I knew I did.

The package arrived a couple days later and, thankfully, I was alone and didn't have to open it in the kitchen with an audience.

I put on my old suit, then stepped into the swim skirt. Forget the size 12. It had the flounce, yes, but the waistband was tight, and it barely covered my upper legs. But when I tried on the size 14, it successfully covered my thighs.

Phew. I would not have to resort to the towel-splash technique. That was an enormous relief.

That Saturday morning, I packed my gym bag with an old bath towel and headed to the Y.

The locker room was mostly empty, but I still went into a changing room and pulled the curtain shut.

I glanced down at my white legs and wondered why in hell I hadn't thought to use some self-tanning lotion for a few days. I could have ordered it on Amazon and had a slight tint by now, except the chlorine would probably wash the color away and defeat the purpose. Oh well.

I gave up trying to tie the towel around my waist and just slung it over my shoulders and went into the pool area.

It was almost humid in the room, which I took as a sign the pool would be well-heated, maybe like bath water. There were kids and their mothers splashing around in the shallow end and I felt my heart wrench, remembering the days when the kids and I played at the town pool. Some of the children were using paddle boards and learning to swim while their mothers cheered them on.

The lifeguards were bored-looking teenagers, all of whom were ridiculously tan for winter, without even a hint of orange color. I wondered what brand of self-tanner they were using.

Someone blew a whistle, and a line of women went to the other side of the pool where the water got as deep as 9 feet.

"OK ladies, let's get started. Use the stairs to get into the water," the woman with the whistle said.

She was a remarkably fit older woman with gray hair that almost looked lilac.

There were 10 of us in the class, and some of my fellow students were wearing bathing caps. I hadn't seen those in years and then wondered if we would be putting our heads under water. Wasn't this mostly a standing-in-the-water exercise class? I'd just had my roots done and my hair was finally growing out. The wet look would not be flattering.

I followed the other women to the stairs leading down to the water. Most looked my age or older; all of us had one-piece, stomach-slimming swimsuits and goosebumps all over our bodies.

I went down the last step, and immediately my foot went numb. The water was absolutely freezing. I hoped there would be a lot of jumping around during the class, because otherwise I was going to die of hypothermia.

"I'm Tildy," the instructor said. "Ladies, please form a line and make sure your shoulders are above the water level."

The ten of us groaned in tandem as we went into the water until we were chest-deep, moving our arms around to try and warm up.

"OK girls, let's get started," Tildy said. She was cheerful because she was allowed to stay out of the cold water and enjoy the balmy humidity in the room.

"Jumping Jacks," she said. "Let's do a set of twenty."

We all groaned again, then started trying to do the exercise.

I'd never taken an aerobics class, though 1 had faithfully done the Jane Fonda workout tape with Maddy when she was a teenager. But I quickly found that moving your arms and legs under water took a lot of energy that 1 didn't have because 1 had skipped breakfast in hopes my stomach would look flatter.

There was a lot of splashing, and 1 could see why the others were wisely wearing swim caps. But theirs were puckered and had flowers on them. If 1 got one, it would have to be something sleek like they used in the Olympics. Or would that kind flatten my hair more?

"Jog in place!" Tildy shouted over the noise of the kids in the other side of the pool.

She was starting to sound like a drill sergeant. Maybe for the Navy, since we were in the water.

Dutifully, we jogged in the water. On the plus side, my limbs were starting to warm up. However, my legs quickly tired out in a way 1 knew would cause lots of muscle pain the next day, maybe even requiring Tylenol.

Well, as Jane Fonda had said, "No pain, no gain."

"Hold your arms out now and twist at the waist. Let's do two sets of twenty!" Tildy hollered.

Was there no floating in water aerobics? Was it all this strenuous?

We twisted. Then we held on to the side of the pool for scissor kicks. I lost track of the number of sets we were doing, but it seemed like we'd been in the water at least 45 minutes, and the class was only supposed to be a half-hour.

"OK girls, let's cool down," Tildy said at last.

Cool down? In a freezing cold pool? I wanted to warm up for god's sake.

Blessedly, the cool down was two sets of neck rotations and shoulder lifting. That I could do.

"You will see a real difference if you practice at home," Tildy said as we half-swam, half-walked towards the stairs to get the hell out.

What? Maybe fill the tub and march in the ankle-deep water?

"I mean, the jumping jacks and jogging in place," she clarified. "It's a great cardio workout."

I was stripped of all my confidence, despite my new bathing skirt, as I got out of the pool. My legs were puckered from the cold, and if possible, even more ghostly white than when I'd gotten to class. Did the chlorine bleach my skin? I didn't care anymore.

I pulled my bath towel off the hook at the edge of the pool and tried unsuccessfully to tie it around my hips. Note to self: next time, bring a jumbo towel.

We walked, shivering, back to the locker room, where I wondered if it would be all right to use one of the hair dryers to thaw my legs.

One of the smart women who'd worn a bathing cap pulled it off, fluffed her hair briefly, and voila! She looked like she walked out of a salon.

I looked in the mirror over the sink. Yup, I'd forgotten to take off my make-up, or for that matter bring anything to wash my face and start all over. It was immediately obvious that my black mascara was not, in fact, waterproof.

And don't even get me started about my wet hair.

28

ONE AFTERNOON IN FEBRUARY, THERE WAS A BRIEF REPRIEVE from winter, and we crossed our fingers for an early spring. I was grateful the slush on the roads had melted, making it less stressful to drive.

I clicked on my Uber app, and what do you know, my first passenger of the day was a clown. I picked up a clown. A flat out, red-nosed, oversized shoe-wearing, wildly pattern-jacketed clown.

"Hi missy," he said, ducking his head to get in the back seat without smushing his clown hat.

"How are you?" I asked, smiling in the rearview mirror and starting to drive.

"Heading to a party," he said. I thought he was smiling back, but with the broadly painted smile, I couldn't tell.

"Kids?"

"Oh no," the clown said. "It's for a fifty-year-old."

Well, that's different, I thought. A clown for the middle-aged.

"I have my own specialties," he said.

"Is   that   right?"

"I'll show you," the clown said.

He pulled out a handful of colored balloons and started blowing up a pink one. It was a long balloon that looked like a full-grown squash when he was done. Then he blew up two small round brown balloons and tied them to the base of the squash.

"How's that for ya?" he said, clearly pleased with himself.

"Huh," I said. "What is it, a sword?"

"It's a dick," he corrected me. "These two on bottom are hairy brown balls."

I knew I would never look at a balloon the same way again.

"Wanna see some tits? You tie the ends in the middle to look like nipples."

"That's OK, I wouldn't want you to waste balloons."

The clown fluffed his curly yellow wig.

"What else do you do; I mean besides the balloons?" I was too curious for my own good.

"Oh, you know, tricks with X-rated playing cards," he said. "Wanna watch me make one appear out of thin air?"

Actually, I did want to see that, but I had to concentrate on driving.

"I also have a bean bag toss with penis-shaped bean bags tossed into vagina holes."

OK, clearly there was a theme here. I'd thrown Eddie a 60th birthday with gag gifts that seemed pretty tame compared to the kinky clown.

We pulled up to a house crowded with cars.

"Looks like a good turnout," the clown said eagerly. "Hey, here's my card if you ever want some unique entertainment."

His business card featured a picture of the balloon boobs. He was right, the knots looked like nipples.

29

"COME FOR WINE AROUND SIX?" NADINE TEXTED ONE AFTER-noon the end of February when I was cursing at the Excel spreadsheet open on my computer.

Ian had helped me learn the basics, but I was still utterly frustrated when it came to merging columns.

I took my phone into the bathroom and stood near the sink. I knew it was ridiculous to hide when texting, but Joe glared at me whenever I took my cell out.

"Taking a break?" he would ask, no doubt thinking he was funny.

"Absolutely." I texted her back. "Want me to bring a bottle?"

"Nope. I'm all set."

"I'll be there at six. Can't wait!"

"See you later. I'm working on an ad campaign for a car-pet company. Wish me luck on this one."

Nadine's house was contemporary with a dramatically angled roof and floor to ceiling windows. I absolutely loved it.

She threw open the door before I even had a chance to knock.

Dustin, her little pug, came running over to greet me. I bent down to scratch his ears.

"Let her come in, Dusty," Nadine said.

Her living room had a cathedral ceiling and hardwood floors. The layout was an open concept with the dining area blending right into the kitchen. A bottle of wine and three glasses sat at the long marble island with silver stools.

"Am I finally going to meet Hunter?"

"How did you know?" Nadine said incredulously.

"Come on, who could the third glass of wine be for? Tristan? Dusty?"

"Tristan is off to a school golf tournament overnight."

"Aha," I said, wishing I'd worn a better outfit than my standard skirt and cardigan. "When is Hunter coming over?"

"Not till 7:30."

I sniffed the air. "I don't smell anything cooking,"

"I didn't want to ruin the night with my cooking!"

I smiled. Nadine and I had many similarities. Among them, a lack of cooking skill. Her favorite was takeout Thai, while the kids, Eddie, and I usually got the good old Bucket of Spaghetti. It was far less refined, but nothing could be better than those meatballs.

"He's taking you out then?"

"Yes," she said, filling our glasses with wine. "I need you to help me pick something out to wear."

"Sure, but tell me first how this happened."

Nadine blushed prettily.

"We have this family tradition, it's silly really, where we make a birthday cake then decorate it with as much candy as we can get our hands on."

"That doesn't sound silly," I said, picturing a cake covered with dark chocolate Hershey's kisses and immediately becoming hungry.

"Anyway, last weekend was Tristan's birthday, and I

made his favorite dinner—beef stroganoff—and then the doorbell rang," she said, smiling radiantly. "It was Hunter, with this enormous cake, covered in more candy than I can even describe. A little house made of Kit-Kats with a licorice fence, a Snicker's sidewalk, Sour Patch kids in the doorway."

"He made it himself?" I was thrilled for my friend.

"Yup, even the cake, which was completely lopsided. The candy almost slid off."

"That's the sweetest thing I've heard in a long time. So, I'm assuming he came in?"

"He did and didn't leave till the next morning."

"Excellent!"

"We both said we missed each other, and it was hard to even remember the things we used to fight about. Neither of us had any interest in seeing anyone else. We hadn't moved on. It was like our life was just put on pause."

We clinked our wine glasses together in a toast.

I enjoyed living vicariously through Nadine's wildly romantic story.

"Come on," Nadine said, pulling at my arm. "Bring your glass."

Dustin followed us up the wide staircase to her bedroom. Nadine disappeared inside the walk-in closet. I sat down on the small beige sofa with her dog, not for the first time feeling a twinge of envy for her home and its furnishings. She and Hunter had a glorious modern house. He had designed it himself and it also clearly showed Nadine's creative flair.

"OK, so of course I want to look young," Nadine called from inside the closet.

"That goes without saying."

She came out wearing high-waisted flared black trousers and a white blouse with a tuxedo vest.

"Wait, look at the shoes too."

Nadine pulled up a pant leg to show black platform heels.

"You look fantastic," I said, admiring her. She had lost about ten pounds since her split with Hunter. Me, I piled on several pounds when my marriages had ended.

"Is it too business-like?"

"Hmm. Maybe a little with the button-down top. What else do you have?"

Nadine modeled clothes for nearly an hour. Cute Levi's with holes at the knees I suspected she had worn in college. A belted pinstriped jumpsuit that made her waist look tiny, but we agreed would make it difficult to pee. A short, pleated plaid skirt with a blue cashmere turtleneck.

At last, she sashayed out of the closet wearing a black satin blouse with a burgundy peplum skirt and gave a little twirl. The blouse tied at the neck and had the perfect combination of sweet and sexy.

"That's it, hands down," I said, getting up to straighten the bow. "How about shoes?"

"Black pumps?"

"Perfect."

Nadine and I didn't hoard shoes; another thing we had in common. OK, I had a large collection of Converse and Vans sneakers. Nadine had more variety, and tended towards boots, but neither of us had accumulated more than a dozen pairs.

After she slipped on the heels, Nadine went into the bathroom to put on more eyeliner and mascara.

Then we heard a man's voice at the front door.

"Dina?"

"Oh my god, he's early," Nadine said, turning pink again. "Can you go down and tell him I'm still getting ready please?"

I grabbed my empty wine glass. I was more than happy to go downstairs and meet Hunter.

He was athletic, with blonde hair and a neatly trimmed goatee. He was wearing a golf shirt and dark blue dress pants.

I liked him immediately.

"Jessica?"

"Guilty as charged," I said, wondering why I always sounded so silly when I was excited.

We shook hands and headed toward the kitchen.

"Dina still deciding what to wear?" Hunter asked, chuckling.

"Sounds like you know her well. But we did make progress and settle on an outfit. She'll be right down."

"I've heard a lot about you," I said, filling the wine glasses.

"All good, I hope."

Nadine had told me about the many good years—and the recent bad year— of their marriage. It had been clear Tristan was their top priority, and like Adam and me, they had put each other second, believing they would just pick up where they left off after Tristan was a teen. It wasn't that simple, they had discovered. Without shared time as a couple, they had grown apart.

"Of course. And Tristan's a great kid. You must be proud of him."

Hunter was beaming.

"I can remember when I first took him out on the course with his little plastic set of golf clubs. He graduated to the real thing fast. Even then he had a natural drive. Me, I'd be chipping away in the rough and he'd be out on the green waiting for me."

We both laughed.

Nadine came around the corner into the kitchen smiling at both of us.

"Hi honey," she said to Hunter.

"Hi baby," he replied.

"So, you met Jess?"

"Sure did. You're right, she's a sweetheart."

It was my turn to blush.

"Damn, it's time to walk Dusty," Nadine said.

"You two get going. I'll walk him and lock up when I leave."

"Thanks," Nadine said, giving me a brief hug and leaving me smelling like her lily perfume.

I could hear them laughing outside the door and down to the driveway.

Dustin was staring up at me from the floor.

"Your parents are back together," I told him as I hooked on his leash. "And all is right with the world."

30

It was March 11, the anniversary of the day we lost Penny. It was still hard to believe she was gone. I saw her everywhere. I saw her nosing around the garden, leaping around in the backyard, waiting for me by the front door every time I went out. I still teared up and my throat closed up every time I thought about her.

She was my girl.

Lucy was a little scrapper, a tomboy puppy who loved to run and chase birds and get her paws dirty. Penny had been angelic and regal. She always tilted her head and studied us closely when we were talking as if she had all the answers. I think she did.

I still couldn't make any sense of her death. Losing her felt like the earth had spun out of orbit and everything was turned sideways. I had leaned hard into my grief. I had cried for five weeks straight everywhere I went: in the grocery store picking out cantaloupe, washing my hands at work, driving, going to sleep.

She was in the wind now, the sun and the rain and the daffodils that sprouted even when it was still cold out.

We had planted a cherry blossom tree on the side of our yard and placed the beautiful mahogany box with her ashes inside the deep hole we'd dug to place the tree. The flowers had bloomed magnificently last spring. I knew it was her.

I had the necklace with a tiny lock of her brown hair in the locket around my neck, a gift from Ian and Maddie. I never took it off.

But as the date came around, I wanted something more permanent to show my love for Penny. I thought long and hard, and I came up with something that seemed fitting. I didn't tell the kids or Eddie or Nadine.

I just did it.

31

"YOU HAVE AN APPOINTMENT?" ASKED THE MAN BEHIND THE case displaying nipple rings, navel barbells and gauges so big you could almost stick your hand through.

"Ah, no, I'm sorry, I don't," I said trying not to look at the array of rings that said "frenulum."

"Eh, we're kinda quiet, we can get you in. You know what you want?"

I did know. I just wanted to stall before they took me back for my tattoo.

"Take a look through them books and see," he pointed to a table with binders that reminded me of the women's magazines set out in waiting rooms at the hair salon.

I sat down on the pleather couch which stuck to the back of my legs. I cursed my choice of a jean skirt.

The pages were filled with scary graphic designs: daggers through hearts, bones in various stages of decay, skulls with slithering snakes, fire-breathing dragons, tribal symbols, and Harley logos. I flipped through quickly. Maybe I'd picked up the book for men's tats, and there was a women's version?

A tall woman wearing combat boots was picking something out from the display case. I didn't want to interrupt to ask for a different binder.

Finally, I found a page of roses. Some had thorns, but I

was relieved they could do non-threatening designs.

"I'm looking for a dog paw with a heart around it," I said to the man, more confidently than I felt.

"Dog paw, yeah, we can do that."

HBased on the size of his biceps, he looked like he would have a heavy hand and I hoped he wouldn't be inking me.

He ushered me through a curtain into a large room with exam tables and I was glad I would be able to recline.

"How ya doin'?" asked a young woman with blue hair. "I'm Lola."

"Good, fine," I said. "A little nervous."

"This your first time?" Lola raised a deeply outlined eyebrow.

"She wants the doggie," the man said before he disappeared back through the curtain.

"The paw and heart? Nice. Have you thought about colors?"

Lola opened a drawer to show me rows of small bottles of ink, some of them fluorescent, of every color imaginable.

I had absolutely no idea there would be a choice of colors. I'd thought black and maybe dark red were used.

I knew immediately what I wanted. Pink. Not like bubblegum pink. Pink like cherry blossoms.

"You a fainter?" she asked, pointing to an exam table.

"No. I mean, I don't think so."

"Let's lie you down just in case," Lola adjusted the table into a flat position.

Did I look like a fainter? How would that look, maybe pale and panicky? I probably was both.

The table was cold, but I was glad, somehow believing it would numb the pain. Then again, if I started to shiver, would that give her a shaky hand and leave me with crooked ink?

"Where's it goin'?"

I held out my right wrist. I'd given it a lot of thought. Putting it over my heart was an obvious choice, but I wouldn't ever see it. I wanted it some place it would always be visible.

"Okey dokey."

"Will it hurt? I mean, does it bleed a lot inside the wrist?"

"Nah. Veins are much deeper under skin than you think," Lola said, getting out tools I didn't want to look at.

"So, all pink, or what?"

"The heart around it can be red."

"Pink and red," she said. "Sit tight."

Lola left the room through the back, and I wondered what she could be doing. Hopefully it was double sterilizing things. Or maybe she was just peeing. Good. I didn't want her to rush tattooing me with a full bladder.

She came back with transparent paper and a drawing in pencil. The heart was tilted slightly to one side and the paw rested in the middle. I loved it.

"That's perfect," I said.

"Thanks," Lola looked pleased. "I've been an artist all my life, ya know."

"I can tell."

"That look about right?" she held the drawing in the center of my wrist.

I squinted. I was already lying down to prepare myself.

"Yes, right in the middle is good."

Lola rummaged around in the drawer. I looked away so I wouldn't see anything that would make me bolt. Did I have to pee? No. It was just my stomach clutching.

"OK, so there will be blood but it's not gonna gush," Lola said patiently. "I'll mop it up as I go along."

Mop? Would it be on the floor? If there was that much blood, I would need more than a prone position. I would need an emergency room.

"Mop?"

"I mean blot," Lola said. "Like, with a paper towel."

Somehow that didn't sound very reassuring.

Lola swabbed my skin with rubbing alcohol that felt cold. Maybe it would numb the area?

When I heard the whir of the ink gun and I looked away, then closed my eyes just in case I might see something from the corner of my eye.

I felt pressure on my skin. OK, not bad at all. Then it turned into a scraping, and it felt like she was working the needle over the same part of my skin over and over, then deeper.

I flinched.

"Hold still," Lola said, bent over her work.

I wanted to ask her to take a break but felt silly since she had just begun. And so, I began something I'd used before to deal with pain: Lamaze breathing. Big breath in, short bursts out. In. Out.

Twenty-five years before, Adam and I had gathered on yoga mats with several other couples, nervous husbands and women who, like me, looked ready to give birth at any moment. The instructor worked hard to make us believe concentrating on our breathing would ease the pain of labor. We had gamely huffed and puffed.

Nothing in the world had prepared me for delivering my

first child. The first contractions were far apart and manageable, then they came rolling in one on top of another, feeling like a truck was driving back and forth over my entire body. I ended up breathing in through clenched teeth and exhaling like a lion, but in the end, only one thing got me through childbirth: epidural.

"That's good, keep that deep breathing," Lola said. "We can take a break if you need to."

I shook my head. Taking a break would just prolong the process. It was a simple red heart with a pink paw inside. How long could it take?

I cursed myself for not looking at my watch before we got started. It seemed to be going on for hours.

I was especially concerned about the amount of blotting she was doing. How much blood was there? Maybe everyone's veins were different, and mine were shallower under the skin.

I focused on my Lamaze breathing.

"Done," Lola finally announced. "Take a look!"

The inside of my wrist was irritated and a little puffy, but I could clearly see the tilted heart and the doggie paw.

"I love it," I said, overwhelmed with relief it was finished.

"Great," Lola smiled. She had an adorable space between her front teeth like Madison had when she lost her first tooth. "Let's wrap you up."

Wrap me up? What?

She pulled out a roll of Saran Wrap and tore off a piece to put around my wrist.

"Take this off tonight, then wash with Dial soap."

"Dial? The liquid or the bar?"

"Doesn't matter, either one," she said patiently. "Then

put on some Aquaphor to keep it clean and hydrated. And no swimming for two weeks to prevent infection."

Well, there was a huge plus! I could skip the next week's water aerobics class.

I had no idea how much it would cost but had put ten $20 bills in my wallet. I fished them all out.

I handed three of them to Lola.

"Geez, thanks," Lola seemed surprised.

What did clients usually tip, $10? For something permanently on their body? For art that no one else had? I had made it through without fainting or bleeding all over the floor. It was well worth a good tip.

"If ya come back, ask for me," Lola called as I went back out through the curtain.

"That's $110," the man at the counter said. "Lola does nice work. She has a light hand so there's not much blood."

I was tired of hearing about bleeding.

My wrist throbbed all day. I gingerly washed it with Dial foaming hand soap that night, then patted it down with Aquaphor.

Success. A tribute to the dogs I love.

32

It didn't take long for Madison to notice.

She was at the kitchen table, and I was microwaving marshmallows for indoor s'mores.

"Holy crap Mombo," she got up and held my wrist to look closer. "Is that real?"

"No. It's temporary. Like we used when you were little to put Jack O'Lanterns on your face."

"Really?"

"No, silly. It's permanent."

"When did you get this done?" her voice rose a full pitch higher.

"Yesterday."

I took out the dish with a graham cracker and warm inflated marshmallow, pressed a square of a Hershey Bar and topped it with a second graham.

For a minute we were both distracted, biting into the s'mores.

"I need all the details," Madd said, wiping a string of marshmallow off her chin. "Certainly I know why. But where? And How was it?"

"That tattoo shop by the yellow barn, near the place with the good ice cream."

"Was it clean?"

"Of course it was clean," I said, licking a glob of

marshmallow. "I wouldn't have stayed if it wasn't."

"OK, well what was it like? Did it hurt?"

I crunched my snack thoughtfully.

"It hurt, but I didn't faint or anything," I said, casually proud. "It felt like digging and the noise was like a dental drill. But it didn't take that long."

"Who did it?"

"A girl with blue hair named Lola," I said.

"Hm. Well, I'm impressed. It just seems so sudden. You didn't tell us."

"I was afraid you two would talk me out of it," I said, standing up to rinse the plate in the sink.

"Looks a little red around the outside," Madd said, sounding concerned.

"I'm using Dial soap and Aquaphor. It itches a little but it's actually fine."

"Well, good for you, Mombo. Very cool. It goes with the Halloween leggings and navy nail polish vibe."

"Thanks," I said, smiling and looking out the window at Penny's cherry blossom tree.

33

"Heard about the fish fry, Missy?" Sal asked one morning the first week of April.

Sal had taped the flyer for the fire company's annual fish fry dinner to the door of the town office almost two weeks beforehand.

"I have."

"Planning to go? All proceeds benefit the firehouse."

I sighed. Certainly the thought of an oversized breaded and fried fish, probably with a side of actual French fries, sounded amazing.

"Reason I ask is that we could use some help in the kitchen," Sal said, smiling in his way that made it impossible to say no.

"Oh sure, of course."

Maybe working in the kitchen would prevent me from stuffing my face. Probably not.

I headed to the firehouse that Friday night. It was already bustling with volunteers doing everything from peeling potatoes for fries in the kitchen to setting up tables and chairs in the enormous empty garage. The rescue trucks were all parked outside.

"Hey, Jessie, come give us a hand over here," Sal called to me from a counter covered in flour and breadcrumbs.

I had brought an apron that I hadn't worn in as long as

I could remember, but I'd kept it hanging in the pantry just in case.

Sal helped me tie the back.

"OK, so we've got an assembly line here. First you break eggs into the breadcrumbs, the next person rolls the filets in the crumbs, next they get popped into the fryer."

I wanted to stay as far from the fryer as possible. Hot oil burns were the worst.

"I'll mix up the crumbs."

There was a huge stainless-steel bowl big enough to bathe a baby in on the counter. I started cracking eggs and dumping breadcrumbs from the package.

Sal hadn't said how much of each ingredient, but my first batch was way too eggy. After I poured in more crumbs, it was too dry.

"Ya got that ready yet?" asked the silver-haired woman next to me wearing plastic gloves, waiting to dredge the fish in coating.

"Uh, yeah."

I handed over the bowl and she frowned, trying to mix it some more with her gloved hands.

"Ya don't got the amounts right. This is too dry."

She reached in front of me to take the egg carton and started cracking them expertly with one hand.

"How's it going sweetheart?" Sal came from where he had been manning the fryer across the kitchen.

"She made it too dry," the mean grandmother said.

"OK, well let's get you over to the potato station."

I washed the crumbs off my hands and followed him to a line of people peeling and slicing the potatoes into incredibly symmetrical long pieces.

Paulie was at the other side of the kitchen stirring pots of boiling water, looking sweaty.

"Can you use the little lady over here?" Sal asked his friend.

"We need all the help we can get."

Paulie handed me an industrial-sized peeler and pointed to a bag of potatoes.

"Better get going. First dinners get served in twenty minutes."

Gamely, I tipped the potato bag and rolled some out onto the cutting board. The first one had so many ruts that by the time I had it peeled, there was practically no potato left. I chopped it into eight small sticks.

The next potato was also uneven all over. Did they give me the bag of hard-to-peel potatoes on purpose?

I peeled the brown spots out of the second-rate potatoes and cut them lengthwise. After 15 minutes, I had a little pile of irregular shaped sticks.

Paulie, who apparently was my kitchen babysitter, showed up again and poked a finger at my potato pile.

"Yeah, you gotta pick up speed," he said, pointing to the other volunteers who were in danger of slicing off a finger with their fast-paced peeling.

"I'll try."

I bent over the counter and concentrated on peeling, but even my best wasn't good enough, apparently, because Paulie was back within minutes.

"This ain't the best job for you," he said.

Paulie handed me an ice cream scooper and pointed to a large vat of coleslaw.

"Just put one serving on every plate, then move them

down to the pie station."

Pie! I was not told there would be pie! I looked over at the table where volunteers were slicing perfect triangles of apple, chocolate cream, and some kind of mixed berry pie, all of them oozing sweet juice.

My first thought was to wonder if there would be any left for the volunteers at the end of the night.

I scooped slaw for three hours, going through five vats. Sleepy Wes, Joe, and his wife came through the line. Joe of course asked for an extra-large serving.

I knew many of the people who came to the dinner from my job at the town hall. It was nice seeing so many community members turn out to eat together at the rows of tables and folding chairs in the firehouse.

All night, I kept my eye on the rapidly diminishing slices of pie.

We stopped serving at 8 p.m., all of us weary from standing for over three hours.

I took off my apron and looked over at the empty pie table. I was hungry from the aroma of fresh fish and fries drifting out from the kitchen.

"Good job, Jessie," Sal said, coming over to pat my shoulder.

"Thanks, it was fun."

"Now comes the best part. We all sit down and eat!"

The volunteers brought out plates of fish and fries and I scooped on servings of slaw. Then, best of all, the silver-haired woman who frowned at my breading came out carrying two fresh peach pies.

"I'm gonna cut big slices for us," she said, and I immediately forgave her crankiness in the crowded kitchen.

We all sat together at one of the long tables and clinked together paper cups of grape juice.

"Sign me up for next year," I said to Paulie, who was digging into his third piece of pie.

34

My April 15th birthday rolled around faster every year, and I was turning 58. How was that possible?

The even numbers didn't sound as bad as the odd ones. But...it was one step closer to 60 and I didn't even want to think about that.

On the positive side, I didn't feel like I was in my late 50s. I still felt 45ish. Sure, Maddie was 25, but I could have had her at a very young age, right? And Ian was still a student living at home. That comforted me as I went to bed the night before the big day.

Madison had texted me Happy Birthday before I even got out of bed the next morning. I didn't want to wear anything special to work and have the Three Stooges ask why. We celebrated the men's birthdays with red velvet cake with cream cheese frosting–their favorite. The cake would beckon me all day long and I usually ended up having at least two pieces.

"Come on Lu," I nudged the sleepy girl with static from the blanket, making her fur all stand up on her head.

I saw the helium balloons floating over the table even before I got into the kitchen. They were purple and orange, the colors of Halloween, with streamers to match. A long silver banner spelled out Happy Birthday and gold confetti cakes were scattered all over the table.

Ian, still in sweats, was at the stove making poached eggs. The toaster pinged to pop up the bread.

"Happy birthday, Mom," he said, serving up the eggs and toast on a birthday paper plate. "How does it feel to be 49?"

We had a family tradition of decorating for birthdays. When they were little, the kids wanted themed decorations, SpongeBob or mermaids or superheroes. The rest of the family would get up extra early and decorate the kitchen, although Adam was never as excited about birthdays as the kids and I were.

When I was a kid, I would invite a few friends to a party and my sister would be the ringmaster. She made pin the tail on the donkey and got out actual potatoes for the hot potato game. We played musical chairs, which always gave me a little anxiety as we scrambled for seats when the music ended. I always had an orange cake with marshmallow frosting and usually got Barbie dolls or clothes for the dolls as gifts.

"Thank you, Ian," I said, picking up my fork. "You didn't have to get up so early for this."

"I wanted to. Madd would have been here, but she had to go into work early this morning."

"This is just the sweetest thing. You really made my day."

"The day's just starting," he said, getting up to pour more hot water into my tea. "We're taking you to dinner at Jalapeño's. Seven p.m. sharp."

Jalapeño's was hands-down the best Mexican restaurant in Ashton, known for their out-of-this-world margaritas.

I finished my breakfast and reluctantly stood up.

"I have to get to the office, but this was amazing honey."

"You're very welcome," Ian said, suppressing a yawn. "As

for me, I'm going back to bed for an hour before my first class."

I was glowing all morning from Ian's thoughtfulness. Even as grown-ups, they kept the celebrations from their childhoods going, and that meant the world to me.

I was reconciling bank statements when a delivery person carrying an enormous bouquet of flowers came in the front door.

"Jess Gabriel?"

"That's me—but what? These are for me?"

"Your name's on the card. Enjoy."

The men woke up Wes and came over to the counter to admire the white calla lilies, roses and mini pink carnations. The smell of flowers instantly filled the office.

I took the little card out of the envelope and read it: Happy Birthday to the most fun Mom in the world! Love, Madison and Ian."

I wiped away tears.

"Aw, missy, what's the special occasion?" Wes asked.

"It's my birthday, actually. These are from my kids."

"Well, isn't that sweet," Sal said. "You never told us it was your birthday. Looks like we've got some celebrating to do!"

"Well, let's take a walk down to Brew Coffee and see what they've got," said Joe, putting on his jacket.

All four men filed out the door.

The phone immediately rang, and right after that a woman came in to dispute her water bill.

Oh well.

The men took their time but came back with four enormous Danishes with cheese, strawberry and apple all braided together. We ate all day, with gusto.

Ian drove me to Jalapeno's that evening. Madison and her boyfriend Billy were already at the table.

"We ordered a pitcher of margaritas," Maddy said, getting up to hug me. "Ian is the designated driver, so drink up."

We had the world's best tortillas and guac, followed by sizzling chicken fajitas, rice, and black beans.

Then the four servers came out with a large deep fried ice cream dessert with flaming sparklers, and everyone sang Happy Birthday to me.

"Best birthday ever," I told the kids as we dug into the ice cream. "I can't thank you enough."

"You deserve it, Mombo."

I went to bed that night a little tipsy, not even caring if I would need Tylenol for a hangover headache the next day.

35

At the time when I least expected it, I hit the Jackpot in my Uber job. A ride to the airport! It was 45 miles from Meredia, and travelers were said to be big tippers if you helped with their luggage.

The rider was a slender woman wearing tortoise cat-eye sunglasses and a black dress. I jumped out to help but all she had for luggage was a small suitcase on wheels that she slung easily into the back seat.

"Heading out on vacation?" I said, glancing in the rear-view mirror.

She took off her sunglasses.

"Not quite. I was here for a funeral. Flying home now."

I immediately regretted mentioning vacation.

"I'm sorry," I said. It was all I could come up with, and, with her glasses off, I could see the dark circles under her eyes and her smudged eyeliner.

"Childhood friend," she said, looking out the window. "Aneurism."

"Oh, that's so awful," I said, thinking about Eddie and how I would feel if anything ever happened to him.

"She went just like that," the woman said, snapping her fingers.

Lights on, lights off. That was what the vet had said the day that Penny died. It was a small comfort on an incomprehensibly painful day.

I touched my paw tattoo and shook off the memory.

"When did you last see her?"

The woman smiled. "Last summer. We brought our kids to Martha's Vineyard for a week. The kids are old enough to run around and do their own thing, so Marcy and I sat on the beach and talked for hours about the good old days in school."

"How wonderful you had that time with her," I said, taking the exit for the airport.

"Yes. That is a bright spot."

"How many children do you have?"

She smiled again. "Three. The older two are in college but my youngest is still in high school. Can't wait to get home and see her."

It was my turn to smile. I felt the same way about Ian. I had missed Madison when she moved out, but I still had a kid home, and I loved all the signs of him living there—even the dirty dishes in the sink and the wet clothes left in the washer.

"Which airline?" I asked, pulling up to the curb at the airport.

"Right here is fine," she said, opening her door and swinging out her rolling suitcase. "It was nice chatting with you."

"Have a safe flight!"

She waved, then went through the automatic doors into the airport lobby.

I looked at the Uber app. The fare alone was $48! It took a minute for her tip to show up, and I couldn't believe it. She tipped $25.

That was a huge haul for an hour's work, enough to quit for the day and pick up pizza for Ian and me. Or go crazy and get Panera gourmet salads with pecans and dried cranberries.

"I'm bringing home dinner," I texted Ian.

"Great. I'm starving."

36

It was the usual dull Thursday night at the end of April and once again, I considered the fact that I had virtually no hobbies.

When I was pregnant with Madison, I took up needlepoint to stitch an intricately designed pair of baby booties on white cloth. The stitches were green and yellow, because Adam and I had always wanted to be surprised about the baby's gender.

Madison kicked and elbowed her way through the third trimester, convincing me she was a boy. Ian was quiet and gentler in his motions, giving us the notion he was another girl. Wrong on both counts.

Raising kids wasn't exactly a hobby. It was my life. It had been a whirlwind of activity, though, and I never planned for my life once they were grown up. If I had thought ahead, I might have taken up knitting, tennis, golf, or maybe tie-dye. I could have been sewing my own clothes or perfecting my sourdough bread recipe. Practicing mixology and making trendy cocktails for Eddie and me. Bird watching. Ballroom dancing with the teacher as my partner. Watercolor. Playing guitar. The possibilities were endless. Sure, I'd taken a jewelry making class and a course on new ways to cook chicken with Eddie, but nothing had stuck.

It started to sprinkle outside, which nixed the idea of

taking Lucy for a walk. Besides, I had shared bits of almonds from my granola dinner with her and she was content and curled up in her dog bed.

A text came through.

"Hey, Jess. Whatcha doing?"

It was Jeremy.

"Not much. You?"

"I'm looking for company."

Well, that was no surprise. What did surprise me was how quickly I found an answer.

"I think I'll stay in for the night."

"Really? You don't want to come cuddle?"

I'd long before learned that "come cuddle" was code for meeting for sex. Which had always been phenomenal with Jeremy, unforgettable really. It was great while it lasted. I was just done. At least for tonight.

"You take care, Jeremy."

"OK, Jess, shoot me a text anytime. I'll be around."

Knowing he was around tempted me. But only for a second, and then it was gone.

37

A FEW WEEKS LATER, I PICKED UP A YOUNG MAN IN A TAN KHAKI suit and red tie. I saw him frown and brush the upholstery in my back seat before he slid in. OK.

"How are you today?" I asked.

"Excellent. Headed to a new job assignment."

"What do you do?"

"I'm a PO," he said, smoothing down his tie.

"PO? Police officer?" I was confused by the suit he was wearing.

"Professional Organizer," he said haughtily as if I should have known what the hell PO stood for.

"Wow, so you organize people's stuff? Have you ever worked with any hoarders?"

"It's not like that," he said primly. "I manage large projects for my clientele. Right now, for instance, I'm overseeing the installation of a baby grand piano in a private home in Scenic Oaks."

Oooooh, Scenic Oaks, I thought. *Big whoop.*

"It's an upscale neighborhood," he said, as if I hadn't known.

"That sounds interesting," I lied.

"I also organize estate sales," he continued.

So basically, he dug through people's old furniture and dusty belongings to sort out what could be sold and what needed to be tossed into a dumpster.

Yawn.

I pulled into the long driveway at one of the largest homes in Glendale.

"You really need to scrub these seats, they have water stains on them," he said as he got out.

"That's from the upholstery cleaner I used a couple days ago after someone spilled coffee back there."

"Well use a different cleaner," he said, frowning. "It shouldn't leave water marks like those. Try a foaming one."

"Will do! Thanks for the suggestion."

I roll my eyes once he's out of sight.

One Saturday afternoon I got a message on the Uber app to pick someone up at Wal-Mart. Their destination was the local private college.

I knew my rider as soon as I saw him because he was standing with two full shopping carts. I sighed. He would need me to open my hatch.

I got out to help him unload his carts.

"Thanks," he said. He was thin and wore thick, black-framed glasses.

"First year?"

"Yeah, how did you know?"

I smiled. He had items so large they didn't even fit in the store's plastic bags. He had a full-length mirror and a yellow beanbag chair that we had to smush down to make room for his cork bulletin board. There was a plaid comforter, green desk lamp and a silver shower caddy. Oh, and a lava lamp because everything old is new again.

"Think I went a little overboard," he said sheepishly.

"Parent's credit card?"

"Yup."

As he pulled the last bag out of the second shopping cart, it ripped down the middle, dropping a silver, economy size box of condoms that I pretended not to notice.

I drove to the college while he texted in the back seat. I thought about how lucky I was that my kids had gone to community college and never made the complicated departure from home. Sure, they spent most of their time on campus and had basically only come home to sleep and do laundry, but my house had been their home base.

"Need help getting stuff to the curb?" I asked when we got to campus.

"Nah," the kid said, getting out and opening the hatch.

I let him struggle a minute before I got out to carry the beanbag chair to the door of his dorm.

"Thanks a lot," he said, holding the door open with his foot.

"Have fun!"

I hoped he would.

The next passenger I picked up was dressed from head to foot in a white suit that made him look like a Hazmat worker. He got in carefully, as if he didn't want to wrinkle it.

"Astronaut?" I asked after he shut the door.

"Beekeeper," he answered. "My hives are out in the woods, and I need to suit up and be ready with the smoker."

"Ah. Kinda hot out there to be in protective gear like that."

"Well, I have nothing on underneath," he said proudly, as if he had come up with a solution that made sense.

Note to self: Scrub back seat with upholstery cleaner

that night. The foaming one.

Most of the riders I picked up were 20 years-old and older, but one day I picked up a kid in a Catholic school uniform who looked around twelve. His destination was a development of pricey condos with private balconies and a huge outdoor pool surrounded by palm trees obviously trucked in from some place tropical.

"Hi," I said, turning off the radio so we could chat.

The kid grunted in reply and took out his cell.

Oh well. I turned the radio back on.

"Where's the water?" the boy asked.

"What water?"

"Uber cars are supposed to have water, and something to eat too," he said, clearly irritated.

I had heard about drivers putting bags of snacks out for riders, but it seemed like it would make a mess and dig into my slim profit margin.

"Sorry," I said.

"Wow, this is one lousy ride," he said, looking out the window.

We pointedly ignored each other for the rest of the 20-minute trip.

"Get yourself some drinks and chips or something," he advised as he got out of the car.

Needless to say, there was no tip from the little snot.

38

"It's been ages since you've come to visit!" my sister Kat texted me in early May.

She was right. I was juggling two jobs and staying close to the kids and Lucy, but there hadn't been much "me time" in recent memory.

Kat lived just under two hours north of Meredia. We saw each other mostly for the kids' birthdays and family gatherings, but when we got together, we huddled in a corner and shared every story about our lives we could think of. Kat is 18 months older than me; our mother dressed us like twins until we were old enough to complain.

Kat and I were best friends for much of our childhood. We shared Barbie doll clothes, even the pink satin ball gown that technically belonged to her. We put the Barbies to bed on Kleenex boxes with tissues for covers, then woke them up to put on party clothes and drive around in the Barbie convertible.

We shared a bedroom until Kat was ten or eleven and insisted on getting her own space. In the middle of the night, I would drag my blankets and pillow into her room and lie on the floor next to her bed. I woke up with a backache, but it was worth it to be near her.

I was always grateful that Kat let me hang around her group of friends when they were newly teenagers and I was still twelve. I'd used my first swear word in front of them, pretended to hate all my teachers even though some were nice, took part in various dares and bets, like who would ring the doorbell at Robbie Briscoe's house and ask if he was home. None of us even made it to the front porch; we all liked him and never wanted him to know. One year, a less kind friend of my sister dared me to open my mouth and close my eyes for a spoon of brown sugar. Kat hollered at the girl when she saw her try to feed me a spoonful of dirt. They ostracized the mean girl after that.

I'd learned a lot from Kat's thwarted attempts to date the high school basketball star, who talked to her only when his girlfriend wasn't around.

"I love him," she used to say, wiping her eyes on the back of her hand.

I never understood why he hadn't loved her back. Kat was everything I wanted to be: smart, funny, outgoing, and loyal. I tended to hide in a book and never tell anyone about my secret crushes.

Kat married Ray when they were in their early 20s. They had two kids, my niece and nephew who I was crazy about.

She and Ray were cruise fanatics; they'd been to every exotic place I could think of, while Adam and I had instead taken our kids on road trips to the Grand Canyon and Myrtle Beach. Maybe that's what sparked the wanderlust in Adam when he moved into the camper and took to life on the road as a vagabond. At least that's what I thought of him. Who knew he had felt so trapped in our life raising the kids? I hadn't.

"Come up this weekend," Kat texted, interrupting my thoughts. "I'll make you lunch. I've got a great chicken salad recipe with walnuts and red grapes you will love."

"In that case, sure. I'll be there at noon."

Lucy wasn't a travel dog. She panted and fogged up the passenger side window or paced back and forth trying to wedge herself under the steering wheel and sit on my lap. I enlisted Eddie and his husband Don to babysit her while I went to see my sister. I still had worries about leaving her alone. My sweet Penny died while she was waiting for me to get home from work, and it felt catastrophic to even think of Lucy home alone for more than a few hours.

The drive to Kat's was a straight shot north on the highway. I brought the cordless earbuds the kids had given me for Christmas to listen to Ayn Rand's The Fountainhead.

Kat was waiting for me in the driveway when I pulled in just before noon.

"Hey sis," she said, skipping to greet me.

She smelled like jasmine, and I wondered why I'd let so much time pass without seeing her. Her hair was tied back with a navy bow that matched her cardigan. She was wearing khakis and red shoes with kitten heels. Somehow, I always felt underdressed around her.

"Like the leggings," Kat said. "Those skulls and mummies?"

"You know me, Halloween is every day of the year."

"You're a kook," she said, ruffling my hair. "Your hair's growing out."

"Thank goodness. It was kind of an impulse cut."

"I understand," Kat said sympathetically.

Kat's house was a modern two-story with an arched entryway. Her hedges were perfectly manicured, and she had flower boxes with red geraniums leaning towards the sun. Her front door was also a gorgeous shade of red that matched her shoes. I tried not to think about my own sagging porch as I followed her inside.

Kat's husband Ray came down the massive mahogany staircase carrying a pair of golf shoes.

"Hey Jess," he said, hugging me warmly. "How's it going? You look great."

Ray was a medical equipment salesman and I always thought he could sell anyone anything in the world. He was as handsome as the Ken dolls that used to date our Barbies: short brunette hair, Polo shirt and ironed plaid golf pants. He had a smattering of silver hair at his temples, which only made him look more dashing.

"I'll be home by dinnertime babe," Ray said to my sister, leaning down to pull her in his arms.

"Be sure you are, it's date night, remember?"

"Always," Ray said, kissing her sweetly before heading out the door.

"Good seeing you, Jess."

"You too."

"Date night?" I teased Kat, following her into the kitchen. "The kids are in college, isn't every night date night?"

Kat smiled and I thought I saw her blush.

"We make dinner together most of the time but go out two nights a week and try new restaurants, see a movie or a show."

Ashton was a cultural hub, with live theater, art galleries and places for a three-course lunch.

Kat opened the fridge and pulled out a pitcher of water with cucumber slices.

"Or did you want seltzer? I have lime, grapefruit, and

clementine."

"Actually, water please for now."

The pitcher had a filter on it. I usually drank from the tap.

She set out a plate of Triscuits and frowned.

"Do we want cheese?"

I certainly did.

"Actually, it will spoil our lunch. Let me get to the chicken salad. You want it on sourdough bread or scoop it over Romaine?"

Was both an option? I had been continuously starving since I started water aerobics. The exercise seemed to make me eat more because I was hungry all the time. The waistbands on some of my leggings still dug into my stomach, making me think I hadn't lost an ounce. I didn't know for sure because I purposefully avoided the scale at the Y. We were not friends.

My sister played tennis in the summer and cross-country skied when it snowed. She had never had so much as a tiny roll around her middle. After she had the kids, she was back on the treadmill a few weeks later.

She served the salad in glass bowls and refilled our water.

Then she sat down and squealed, grabbing my arm to look at the dog paw tattoo.

"What's this? Is it permanent? When—"

"Yes, it's permanent, and I got it about a month ago."

"Wow, good for you sis. Did it hurt?"

"Not as much as I thought it would!"

"So, will you get more? I always wanted to get a tat but never had the guts."

I laughed.

"One at a time. I think I'm good for now."

"So, are you still friends with Bryan?"

"Oh yeah, we're still friends. He's doing great. Remarried actually," I said, spearing a grape with my fork.

"Already?"

"Well, it's been over a year."

Kat stirred her cucumber water.

"And Adam? Do you hear from him?"

I cleared my throat. "He keeps in touch with Ian. They meet up a couple times a month. Actually, he sent a nice condolence card for Penny."

"That was nice," she said, putting her hand over mine. "And how's little Miss Lucy?"

"Amazing," I said, smiling broadly.

She cleared the salad and pulled a bowl out of the fridge.

"Remember our favorite when we were kids?"

"No way, you didn't make—"

"Raspberry Jell-O," she said proudly. "And not sugar-free either. I went wild and got the kind with sugar."

We heaped our bowls and clinked our spoons together.

"To us," she toasted.

"What's up with you guys?" I asked.

"Well, we're cruising next month for our 35th anniversary. *Alaska,*" she beamed.

"Holy shit, 35 years? Hard to believe; you two look so great."

"Ray said he's had enough of the party ships with the endless buffets and Pina Coladas all day long—"

"All day long?" I couldn't picture my sister and drinking out of pineapples through straws at 11am. I thought of them as more of a Manhattan at cocktail hour kind of couple.

"Yeah, I still won't let him live down doing the limbo under a bamboo branch when we cruised to Cancun. He went too low and landed on his ass. He just stayed down, long enough for me to take pictures. Told him I was gonna post them on Facebook and he said, 'go ahead.' He has never had any inhibitions."

"Wow, I never saw them online!"

"I didn't want to embarrass the kids," she said, breaking a cracker in half and nibbling on it, skipping the cheese.

I pictured my sister and Ray with their arms around each other, under a sky turned pink by Northern lights. Wasn't the sky over Alaska always glowing magnificently?

Thirty-five years. Unless I lived to be 90, I would never have that history with any man. I pictured the older couple that walked down my sidewalk in spring, holding hands. She was always talking, and her husband would be leaning in so he didn't miss a word she was saying. The old woman could have been reminiscing about any part of their lives: their honeymoon, a trip to Vegas, the days their children had been born, anniversary parties. Of course, there would have been bad times too: lost jobs, scrambling to pay the bills, illness, tears. But they had made it, still together holding hands.

I didn't have that shared history with anyone now except my kids. I remembered how Adam had laughed joyously and spun me around in his arms when we found out we were expecting Madison. We had done all the silly things expectant couples do: taking turns reading stories to my growing belly so the baby would recognize our voices, playing classical music while holding headphones nearby, the Lamaze class. I was the keeper of those memories now. I didn't have Adam to talk to about the old days when the children were small, and we were exhausted but happier than we'd ever been. Or I'd been.

I remembered Adam pulling into our driveway in the enormous RV, being so proud and asking me to take photos for Facebook. Our neighbor spying at us from behind his living room curtains. Having to sit down, hard, on the lawn because my legs felt shaky. I remembered my rising panic as Adam had talked excitedly about a new life on the road, a life that had nothing to do with raising kids in a nice neighborhood where their house was always in the same place.

I hadn't actually believed he would leave, until he did.

"Here," my sister said, interrupting my thoughts. "I made some quinoa berry muffins to snack on while you drive home."

They looked Martha Stewart perfect.

"Sometimes I envy your freedom," she said, smoothing her hair back into her bow. "What's it like being single?"

How to answer? That I squeezed the toothpaste from the center because no one else was there to complain? Texted the kids too much? Gossiped with four codgers at work about who was sleeping with the fire chief? Ate dinner standing up at the kitchen sink so I didn't drop crumbs?

"Sometimes I want to run away," Kat said quietly. "I wonder how it would be if I had a different life that didn't revolve around being a wife and mother."

"Oh, Kat—"

"Never mind me," she said, waving her hand as if to take back the words. "I have the life I wanted. You know, the grass is always greener, as they say."

"That's what they say," I agreed.

"Better get on the road," she said, smiling brightly. "Hug the kids for me."

The muffins were gone before I went through the toll booth.

I once had the life my sister had with Ray. Adam and I had the quintessential adult life I always imagined: a perfectly nice house with friendly neighbors on a quiet cul de sac where the trees were just starting to mature. Having a glass of wine on the porch with Adam. Kissing him at the stroke of midnight New Year's Eve. Making confetti cupcakes for the kids' birthdays. Sending photo Christmas cards. Putting their artwork on the fridge with alphabet magnets. Reading *Charlotte's Web* to the kids. Swimming. Ice skating. Taking turns bringing them to the dentist. Building a snowman and using one of Adam's baseball caps for a hat.

That life was fractured and swallowed whole by deep cracks like a home with a shaky foundation when Adam left. It hadn't been enough for him, he wasn't satisfied, he had other plans for his life.

I pictured my sister and her husband skiing side-by-side.

After I pulled in my driveway and greeted my thoroughly ecstatic puppy, I texted Nadine.

"Wanta go out for nachos? I have a craving for salsa and some girl talk."

39

One morning in the middle of May, I picked up a grand-motherly woman wearing a cardigan with pearl buttons, carrying a handbag covered in white seashells.

She walked daintily in her strappy sandals over to my driver's side window.

"This is my first Uber ride," she said excitedly. "I don't know what to expect. For one thing, where do I sit?"

"You could sit up front with me, but most people are more comfortable in the back seat."

"Oh good, I can stretch out," she said, opening the door and settling herself in.

The scent of lavender and talc powder filled the car.

"I'm Jessica."

"What a pretty name, sounds like a Hollywood actress. I'm Loretta."

Her destination was a street address in a development with mansion-size homes and impeccably groomed landscaping.

"So, what are you up to on this beautiful day?"

"I'm paying a visit to my boyfriend," Loretta said, turning a faint shade of pink.

More power to you, I thought.

"Good for you!"

"Thank you," Loretta waved a hand. "It's nothing really

serious. We're mostly friends with benefits."

I did a half-laugh, half-cough.

"Days like today make me feel invigorated," she said, raising her face into the sun. She had high cheekbones and a little bow mouth outlined in just the right shade of toffee lipstick.

"It is a great day."

"So, tell me dear, how long have you been driving?"

"Several months," I said, adjusting the visor because the sun was making me squint.

"Well goodness. How do you like it?" I thought for a moment.

"You can tell me," Loretta said. "Are people really gross? Smelly? Impolite?"

I laughed.

"Some of them are just in their own world," I said. "The young kids have their ear buds in for the entire ride. When I drop them off, they jump out without having said a single word."

"That's no fun," she said.

"Other people are really chatty."

"I enjoy meeting new people and getting a chance to know a little about them," she said. "So, are you married?"

"Divorced actually. Twice."

"I hear you," Loretta said. "I've been married three times and it never stuck. Hal wants to get married, or at least live together, but that just doesn't appeal to me. I like my independence."

"Sure. I understand."

"It's the sex I can't live without," Loretta opened her shell purse and pulled out a compact to check her lipstick.

You go, girl.

"Not to embarrass you, but just between you and me, Hal is really built, if you know what I mean."

Ah. I did know. I just had nothing to say in response.

"He's younger, of course, couldn't keep up with me otherwise," she said. "I've always had a very high sex drive. Hal is the first man to give me multiple orgasms."

I was officially jealous.

"Do you have kids?" Loretta asked.

I was sorry we were off the subject of sex, because I was always ready to hear more.

"I do. And you?"

Loretta shook her head and furrowed her elegant eyebrows.

"No," she said quietly, looking out the window. "Wasn't meant to be."

She took a tiny lace handkerchief out of her purse and dabbed her nose.

We were silent a moment.

"Tell me about your children," she said.

"Two. Daughter and a son. My daughter has her own apartment, but my son still lives with me. Tell you the truth, I don't see much of him, but I know he's around if I need him. Keeps me from getting lonely."

"And some day you will have grandchildren."

I gave a short laugh. "Not anytime soon. Neither of my kids are anywhere close to ready to think about that."

Madison and her boyfriend Billy had been dating for more than a year, but Billy had to finish med school, and they had plans to travel Europe. They weren't looking to put down roots. They didn't even have a dog.

"Have a good time," I called after her when she got out in front of the house. I knew she would.

40

ONE FRIDAY IN MID-MAY, I WAS PLOWING THROUGH A HUGE stack of invoices Joe had stuffed into my In basket, debating whether I should Uber that night.

It was Friday and the college kids and young professionals would be packing bars into the wee hours of the night. My earnings from the last weekend were a paltry $114. It was never clear whether it would be a good night or not. It was a roll of the dice; I could get a 10-minute drive for a passenger to go to their bank, or a 35-minute commute home for someone whose car was in the shop.

The men were knee deep in a debate about the annual Rotary Club car wash.

"I tell ya, it's not worth the money," Wes argued.

"It's $20!" Paulie said, snorting. "And it's for a good cause! That club put up the American flags on the lamp posts lining the entrance to town. You know how good they make us all look, very patriotic."

"Right, and a car wash at one of them automatic places these days is a rip-off," Joe said, reclining at his desk, where no work interfered with his daily gossip session with his three cronies.

"I wash mine myself with a garden hose. Or just wait for it to rain," Sal said mildly. "I find a good downpour cleans everything but the tire rims."

"Doesn't wash off the bird poop," Paulie reminded the men.

And it was official. The men were talking shit.

The phone rang a couple times with disgruntled people complaining about their water bill. The worst part of the job was dealing with residents whose irritation escalated when I explained for the millionth time the town's rates were the lowest in the county. It was $112 twice a year. What I wanted to say was, "If you don't like it, move."

"Who's up for a donut run?" Paulie asked, scratching behind his ear like a sleepy pup.

Wes had dozed off. He really needed to have his sleep apnea medication checked.

"It's almost lunchtime, someone go for paninis," Joe said lazily.

I prayed he wasn't looking my way.

"Paninis? What's a panini?" Paulie said.

"It's one of those grilled sandwiches, ya know, they take turkey and cheese and some roasted red peppers—whatever you want, really—then pop it in a machine like they make waffles," Joe said, his eyes lighting up. "Makes them hot and melty."

Jerky bounded off his seat at the window as if he sensed that food would soon be arriving.

"I'll go down," Sal offered. "Dog could use some fresh air anyway."

"Someone wake up Wes and see what he wants," Joe said.

Paulie shook his shoulder. Wes snorted and looked around.

"Lunchtime?" he asked hopefully.

Sal wrote down everyone's orders on a piece of their morning newspaper. I passed on a panini, already fighting a losing battle with the tight fit of the waistbands of all my skirts and even my leggings.

"You want some money?" Wes said.

Sal waved a hand. "I've got it. You can get it next time."

The heavy front door to the Town Hall shut hard behind Sal and Jerky. As soon as they left, I regretted passing on a panini.

Wes went back to sleep while Paulie read baseball results aloud to Joe. I shuffled spreadsheets around, my mind returning to Uber driving that night.

Quite some time passed.

"Geez, what's taking Sal so long?" Paulie said.

"Probably a long line," Joe said. "You know those newbies found our little spot and have overrun the place. Last week I was in there, I had to take a number and wait. And they forgot what my regular order is!"

I smiled. The guys called anyone working downtown new to Meredia if their grandmother hadn't been born and raised there. They still considered me a newbie.

"I got his cell, I'll text him," Paulie said.

When Sal didn't return the text, Paulie woke up Wes.

"Let's take a walk down; maybe Sal needs a hand carrying everything back. We did order a lotta food."

I heard Jerky barking even before the sound of sirens coming around the corner.

We all raced to the window.

Out on the sidewalk, a hundred feet from our building, Sal was lying on his side, knees pulled up to his chest, a paper bag from Brew Coffee still in his arms.

Jerky was barking furiously, running in circles around his owner.

Within seconds, someone was leaning over Sal, blocking our view, and we couldn't see him anymore.

"Move, man, move," Paulie said, elbowing Wes out of the way to get to the door.

Paulie sprinted down the sidewalk with Wes and Joe close behind him.

I stood frozen by the radiator. There was a growing crowd on the sidewalk and in the street.

Within minutes, the emergency corps ambulance came roaring in and three EMT's jumped out and pushed through the people to get to Sal.

One sat right on Sal's chest to perform CPR. The other was doing mouth-to-mouth resuscitation.

The third paramedic took Jerky's leash and got on his knees to soothe the dog. Jerky began to howl.

I watched from the window as they loaded the stretcher into the ambulance. A couple of police officers talked to Joe, Wes, and Paulie, then the paramedic handed over Jerky's leash.

Then the men were alone, and one by one, they began to embrace each other and put their heads down to cry.

41

Sal's funeral was the following Sunday.

I asked Eddie to go with me. We walked downtown to the ornate Catholic church under a sunny sky so bright it was painful. By rights it should have been a terrible, overcast day.

A park near the church was full of children swinging and going down slides. We stopped for a minute to watch them. Two little boys were pretending to sword fight on the top of a wooden ship with a pirate flag. A girl was sipping from a juice box with her family eating subs at the picnic table. Birds swooped overhead hoping for breadcrumbs.

It was an ordinary weekend for everyone but the people who had known and loved Sal.

I heard a bark and turned to see Wes with Jerky on his leash, walking with his head down slowly as if he didn't want to go to the church.

"Had to bring him. Didn't seem right not to have him here."

I knelt down to rub Jerky's neck and he leaned on my shoulder.

"We'll stay outside with him," I said, taking the leash from Wes.

"Would you, sweetheart?"

"I'm happy to."

Wes walked just as slowly up the steps and disappeared into the church. Several people had parked and were starting to congregate ono the sidewalk.

"Let's go over to the park," I said to Eddie.

Jerky followed quietly and showed no interest in the children playing at the park. We led him over to a picnic table where he lay down under the bench.

"Poor guy," Eddie said.

"He and Sal went everywhere together."

"Does he have family around to take him?"

"I'm not sure. His wife passed a few years ago, and they never had kids."

A little boy around seven or eight came over.

"Can I pet your dog?"

"Of course. He's friendly."

The boy kneeled down and rubbed Jerky's back. Jerky's tail started to thump and his ears perked up.

"Good doggie," the boy said before scampering away.

Jerky put his head down in his paws.

"You OK?" Eddie asked.

"Yeah. It just won't be the same without him."

"I understand."

"Did I ever tell you about the time Sal came in disgusted about his smoke detector because something was wrong with the batteries and it kept going off?"

"Yup," Eddie said. "It made Jerky go ballistic."

"He could not get it to shut off, so he finally got a yard stick and whacked it off the ceiling," I said. "Broke the whole thing into pieces and had to get a new one."

It was just one of the many stories about Sal that made me smile.

I thought of Sal holding the door for me and helping me down the steps when my wrist was sprained, eating pie at the firehouse with me, how he loved his dog as much as I loved mine, and my heart lurched.

The next morning, Paulie and Wes arrived at the town office at the same time. Jerky was not far behind them.

"His kids wanted me to have him," Paulie said. "Figured it would be good for him to keep things in a routine."

But when he let Jerky off the leash, the dog did not bound to his usual seat at the window to watch pigeons. Instead, he settled on Sal's old chair at the table, looking around at the men as if that was where he belonged.

42

"COME OVER AFTER WORK FOR PIZZA?" MADD TEXTED ME ONE terribly dull afternoon in the end of May as I was trying to reconcile a particularly complicated bank deposit.

"Sure! What can I bring?"

"Just you and Lucy."

Madison and Billy's apartment was in a new development just outside Meredia. There were two entrances, and I usually took the wrong one and ended up circling back.

I parked in a visitor's spot and put Lucy on her leash to let her wander around a bit and pee.

When she was done squatting and dribbling, we went to the door to be buzzed into the lobby.

"Come on up," Billy answered the intercom.

Elevators made Lucy nervous, so I held her on the way up to the fourth floor.

Madison had always been scared in elevators, particularly because Ian, in his taunting years, would jump up and down and make it lurch slightly. He also would push all the buttons so that the elevator stopped on every floor. Ian had his share of days when all he wanted to do was taunt his sister. One memorable April Fool's Day, he had filled Madison's car with helium balloons. It had actually been kind of pretty when she opened all the doors and the balloons soared skyward and away. She had gotten him back the next year by putting Saran Wrap over the toilet, causing a mess I didn't care to think about ever again. Fortunately, my kids had never pranked me.

Madison and Billy's apartment had a dramatic open floorplan. On one wall was a walk-through kitchen with an enormous island and four brushed bronze stools. The rest of the room was a spacious living area. Their cream-colored couch with large linen pillows delineated the TV corner from the dining area. They had found a knockoff Oriental rug with deep burgundy and navy tones that they laid down over the very cool cement floor. It was sort of industrial meets homey, a contrast of styles that worked for them both.

Lucy ran straight to Madison.

"Wine?" Billy asked.

He was always the consummate host.

"Yes, please."

Although they had me over for dinner on a regular basis, I suspected they had a reason for tonight's invite.

"Cheers," Madison said.

We clicked glasses and sipped the red wine.

"So, are we celebrating?" I couldn't contain my curiosity any longer.

"We are," Madd beamed. "We have something to show you."

It had to be an engagement ring! They had been dating almost two years and were one of those couples that finished each other's sentences and had adorable nicknames like "Lovey" and "Sweet cheeks" for one another.

Madison opened the door to the bedroom and a little flurry of fur bounded out.

"A puppy?" I exclaimed.

"Meet Rogue," Billy said, bending down to pick up the tiny Corgi.

"Well hello, Rogue," I said, scratching the puppy under the chin.

The dog tilted his head to the ceiling to give me more room to scratch, and his leg started thumping.

"When did you get this little cutie?"

"Just yesterday," Madison said.

Lucy ran to the puppy, and they circled each other, nosing and sniffing one another.

Then Rogue licked Lucy's nose, sealing the deal. They were already fast friends.

The oven timer went off, and I realized in all the excitement, I hadn't even noticed the delicious aroma of pizza.

Billy put on potholders and opened the oven to pull out a round pizza stone with a sizzling pie smothered in cheese just beginning to brown.

"That looks amazing," I said, ready to start drooling.

Madison set out plates with Day of the Dead sugar skull designs (she was my daughter, after all) and we sat down to dive into the pizza.

Lucy and Rogue lay down next to each other to doze.

All was right in our world.

43

ON A SATURDAY MORNING IN MID-JUNE, I GOT HOME FROM A particularly exhausting hour at the gym wanting nothing but a refreshing shower and maybe some cookies, but that would defeat the workout.

Ian was waiting for me at the kitchen table, watching the front door intently.

"Mom, I need to talk to you," Ian said.

Shit, I almost said out loud. This did not bode well for whatever was coming.

"Um, you should sit down."

I had that feeling of dread that starts in the pit of my stomach and winds its way up my esophagus to the back of my throat, making it hard to swallow and wonder where the Pepcid was.

"OK," I pulled out a kitchen chair and sat at the table.

Ian sat across from me. He looked flushed and wasn't meeting my eyes. All bad signs.

"So...." He started to talk then stopped as if he couldn't find the words.

"Ian what is it? Are you OK?" I asked, suddenly in alarmed-mother mode.

"No, that's not it," he picked up a napkin and wiped his upper lip.

"Then say it. Just say it."

"I'm going to live with dad," he blurted out.

Wait, what? I took a deep breath then exhaled in a way that reminded me once again of my Lamaze breathing when I was in labor for Ian. Inhale slowly. Hold it. Breathe out like a lion's roar. I hadn't done the slow breathing since my tattoo, and it hadn't really worked then either.

"What do you mean live with Dad? He doesn't have a house."

"He has the camper," Ian said, finally looking up.

"The camper. You want to go live in the camper?" I put my hands on the table to steady myself.

I swallowed hard and studied my son's face. His jaw was tense the way it used to be when he was arguing with me as a teenager about curfew, or something else that now seemed incidental. In the same way I'd felt when Adam said he was taking to the road, I felt the wind knocked out of me, making it hard to breathe or even begin to process his words. My ears were ringing and I desperately needed water.

"I want to go out on the road with him. He said I could pick the places I want to see. I haven't been anywhere but Meredia my whole life."

"That's not true. We took you and Madison to see the Grand Canyon when you were nine."

It was a moot point and I knew it, but I would use anything I could come up with to make him stay. He probably didn't even remember the trip out West.

"OK, well that doesn't really count," Ian said, tearing up the napkin into small pieces on the table.

"Are you serious about this?"

"Yeah, Mom, I am."

I listened to the kitchen clock tick, looked over at the

dishwasher and had the sudden urge to put away the silver-ware and pretend what Ian had said was a joke. I thought his home would always be where I was. I never expected him to live with me until he was thirty, but at least until he graduated and found a good job. Ian would graduate and to earn his degree in electrical construction later that month.

It would all make sense happening gradually that way. This seemed painfully abrupt. I had a somewhat ridiculous but still possible idea that Adam had talked him into it, promised him the world, told him all the good parts of living wildly, skipping the parts like drying their socks and underwear on a makeshift clothesline strung between trees at a campsite and eating too many dinners of canned beans and hot dogs.

"You mean after graduation, right?"

"Well, I'm done with all my classes, and I don't have to be there for the actual ceremony," Ian said.

I closed my eyes, thinking of the chance for photos of my son in a cap and gown fading away.

"All right, so you want to spend the summer with Dad?" I said, trying not to use my bossy-mother voice.

To hell with that. I was upset, no, I was pissed, stunned, off kilter, I would use my bossy voice or anything else that would make this situation better.

I was still haunted by the way Adam had left, so abruptly, with such flimsy reasons. He wanted to see the country, he'd said, when what he really meant was that he didn't love me anymore. He didn't love the life we had built, the Sunday pancake breakfasts, cheering Ian at soccer games, trips to the aquarium, our favorite movie night snack of peanut butter and jelly on Saltine crackers. By leaving, Adam had made our life seem irrelevant.

"Well, we're kind of making it open-ended. We don't have a set timeline. I can find electrical work on the road."

He picked up the pieces of napkin and let them drift back down to the table like snowflakes.

I tapped my nails on the table. My navy polish was chipped and needed touching up. So much for the chip-proof topcoat. It was far easier to think about my nail polish than to let his words, his terrible words, sink in.

"Ian, I just don't know if this is such a great idea—"

"Mom, I've made my plans with Dad. I'm going with him at the end of the month," his voice rose and became almost shrill.

Ian and I never argued. Maddie and I, we were a different story because were both hotheads and lacked impulse control. But Ian was mild and patient in a way that sometimes made me wonder if he was switched at birth. He spent most of his time out of the house, but when he was home, he liked his solitude, listening to music or reading.

Lucy would tread up the stairs to see him, or he would visit her in the family room, but he had his space and I had to respect that, even though I missed spending time with him terribly.

Still, knowing someone was living with me, sharing space, was what made it feel like home.

When Ian was little, his Lego table was set up in the middle of the living room and he spent hours in the small red plastic chair building castles and bridges and robots.

"Can you do Legos with me?" he would ask plaintively, and most of the time I put down the laundry or closed my computer to sit in the other little chair and make a lopsided car. His creations were always far more intricate.

When he finished a new project, he would hold it up proudly and I took pictures and pasted them into photo albums. He had a pail of Legos in the bathtub and by his seat at the dinner table and in his backpack to take to school. I had snuck some of his creations away to save in the glass-front hutch, because I never wanted to forget his Lego days.

Funny how mothers cherish all the days the kids don't even remember. I never really learned how to let go.

Now I needed to do exactly that. He wasn't asking for permission; he was asking for my support.

I looked down at my hands. I didn't want to argue. What I wanted to do was throw myself at his sneakered feet and ask him to stay, maybe just for the summer, or at least for his graduation. Or make a better choice than living in the camper like a vagabond with his father.

"It's my decision. Mom, I'm a capable adult. I'd like you to treat me like one."

"Ian, the camper? Do you really think you'll be comfortable living in that—"

"He's made a lot of improvements in it," Ian said. "It looks like a small apartment inside. You should see it."

Oh yes, sign me up for a tour. Maybe Adam could park it in the backyard like he did the summer before he packed up and left. Maybe he could start small campfires and play Bob Marley songs and just chill, as if he weren't renouncing his suburban life with his wife and kids.

"I know I can't stop you but—"

"I'm sorry Mom, you can't, and I've made my decision."

With that, he got up and left the kitchen to go up to his room, where I heard his door close in a way that wasn't quite a slam, but almost. Would he even have a room in the camper? Probably just a bunk bed. How could it possibly look like an apartment?

I've made my decision, his words echoed in my head. It wasn't like Ian to be so obstinate.

I sat for a moment at the table, resuming my unhelpful Lamaze breathing. I knew it was time to call in the troops for this most recent calamity.

44

I called Eddie and he knew from the sound of my voice to get there right away. Ten minutes later, he rushed in my front door.

"What is it, sweet pea?" he opened the fridge and took out a bottle of wine.

"No wine," I said. "I need to think."

Eddie furrowed his brow, then took out mugs and green tea bags and put the kettle on to boil.

"So, Ian just gave me some news."

"Yes? What could be so bad? Was he dyeing his hair orange again? Got detention? Do they even do that in college?"

"He's going to live with Adam," I interrupted.

"In the camper?" Eddie said incredulously.

"That piece of junk Adam calls home, yes. He wants to go on the road with his father and see the country, apparently."

Eddie got up to pour tea and brought the mugs to the table. We both picked up our cups and blew on them, watching the steam rise.

"Well, this is new and different," Eddie said at last. "How do you feel about it?"

Tears formed in my eyes, and I wiped my face on the back of my hand. Why were there never Kleenex in the kitchen? This is where everyone ended up crying.

"Terrible. Sick. Furious."

"Ok, well I can understand terrible and sick, but why would you be furious?" Eddie asked gently.

I gulped my tea. Why was I so angry?

"Because Adam is taking him," I said. "Ian is the last child I have here with me. When Adam left, he abandoned all of us. I've been Ian's parent for 22 years. Now, it feels like his father is winning."

"Ian isn't a commodity, chickie," Eddie reached across the table to take my hand in his. "There's no winning or losing here. Ian's an adult, and he can make his own choices. You have to let him do that, whether you agree or not."

Crap. Eddie was being logical, and I was a blubbering, overly-attached Lego Mom.

I had based so much of my value on being a mom to Madd and Ian. Raising them had been the center of my existence, my heart, for 25 years. I had thrown myself into parenting with unparalleled enthusiasm. It was who I was.

Even married to Adam, and then Bryan, the kids came first, without question.

Madison had moved out after college. It was a planned, organized exit. She didn't just slam me with the news at the kitchen table. Luckily for me, she had stayed nearby and stopped over regularly.

Ian was a bit of a late bloomer who was not as independent as she was. Of course he wasn't going to stay forever. I never asked him to. But in a million years, I had not expected him to drop a bomb like this on me on an otherwise ordinary Wednesday.

"You gotta let him go," Eddie said quietly.

I knew that. I did. I just had no idea how I would do it.

I also knew I would be pissed at Adam for quite some time. Years, maybe. Forever.

"You and I have had this discussion before, babe. Part of the problem seems to be you don't want to be alone."

"I've been alone," I said indignantly, reaching down to scoop up Lulu, who had been dozing at my feet. "After Adam and I divorced, and then also after Bryan left."

"Sweetie, you rebounded to Bryan within a few months, and then after Bryan, you started with the online dating—"

"I was still alone! I fixed a broken toilet! Did my own taxes! Snaked the drain with that snaky thing! Snow-blowed the damn driveway, and there was a shitload of snow that year!

"I know that. I'm not saying you weren't independent," Eddie said.

"Look around, Eddie. Most people are partnered. Sure, single people can be strong and manage our own households, but it stinks coming home and eating dinner alone! You know what I did the other night?"

"Screamed into a pillow?" Eddie said.

"No. I ate my entire chicken dinner with my fingers. Even the asparagus."

Eddie chuckled. "Bad table manners aside, I see nothing wrong with that. Who's to say asparagus isn't finger food?"

I smiled in spite of myself.

"Ian was always on the go or holed up in his room anyway," Eddie said. "You probably hardly ever saw him."

"True. But I knew my house was his home. I always had an idea where he was or what he was doing. Now what?"

"You know the drill," Eddie sighed. "Pick yourself up and dust off."

I didn't feel like dusting.

"Freaking Adam, taking him into to a life of homelessness," I said, still upset.

"You gotta take Adam out of the equation Jess. It's Ian we're talking about."

I handed Lucy to Eddie and went over to the sink to look out the kitchen window.

It was the quintessential perfect summer day in June. Couldn't it at least rain?

I wiped my hands on a dishtowel.

"I love him," I said after a moment. "I support his choices. But why he would choose to be a vagabond is beyond me."

"Because his father chose it," Eddie said, stroking Lucy under the chin.

"I know. Something else I will never understand."

"It's going to be OK."

I looked back out the window. I had never thought about what to do when I arrived at a place like this.

45

I WAITED ONE DAY UNTIL I COOLED DOWN A LITTLE TO TEXT Madison, who I realized had probably known about Ian's plan long before he told me.

Madd had already texted first thing that morning, saying she was coming over with donuts. I felt momentarily cheered up.

I was making coffee when she bustled in with the box of donuts, then came over and put her arms around me as I stood at the sink.

Aha. So she did know.

"What kind did you get?" I asked, flipping the switch on the coffee machine.

"Chocolate frosted, chocolate glazed and those Boston creams you like," she said, getting out plates.

"So, basically all chocolate," I said, pulling up a chair. "You know me well."

We ate the sweets in silence, licking our fingers.

"So, you know about Ian?"

Madison put her donut down.

"Yeah. He's been thinking about it for a while, Mom. He really didn't know what to do. He didn't want to upset you."

I smoothed back a stray hair from the ponytail I'd thrown my hair into, because I could not have cared less how I looked. I was still in pajamas. Not even a matching set.

"Well, he wants to, you know, discover the world," Madison said gently.

"I understand that."

"So, you're not upset?"

"The only thing that upsets me is his decision to leave school," I lied.

I was upset about the whole thing, skipping graduation (though at this point that was a minor detail), moving out, taking to the road with his hobo father. Choosing Adam over me.

"More coffee?" Maddy said, wiping chocolate crumbs from her chin.

"I'm good."

Madison got up to refill her mug.

"You're good? About the coffee, or about Ian moving out?"

I sighed. It was another one of those intense talks that always ended up happening at the kitchen table.

Wasn't a kitchen supposed to be a place for the family to gather for spaghetti dinner, with the sauce Mom made from her grandmother's recipe, which was also learned in a kitchen? Or at least share a takeout Bucket of Spaghetti? A place to joke about their days? Maybe linger and play some board games?

My kitchen was the fallout zone for sad news. Maybe it was time to start using the living room more.

I looked around for Lucy, my buffer against discomfort. She was asleep under the table, and I didn't want to wake her.

"You know you can text me any time to come over, or

maybe go out and do some shopping. That is, if you do any actual shopping anymore besides online."

"I shop!"

"What was the last thing you went shopping for in an actual store, besides groceries?"

I had to think.

"Notebooks and highlighters," I said, feeling vindicated.

"That hardly counts," Madison said, laughing. "It has to be shoes, or make-up, or even dog toys for Lucy."

I bought those items online too, but I wasn't going to admit it.

"Whoops, gotta go," she said, looking at her watch. "Billy and I got permission from the landlord to paint the walls, so we're going paint shopping. That's right, shopping. In a real-life store."

Madd's face lit up whenever she talked about her boy-friend, and that cheered me up.

"So, you're sure you're OK?"

She bent down to hug me.

"I will be."

"Bye Mombo," she blew me a kiss at the door.

The sound of the door shutting woke Lucy. She stretched, then put her paws on my leg to get picked up. I snuggled the back of her shoulder.

"These are strange times Lu," I told her. "I hope to get through it gracefully. Or at least not fall apart."

I wasn't making any promises to myself.

46

"Dad's coming to help me move my stuff into the camper," Ian said two weeks later on Saturday morning.

I could tell he was trying to sound casual. Nevertheless, I was startled. Ian had spent the days since he broke the news pretty much avoiding me, evidently fearing I would break down and beg him to stay. Which was a true possibility.

I tried hard to etch those final days into my heart, to remember the feeling of Ian being at home, of having him home with me.

He hadn't come downstairs for breakfast wearing the sweatpants and well-worn t-shirt he used for pajamas. Hadn't lingered at the kitchen table to tell me about his day. Or added anything to the grocery list. He was already a ghost.

"So, he's coming around noon," Ian continued.

"Thanks for the warning."

I immediately regretted my sarcasm. Of course, it was inevitable that Adam would show up to help Ian move. Ian needed help. And he didn't want mine, which was for the best, because I would have cried into all his clothes as he packed.

I remembered packing up Bryan's clothes after we agreed the marriage was over and he decided to move south. We sorted through wool sweaters, thick socks, jeans lined with red flannel, putting them all into a donate pile. He searched for his golf shoes, which I found months later and mailed down to him in North Carolina. Bryan kept the hooded robe I had gotten him right after we were married. He used to put it on and pull the hood up and I would hum the song to "Rocky" while he shadow boxed like Sylvester Stallone.

It was probably too warm in North Carolina to wear the robe; maybe he had gotten rid of it by now when he combined houses with Sarah.

As if he knew it would be hard for me, Bryan didn't send as many beach pics as he had when he first moved down. We texted from time to time to update each other on family news: the time his grandson Ben made a Father's Day card for Bryan because that's how close they were now; how they spent Christmas at the ocean. I told him about my raise and funny stories about the guys at work.

I'd texted him the very sad news of Sal's death, something that still hurt. All of us at the town office had lost a friend, and we felt that loss every day when conversation dwindled and Sal would have told a knock-knock joke.

Jerky was more subdued, although we brought in dog toys and chewie treats on a regular basis. He mostly sat under Sal's chair at the table, no longer interested in barking at pigeons from the window. We took turns sitting in the chair to scratch Jerky's ears and under his chin, which seemed to cheer him up for a while. Ok, so it was mostly Joe who petted the dog, since it gave him an excuse to leave his desk and avoid the ringing phones.

I missed Bryan, but I knew he was happy. Sal took a heart full of memories with him when he left, and was never forgotten. I had survived losing my ex and Sal, one of the kindest people I had ever known. Would I be able to do this when I lost Ian to the life of a wanderer?

Now Adam was coming to help Ian pack up and leave. Just like he had done.

I sighed and drained my coffee. I had several options. I could go out and avoid the whole thing. Or ask Eddie to come over to be a buffer if I started arguing with Adam. Or maybe we would just stand in stony silence.

I straightened my shoulders, determined to take the high road. I didn't want Ian's last memories of home being his parents fighting.

And I needed to be there when Ian left, to say good-bye.

The doorbell rang an hour later. Lucy started barking and growling.

"You go right ahead and bark," I told her. "Nip at his ankles if you feel like it."

Ian didn't come downstairs, so I went reluctantly to the door.

I was startled when I opened the door. I don't know what I'd expected. I guess I'd thought he would be a complete stranger to me.

I wasn't facing a stranger. I was facing Adam.

Yes, he had changed in the four years since I'd last seen him. It felt like forever; it also felt like no time had passed at all.

He still had a full head of thick hair, but it was salt and pepper. He had always been clean-shaven, but now he had a goatee. I had never been a fan of facial hair, but it was neatly trimmed. There were creases around his mouth I had never seen before, and deep lines around his eyes when he gave me a shaky smile.

It was the same nervous smile he'd used whenever I had asked him, years before, to go apple picking or to the town pool or any other of a million family activities. It was a forced smile, because he was already planning to leave us. I had suspected another woman, but the truth was, he had wanted a different life than the one we had built together for 22 years.

I swallowed hard.

"Hi Jess," he said, and it was the familiar voice that had asked me to marry him, soothed me when I needed comfort, cheered on the kids from the sidelines of soccer games, wished me Happy New Year.

It was Adam. Still Adam.

I took a step back and bumped into a kitchen chair.

He was waiting for me to invite him in, because it wasn't our house, it was mine, and he was a guest.

I opened the door wider to let him inside, quickly wiping my eyes on my sleeves because I was tearing up and if I didn't stay strong, I would start sobbing and maybe not be able to stop.

He was wearing a faded blue t-shirt with the name of a band I didn't know on it and broken-in camo cargo shorts. On his feet were well-worn hiking boots with leather shoelaces.

Reflexively, I glanced down at his left hand where his wedding band once was. It was deeply tanned, but no ring. I had held that hand on long walks, in movie theaters, while I was struggling to breathe and push during childbirth. I had always felt safe. I had believed we belonged to one another.

I realized I had put my despair over losing my husband

into a locked vault, pushed down somewhere beneath my heart where I thought it would stay shut forever.

Everything came flooding back as Adam and I faced each other, less than a few feet apart in my kitchen.

When he had come home with the RV, he asked us to go on the road with him, which was wildly unrealistic because the kids had been in junior high, and anyway, we had a family life that was stable. Until it wasn't.

For months after Adam left, I had waited to hear the screech of the brakes on the RV as he pulled hastily into the driveway. He would rush in and tell me he'd made a mistake, that he loved our life together and would never leave again.

That hadn't happened. It hadn't happened after months or even a year, then I met and married Bryan. Adam had sent me messages apologizing for hurting me. I had deleted them immediately. Because he had never come back.

Adam had stayed close to Ian. Madison hadn't ever really forgiven him, but I hoped one day she would come around. Adam loved the kids, I knew that. What I didn't know was if he had ever loved me. And that was important because I had loved him with all my heart. And always would.

Adam stood awkwardly in the middle of my kitchen. He didn't meet my eyes, which was an old habit of his when he was hiding something from me. What was it? Could it be regret?

I knew I should offer him coffee, but all I wanted to do was look at him. I needed to see if there was any hint of who he once was; a husband and father living a regular life in middle-class suburbia. Relatively satisfied. Going out Saturday mornings and taking photos he might one day submit to magazines. Nuzzling my neck when he wanted to make love. Looking forward to retirement to spend more time with me when the kids were grown.

It was the worst of the unavoidably uncomfortable times in my kitchen.

Then Adam took a step towards me, and time fell away as we met halfway and clung to each other. I put my arms around his neck and leaned my head on his shoulder, as naturally as it had been before he left us. He felt like Adam. He felt like home.

Then he stroked the back of my hair, quietly shushing me, and as I cried into the neck of the t-shirt I didn't recognize.

Adam pulled me closer to his chest and it was if he had never left, that he was still my partner, still mine.

"I'm so sorry Jess," he breathed into my ear.

What was he sorry for, exactly? For abandoning his wife and two children? For mailing divorce papers from another part of the country? For never, not even once, turning around and coming back?

"I'm sorry for everything," Adam said, as if he'd heard my thoughts.

We were holding each other when Ian came into the kitchen, stopping short when he saw us.

"Ah, let me give you guys a minute," Ian said, starting to back away.

"It's all right," I said, stepping back from Adam and wiping my tears on the back of my hand.

Ian put down the backpack he was carrying and went back up the stairs.

It was quiet in the kitchen. Neither of us had moved away from one another.

"I guess I'll go up and help him bring his things down," Adam said at last.

"Of course," I said, turning back to the table and almost stepping on Lucy, who had been watching us embrace, as if it was the most natural thing in the world. In many ways, even after all the time that had passed, it still was.

Adam turned to follow Ian, then stopped in the doorway, hesitating.

"I promise I will bring him home to see you whenever he wants."

I had no idea if and when Ian would want to visit me.

"OK," I said at last.

Adam went upstairs, and I could hear their excited voices as they finished packing.

Lucy came over and brushed against my leg. I picked her up, then went to the window to see the RV Adam now called home.

It was a larger camper than the one he had left in four years ago. He must have been making hefty commissions in his sales job to afford it.

I shook my head to clear my thoughts about Adam's new life. The RV was shiny and clean and had light blue gingham curtains on the windows and a rolled up green awning on the side. Even the tire rims were spotless.

My throat was closing up again and I felt the anger rolling in when Ian said he was leaving. The RV wasn't a home. It was never in the same place, never rooted. And who knew what it looked like inside? Ian wouldn't even have his own bedroom. He would probably sleep on a foldout couch with a thin, bumpy mattress. Some kind of futon. Or maybe a table that turned into a bed.

Maybe they would use sleeping bags and lie outside by a fire under a canopy of stars like cowboys.

I heard Ian come bounding down the stairs. He carried a laundry bag stuffed with clothes and a backpack with his laptop and assorted chargers hanging out. I wondered for a moment if the trailer even had Wi-Fi. They would probably have to stop at coffee houses to use their internet.

I remembered when Ian was a young teenager into Nintendo and Yu-Gi-Oh! cards. He would pester Maddy to play and sometimes she would cave and race carts with him or help Zelda find his way. The PlayStations had been put away long ago, replaced with laptops and social media. At the time, I'd been relieved they weren't going to turn into professional gamers, but now all I wanted was for the two of them to be on the couch, whooping over the videogames, laughing, laughing, laughing. Home.

It took Ian and his father less than two hours to move him out.

I tried to stay busy by cleaning out the fridge but did little more than throw out some old cheese.

"Well, I'm all set," Ian said, coming into the kitchen wearing two knit Carhart hats.

"Planning on being cold in the camper?"

"Nah, just didn't want to forget them."

"So where are you guys headed?"

I flinched when I saw Ian's eyes light up.

"Yellowstone."

Of course. Freaking Yellowstone, possibly the most beautiful spot in the country.

He came over to hug me. I didn't want to let go.

"I'll text you."

Ian had always been a great texter. He texted me stories about his day. He texted at the gym. He even texted when he was up in his room and had something to share but was too lazy to come downstairs.

"I need to go to bed early," he would text me.

Or, "I had bacon on my turkey sub for lunch."

Or even, "My shoulder hurts from lifting at the gym."

He had never been overly chatty—but I could always count on his recurring updates. Over time, I had relied on them to keep him close to me. I didn't have to know where he was every second of the day after he got older, but he would share entertaining snippets with me.

I knew those days of constant contact with Ian were over, and it would never be the same.

Adam stood by the front door. It was his turn to look down at his scuffed hiking boots.

"See you, Jess," he said at last.

We both knew he wouldn't be seeing me any time soon.

I didn't walk my son and former husband out to the driveway. I didn't go to the window to watch them drive away. I put my head in my arms on the kitchen table and cried, this time harder because there was no one to hear me.

47

By Sunday night, Ian's room had an echo.

He had left his bedroom door open, which already felt wrong. Ian had always been a private kid, closing his door and turning on music to indicate he needed his space. Now his open door stunned me with the realization that it wasn't his space anymore; he had vacated.

I knew Adam would keep his word, just like I had to believe Ian would miss me and still text, maybe even visit regularly. But he wouldn't be back, not the way it had been anyway. He wouldn't come downstairs in his red flannel robe and make toast, nearly burnt, the way he liked it. His hoodies wouldn't hang off the stair rail. The upstairs shower would not be continuously running. He wouldn't bolt out the back door and gun his engine as if he couldn't get to the gym fast enough.

I looked around the room. He'd had to downsize considerably to live in whatever his space was in Adam's camper. Basically, he took clothes and his electronic devices.

It was fine with me that he had left belongings behind. I would gladly be his mom self-storage unit.

He'd left his 21 Pilots framed poster, the shelf Adam had built for his collection of miniature Buddhas, his pink Himalayan salt lamp, a pair of child-sized binoculars he used to spot birds and spy on neighbors when he was in grade school. There was the little porcelain leprechaun from a thrift shop that he always believed was haunted because the eyes seemed to follow him as he moved around the room. A couple of times Ian and Madd used a Ouija board to try and contact the leprechaun's spirit and claimed it had spoken to them. Leery, they put the board away, but the little Irish doll stayed on Ian's shelf, where they swore it was watching him.

For much of his childhood, Ian wanted to be an astronaut, so he spent his birthday money on freeze-dried meals. The little pouches of beef stroganoff and chicken noodle soup were stacked in neat rows inside a small cabinet near his bed. Funny that he didn't take them. They might have been dinner some night around the fire with his father.

Ian left two boxes of books with the word DONATE on them in his familiar scrawl. I ran my hand over the packing tape, then opened one of the boxes. On the top was a well-worn, large hardcover book about the world's natural wonders, from volcanos to hurricanes. He had always been fascinated by the weather. When the dream of being in space died, Ian said he would be a storm chaser when he grew up. During the occasional hailstorm in New York, he would run outside and catch some of the ice pellets to try to measure them. He had waited for hail as big as pennies to come down.

He left behind his high school yearbook. Several books about haunted places in upstate New York. A guide to organic gardening, because he had the idea of selling tomatoes to make money one summer when he was twelve. A program for a Blue Man Group show we'd gone to in Boston several years ago.

I would never donate the books. In fact, I would move

them into my closet to make sure no one else ever did.

Ian's bed was still made with his hunter green comforter. Apparently, he didn't need bedding in his father's camper. Or there was some kind of small sofa that opened into a bed with a thin foam mattress. Or the kitchen table transformed into a cot. I shook my head. I had just no idea where he would be sleeping.

Several boxes of clothes were stacked by the closet, things he wouldn't be able to fit in the camper.

"You can donate these too, Mom," he had said.

Not in a million years. I wanted to know his Maroon 5 band T-shirt, Nike shorts, and running shoes were still in the house. I hoped the day would never come that I went upstairs and looked through his things, just for the memories, but I knew it might.

I was a sap; I knew it, but sappiness had been a career for my kids' entire childhoods.

A lone green plastic soldier the size of a thimble stood on his bookshelf, the last man standing after what must have been an epic battle. At one time, Ian had dozens. He would line them up on the stairs and make loud tank engine noises, hurtling them down the steps to the bottom to lie sideways and forlorn.

The soldiers were Ian's first choice when we went shopping at Quik Stop during long, glorious summer vacations from school.

"Can you take us to the dollar store?"

Madd always had Ian ask because he was smaller, and she believed him to be more likely to get a yes.

Not everything at Quik Stop was a buck, but pretty close. I gave the kids a budget of $5 each. Madd would deliberate for 20 minutes over pink butterfly nets, green sand toys shaped like frogs, rubber fish to float in the tub, knock-off Barbie dolls, balloons filled with fluorescent yellow water, fake moustaches or a zillion other items that caught her eye.

Ian would head right to the shelves of soldiers. There were different troops, air fighters, battleships, little figures with grenades.

One day when he was about four, I heard Ian calling for help from the stairs. I dropped my mug of tea on the kitchen floor racing to get him.

But it was the little soldiers crying for help. Ian had borrowed Madison's cheerleader Barbie to join the battle, and she kicked all the soldiers' butts. They were all in a heap at the bottom of the stairs.

"So Barbie won?"

"Course, Mom. Do you see how big she is?"

Now there was just one plastic soldier, knocked on its side. I stood him back up on the shelf.

I left everything as Ian had, the stacked boxes, the lone sock on the floor by the dresser. The creepy leprechaun did seem to follow me with his squinty green eyes as I quietly closed the door.

48

DESPAIR HIT HARD AFTER LOSING IAN, JUST LIKE WHEN ADAM left and when Bryan moved south.

I fought the urge to take to my bed. Those first few days, I just kept putting one foot in front of the other. I wore the same blouse three days in a row because I lacked the energy to come up with a new outfit. I turned down chocolate chip scones when the men were making a coffee run. I relied on dry shampoo for several days in a row. Lucy scooted next to me as I sat on the couch at night, leaving the lights off as it got dark.

Nadine and Eddie texted but I told them I was fine and didn't need them to come over. Eddie offered to bring takeout Asian food, but everything tasted like cardboard to me. Nadine said she'd bring Moscato, but even wine didn't appeal to me.

I willed myself not to get down the photo albums and go through Ian's baby pictures. But memories washed over me before I could stop them.

When Ian was an infant, he slept in a tiny wooden cradle near my bedside, and at night when he started fussing, I would lean a leg out to rock it with my foot, still mostly asleep myself. But when he started balling up his little fists and getting worked up, I would bend over the cradle and pick him up, a swaddled lump of baby starting to squirm and get red in the face, my little monkey boy. I would lay him in the warm spot next to me to nurse him. He would latch on immediately, and I would feel my milk coming in, and we fell into a perfect rhythm of giving and taking nourishment. His face would relax, and he would suckle until he was milk-drunk, lulled back to sleep, a faint dribble coming from the corner of his little bow mouth. Even then, so tired I could barely see straight, I knew to keep the memory safely in my heart and hold it there, even as it hurt to know the time when I could give Ian everything he needed would be fleeting and finite.

A week later Ian messaged me a photo of Yellowstone, with its gorgeous mountain ridges and perfect blue sky.

"It's great to be traveling," he texted. "Feels like a different world."

"You've traveled before. Remember when we took you and Madd to see the Grand Canyon?" I texted back, mentioning the trip again because it was imperative to me that he remembered we had travelled as a family. "You were about nine?"

"Nope, but you've shown me pictures," he texted back.

We had driven west across the country in the springtime that year. Adam told the kids it was cowboy land, and they stuck their faces on the windows in the back seat, fogging up the glass while they waited for a rancher on a horse to ride up to the car.

We'd had Western omelets even though neither of the kids liked peppers or onions, stood at the railing surrounding the canyon and hollered into the abyss. Ian and Maddy wanted to take the mule ride down the rough paths into the canyon, but Adam and I had quickly refused, distracting them by saying we were headed to a ghost town.

The kids had been disappointed there weren't any ghosts; after all it was mid-day under a scorching sun. We told them the spirits mostly came out at night, which made Ian run over to hold my hand.

Then they chased down tumbleweeds and we took pictures of them standing in the swinging doors at the entrance of an old saloon, which thrilled them.

The memory was another picture in the slide show of our lives, imprinted on my heart, now bittersweet.

49

ONE DAY IN THE MIDDLE OF JUNE WHEN I WAS WALKING LUCY, I took a close look around and realized my lawn was the least green on my street. Why was I even calling it grass? It was straw, burned out right down to the dry soil.

I had seen homes with lawns that looked like golf fairways, most of them mowed diagonally.

I wasn't looking for that kind of perfection, and I didn't have the money to hire a landscaper. I just wanted to be able to walk on the lawn without burning the bottoms of my feet.

If Ian was there, he would have rolled up his sleeves and helped me out with the project. He would have made it fun. But he wasn't, so I was on my own. And I desperately needed a project to throw myself into.

Besides, how hard could it be to sprinkle some seed and turn on the hose?

Gamely, I headed to the garden store.

I had not anticipated whole aisles of lawn prep items I would need to grow grass. I looked around and then got distracted by the dog treat display. Lucy would love the turkey chews.

"Can I help you?"

It was the type of guy I imagined working at a greenhouse: overalls, well-worn muck boots, a straw brimmed hat.

"You can. I want to start a lawn."

"Got your work cut out for you, this being a hot summer already," he said, rubbing his face as if I'd already given him a headache. "You're going to need everything from A to Z."

I had no idea what that meant, but it sounded like he did.

"What kind of soil you got?"

"Um, medium brown?"

He suppressed a laugh. Well, he tried to anyway.

"I mean, sand or clay?"

"It's not clay," that much I did know.

"So, let's get you started with topsoil," he said, walking away.

We passed a display of wind chimes made with forks and spoons. I paused momentarily to check the price.

"Come on," the lawn guy called to me.

There were at least a dozen kinds of soil, all in enormous green bags and nearly indistinguishable.

"How many square feet?"

I was stumped. How exactly would I have measured that?

"It's a regular sized front yard."

I held out my hands as if that would give him an idea about the size of my lawn.

He grunted.

"Gonna need a shopping cart."

I hurried to the door and wheeled one back, then stood by as he loaded it with bags of topsoil, grass seed, fertilizer, and a huge bale of straw. I could barely see over the top of everything to push the cart.

"Soil goes first," he said patiently. "Then seed, then fertilizer, then put down straw. Not too heavy or it will smother the seed."

I nodded. Smothering sounded bad.

"Good luck," he said. "Remember, there's no such thing as over-watering."

I grabbed a bag of turkey treats for Lucy on the way to the register.

"That's $127.49," said the bored girl who rang me up.

Seriously? Had I heard her right? But my heavy bags were already on the checkout counter, and I couldn't see any way to bolt for the door without buying anything.

I paid and wheeled my cart out to the parking lot. The bags were 40 pounds each, but I mustered the strength to haul them into my hatchback. I was surprised I was able to carry them; maybe the water aerobics had paid off and I'd built some muscle!

I was going to grow a lawn, dammit. Might not be the lushest green in the neighborhood, but I was going to do it.

50

THE NEXT DAY WAS INTOLERABLY HUMID. BUT I HAD MADE A commitment to plant grass seed and was determined to follow through.

The first challenge I encountered was not having a wheelbarrow. I seemed to recall having one earlier; it was red and had one unstable back wheel. Had Adam taken it? In the RV? Not likely.

I found a non-snow shovel in the shed and spent most of the afternoon laying down topsoil. I was certain I had as much on my face and in my hair as I had put down.

After I raked it out smoothly, I took a moment to admire my work. It was dark and earthy and didn't have any worms or stink bugs. Perfection!

Lucy was scratching at the door to get outside. I took off my filthy rain boots and went inside to pet her with my soil-encrusted and newly calloused hands because I had taken off the gardening gloves when my palms began to sweat.

"A farmer's gotta do what a farmer's gotta do," I told her as I headed out again.

It took the rest of the afternoon to sprinkle seed and fertilizer, then blanket it with straw.

The sweat was running down my face as if I was crying. If anything, they would have been tears of joy that I finally finished.

I had two bags of seed, a bag of fertilizer and half a bale of straw left. Clearly the man over-estimated the size of my lawn. Note to self: figure out how to measure square footage.

Two old sprinklers were in the very back of the shed. One had been the kids' favorite because of the long sweeping streams of water they could jump over. I had tons of video of Ian and Madd running through the sprinkler and daring each other to drink out of it. Madison had convinced Ian hose water came straight from a dirty river bed.

The other was a rotor sprinkler I had never seen before, but it looked like a better candidate. It was rusty, though, and it took some patience to attach to the garden hose.

The sprinkler didn't quite reach the middle of the lawn. I was sure there was some extra length in the hose around the corner, so I yanked on the sprinkler. When it disconnected from the hose, I fell backwards, somehow tucking into a roll to avoid a head injury.

"Shit!"

From the dirty ground, I looked around stealthily to see if anyone had witnessed me falling on my ass. Then I waited to see if there was any pain in my body from injuries. Nothing but wounded pride. I got up carefully, covered in topsoil and straw.

But I was in my glory when the sprinkler was on, spinning water and making muddy puddles all over the soil.

"Whatcha doing?" Lily had scootered up the sidewalk silently.

I wiped my sweaty forehead with the back of my dirty hand and wished I'd brought out a bottle of water.

"Oh, just growing grass."

Lily contemplated this while she looked around my patchy front lawn.

"So, how's it going?" she asked politely, clearly able to see it wasn't going well.

"Oh, I'm getting there. Takes a while."

Lily looked up at the sky.

"Grandpa said rain is coming. Maybe that will help."

Even after all the months since Sawyer and I called it quits, it was jarring to hear Lily mention him.

"He's probably right," I said.

"Yeah, he's right about everything," Lily said matter-of-factly.

I smiled at my little friend.

"So what color green is your new lawn going to be?"

"Like the spring green crayon in your big collection," I said, reaching down to ruffle her hair.

"That will be pretty," Lily said, smoothing her hair back down.

51

AFTER A WEEKEND OF RUNNING THE SPRINKLER, THE SEED was washed into clumps in small puddles, swimming on the surface mocking me.

Maybe everyone had their own opinion on grass growing, and there was no right way. But clearly, mud puddles were not going to sprout.

Turned out, everyone did have their opinions, and the office men were all too happy to share their unsolicited advice.

"You only water first thing in the morning and last thing in the evening, round bedtime. Too much water will drown the seeds," Wes said the next day at Danish time.

"Did you fertilize? Lay it down too thick and it will choke out the grass when it just starts to sprout," Paulie said.

"It's the soil in town, all sand, doesn't hold the water," Joe said, swiveling his chair towards me. "You being a newcomer wouldn't know that."

"I'll tell ya who knew best how to tend a lawn, it was Sal," Paulie said sadly.

"You got that right, remember how pretty his front lawn was? Looked like artificial turf," Wes said, looking down at the moons of dirt under his fingernails.

We all fell silent for a moment.

I switched it up to morning and night watering. The sprinkler, with its unpredictable direction, doused my clothes most of the time I tried to move it. My rain boots were beyond hosing off. There was straw on the welcome mat, the kitchen floor, and Lucy's dog bed.

Against all odds, ten days later, I had a ground cover of green fuzz. Some of it was crab grass, and there were patches where I'd layered too much straw, but it was a long way from the trampled, burned-out mess I'd started out with.

I called Madison to come admire it.

"Well look at you," she said when she arrived. "Next thing you'll be planting an apple orchard. Or peaches! Can you do peaches? I love them."

"You love all fruits, honey," I said, ruffling her hair. "It all started with Gerber strained pears."

After Madd left, I pulled out a lawn chair and set it up in the shade of Penny's cherry tree. Lucy dozed on my lap.

I wished Ian had been there to share my triumph, but instead, I took a picture to text him later.

Ian still texted, mainly one or two sentences like "Hiked Terrace Mountain today," "Forgot sunscreen and got sunburned," or "Caught a trout in a little stream."

He sent pictures. I knew I was still very much a part of his life, but the house felt as empty as a ghost town.

52

"JESS? YOU HOME?"

It was a hot July morning. I was filling the washer with sheets and towels when I heard my sister's voice at the kitchen door.

"Kat?"

"Can I come in?"

"Absolutely, of course, what are you doing—"

I stopped talking when I saw her face. She looked sad beyond sad, her hair was pulled back in a messy ponytail and her merlot lipstick was smeared. She was wearing jeans with frayed hems like she did in high school and blue striped canvas sneaks. Her yellow blouse was buttoned wrong.

"Sorry to just show up," Kat said, putting her suitcase-sized leather purse on the floor and plopping down on a chair at the table. "I meant to text you on the way here."

"Don't apologize. I am thrilled to see you—but I don't have lunch ready. I can make something—"

"I can't eat right now," she waved a hand at me, and I could see how exhausted she looked.

"What's wrong? Are you all right?" I asked, immediately alarmed.

"Yes. No. I don't know actually," Kat said, raking her fingers through her hair in a way that made it messier, but in a cute, forlorn way.

"Is it something about the boys?"

"No. They're fine. They're good. It's me. I'm upset."

That much I could see. I got up and opened the fridge to pour us both lemon seltzer, wishing I had real lemon to slice for the rim of the glasses. Why did I never have garnishes? One of my shortcomings as an unprepared host.

But I did have paper straws with little watermelon designs, so I plopped one in each glass.

"So, what is it?"

Kat sipped her drink.

"It's Ray."

"Oh my god, is he OK? Is he sick?"

I felt panicked. Ray was a stellar husband to Kat and great father to their kids.

"No, he's not sick. He's just a terrible person."

Lucy padded in and sniffed at my sister's ankles until she bent down and scooped her up.

"What happened?"

Kat held Lucy up on her shoulder the way you would when burping a baby. She had always been a natural with children and dogs.

"Lu smells great—is she wearing cologne?"

"What? For a dog? Does that even exist? No, she was just groomed the other day and they bathed her with some kind of strawberry shampoo."

Lucy gave a little belch.

"So back to my question, what happened with Ray?"

"It's such a classic man-thing to do that it's almost a cliché. He forgot our anniversary."

"Like, completely? It was just a couple days ago, wasn't it? Maybe he has something planned?"

"No," she shook her head and put Lucy down. "He doesn't have anything planned."

"How do you know?"

I got up and started rummaging through my kitchen cabinets for Cheez-Its or Doritos or something to eat as we went through the impossible scenario of Kat's husband forgetting their anniversary.

"Because I asked him. There was no plan."

"Maybe it's a surprise! The kids and I gave Eddie a surprise party for his last birthday, and he knew nothing about it until he walked in the door!"

Kat slurped miserably through her straw and watched me pour Chex Mix into a bowl. She had a yellow gold ring on every finger including her thumb, some of them sapphires, some emeralds, one a champagne diamond, many of them anniversary gifts from Ray. Me, I was more of a sterling silver bracelet girl.

"It was the worst anniversary ever," she said. "Thank you for the card by the way."

"You're welcome. And it wasn't the worst anniversary ever. Remember in tenth grade when you'd been dating Danny Lyons for six months and he gave you a Tom Petty album and tried to get to third base—"

"Which I never let him."

"I know that, silly. But do you remember what happened the next day?"

"He broke up with me in study hall."

"That's right. Then you came home and smashed the album on the driveway," I reminded her with my mouth full of the little waffle pretzels I was picking out of the Chex Mix.

"Yeah, that was dramatic, wasn't it? And I really liked Tom Petty."

"Whatever happened to Danny Lyons?"

"I Facebook-stalked him," Kat admitted. "He's still single, as far as I could tell."

"See?" I had gotten off track. What was the correlation between Danny never getting married and my sweet brother-in-law? What was the point I was trying to make?

"Look Jess," she said, slurping through her straw. "I know you want to make this better for me, but he forgot. Plain and simple."

"All right. Do you want to know what I think?"

"Uh, yea, that's why I drove two hours to get here. Of course, it's always good to see you, but I need some sisterly advice."

"Here's my suggestion: go out and buy yourself something amazing. Maybe another ring. Go home, put it on, and thank Ray for the gift. Done. Disaster averted."

Kat reached into her bag and pulled out a compact to check her lipstick, which was a good sign. She cared how she looked.

"Jesus, couldn't you tell me I had messed up my lips? I look like I just drank cherry Kool-Aid!"

"Can you believe moms ever gave that stuff to us? Wasn't it, like, a little packet of powder and a cup of sugar?"

"It's a miracle we have any of our teeth left," Kat said.

"Life was so much less complicated when we were kids. Remember every summer the ice cream man drove through our neighborhood, and we elbowed our way past all our friends to get in line because he always ran out of fudgesicles?" I said.

"Yes! And remember you got that burn from the hot tar they were using to patch the road and had to sit with your foot in a bucket of ice for the rest of the day?"

"Remember? I think I still have a scar."

I hadn't looked at it for decades, but I imagined the little burn mark was on the sole of my left foot.

"Good times," Kat said, finally eating some Chex Mix.

"Great times."

"So, if I'm gonna buy myself a gift, it's gonna be a helluva lot better than another ring. I'm thinking maybe Lexus."

"Now you're talking! What color?"

"Red," she said smiling in a way that made her dimples deepen.

We had finished the bowl of Chex.

"Want some lunch?" I asked, standing up and going to the fridge.

"Can you make my favorite?"

"Grilled cheese it is. I even have dill pickles somewhere in here."

My sister put her feet up on another chair and stretched her arms over her head.

"So, now that we've solved my problem, what's new with you?"

I flipped the sandwiches in the pan with a spatula, glad to see they were golden brown and not burned.

"Nothing much, sadly." I got plates out of the dish drainer. "Just glad I have Lucy to talk to."

"How's Ian?"

"Ian is–," I took a breath and set her plated sandwich down in front of her, with the pickle on the side. Garnish!

At last, I had come through with garnish!

"Ian is good, as far as I know," I said, sitting down and pulling the crust off my grilled cheese to eat first. "I mean, I guess I was hoping to hear from him more often."

Kat reached across the table and squeezed my hand.

"You know Adam is taking good care of him," she said gently.

I bristled at the sound of Adam's name. Of course, I knew that. Adam probably needed more taking care of than Ian.

"It's better for him to know his father," my sister said. "He wasn't exactly Father of the Year when the kids were growing up."

I was surprised to see Kat had noticed Adam's absence from our life, even before he left us for life on the road. I think he had always been distracted by the life he wanted for himself; it made our life together pale in comparison.

"Another round?" I changed the subject back to lunch.

"No thanks, but have any cookies?"

I loved my sister. "Oreos or Chips Ahoy?"
"Both?"

"Perfect," I said, getting the cookies down from my stash.

"Hey, you know, for what it's worth, I think you're handling all this really well."

I scoffed. Well, it was more of a snort.

"Ha-ha. Kidding right? I'm a mess."

"Actually, I think you're really brave, Jess."

I held back another snort and looked at her as I bit into a cookie to see if she was being serious.

"I couldn't do it," Kat said, prying open an Oreo and

licking the middle. "I don't have your independent streak."

I was startled. Even at my obvious low point, I was a role model? Didn't seem possible.

"Sure you do. Remember when we were on that Girl Scout camp out, and you were the only one who could follow the map? Make a fire? Pitch our tent?"

"And almost lit my hair on fire? Yeah, I remember."

I still had my scouting sash somewhere with the iron-on badges for sewing a Christmas tablecloth, making a birdcage from popsicle sticks, and cooking a piece of chicken over a tin-can grill. Madison used to wear it for dressing up, although she was never a Girl Scout because she said it was no longer cool.

"I give you credit for 35 years of marriage. It can't be easy."

"No, it's not, but then again, being single has its ups and downs, right?"

"Well on the plus side, it's easier to pick out furniture and buy groceries and I have been known to frequently have chocolate muffins for dinner. While standing at the sink."

Kat laughed.

"But seriously sis, you're just as strong as me," I said.

"The grass is always greener, as they say," she sighed.

Kat leaned back in her chair and rubbed her stomach.

"That lunch hit the spot. Now, where's your computer? Let's look at the Lexus dealership."

"I'm all in for online shopping."

53

"Jess?"

I was just climbing into bed when I got Bryan's text. It had been too long since I'd heard from him, and I was delighted.

"Bryan! How are you? How's married life?"

"Great, really great."

"Same here," I lied. My emotions were a roller coaster that showed no signs of slowing down.

"So, I have news. Sarah and I are adopting a child."

My breath caught in my throat. Well, of course they would want to be parents after getting married. It shouldn't have surprised me.

I knew Bryan would be a natural father. He had always goofed around with Ian, especially in the summer when he hauled all the yard games out of the shed. Madison and I would pull up chairs to watch their version of ultimate Frisbee or cornhole. One year they put up an inflatable pool and played volleyball over a mesh net and shot beachballs into a floating basketball hoop.

Ian had been a teenager when I married Bryan, and with his father out on the road, I always thought of Bryan as a fun guy presence in his life. But I could picture Bryan with a child because he found so much joy with his grandson Ben.

"Congratulations to both of you," I texted back.

"Thanks Jess. We'll send pics."

"You better!"

Lucy bolted into the kitchen to yip happily at the door just as Nadine came in balancing a drink tray of chocolate milkshakes topped with whip cream.

"Hey lady," she said, putting down the drinks and scooping up Lucy.

"How did you know I needed chocolate?" I said, reaching for a shake.

"Whatcha doin`?" Nadine settled in the other chair at the kitchen table.

"Well, I just heard from Bryan," I said, slurping my shake.

"That's great! How's he doing? Spending all his time on the beach with the swimsuit model?"

"Probably. But he texted to tell me they're adopting."

"Hmmm," Nadine said. "A baby, or an older child?"

"They don't care either way, they just want to be parents."

"So, how do you feel about this news?"

I sipped my shake. "Well, obviously I'm happy for him. For them."

"And what about the less obvious?"

I stood up and went to the window. Not for the first time, my heart lurched as I thought about Lily riding her scooter up the sidewalk to my house. She would draw a smiley face on my driveway or write "Welcome" to encourage visitors, tell me stories about third grade, show me her sparkly nail polish. I had been teaching her to French braid her hair.

I hadn't seen Sawyer since the break-up in my kitchen. He never walked as far up the street as my house. I knew he was purposefully avoiding me. Which was just as well. But I rarely saw Lily, and I missed her.

I turned back to Nadine.

"Bryan will be really good with a kid. And of course I want him to be happy."

Nadine slurped down the last drop of her milkshake.

"Well, shall we go online and shop for little kids' clothes?"

"As much as I love Amazon, I'm not quite ready for that yet. But soon."

54

By mid-July, I had to get out of the house because it was starting to feel more and more like a tomb. The silence was overwhelming.

I missed Ian coming in the back door with his gym bag and heading straight to the fridge. Pulling up a chair to join in conversation with Maddie and me. I missed Ian's loud music coming down the stairs. I missed Ian.

I took Lucy to browse chew toys in PetLuv on a Sunday afternoon.

I was happy to see there was a skeleton squeak toy wearing a cloth tuxedo. We were buying that one for sure.

A dog bounded around the corner into our aisle even before its owner, a man my age who was a couple inches taller than me with bluish-green eyes and a newsboy cap.

"So sorry," he said. "Sadie, stop!" The man had turned a little pink with embarrassment.

But Lucy and Sadie were already immersed in doggie introductions, sniffing each other's butts and bumping noses. His dog, a Corgi, lay down and showed Lucy her belly.

"Looks like they're best buds already," I said, bending down to rub Sadie's tummy.

"Looks like it."

"I'm Jessie," I said, offering my hand. "And that's Lucy."

"Luca," he said, shaking mine.

We stood in awkward silence, watching the dogs play.

"So, what are you here for?" I asked, as if it wasn't clear he was looking for dog items.

"Food. She's been on a hunger strike since I haven't been able to find the beef stew she likes."

"Pretty smart."

"That's right. You on the hunt for new chew toys?"

"Yup. She's torn apart most of her old ones, but it's better than gnawing at the furniture."

"Sadie used to do that when she was a pup."

"How old is she now?"

"She's 11."

"She looks good for her age."

Like me, I hoped.

The awkward silence set in again. Both dogs had plopped on the floor after the frenzied excitement of meeting.

"OK, well, have a good one," I said. "Come on Lucy, don't be lazy."

"You too. Come on sweetheart," he said to Sadie.

We went in opposite directions in the aisle.

Before he turned the corner, Luca called back to me.

"I like your leggings."

I smiled. The zombies chasing people were one of my favorite patterns.

"Thanks."

A week later, it was time to change Lucy's tick and flea collar, so I made another trip to PetLuv. I parked at the far end of the lot for the extra walk that would probably burn about four calories. Oh well.

Lucy made a beeline for the fish tanks housing the

guinea pigs and started barking.

"Oh come on," I said, leaning down to pick her up. "They aren't for lunch."

"Hi Jess."

I turned and saw Luca pushing a green shopping cart. He had put down a pink blanket so Sadie could sit inside comfortably. It was quite adorable.

"Oh, hey Luca," I said, struggling to hold Lucy as she spotted Sadie and tried to get to her.

"I hope you don't think I'm stalking you," he said, looking a little sheepish.

"Of course not," I said, finally putting Lucy down and holding the leash closely.

"So, you come here every week like we do?"

"Pretty much. We like it here, except for the fish and parakeets."

Luca laughed. "Yeah, we steer clear of them."

He had on a faded green T-shirt, and this time without the hat, I could see his neatly shaved head. No problem there. Bryan had been bald and I always found it sexy.

Trying to be furtive, I glanced down at his hand for a wedding ring. None.

"Do you live around here?" Luca asked, turning pink again.

"Yeah, on Glen Street."

Lucy was starting to pull on the leash to get moving.

"You ever go to Ashton Park? We like to walk there and look at the flowers."

I closed my eyes for a moment, remembering the debacle of snow shoeing in the park. But I had conquered the sport by the end of the winter. So there!

"Sure, I love that park."

"Maybe we can get together—I mean, get the dogs together for a walk sometime."

"I'd like that," I said, desperately trying to stand still as Lucy pulled harder.

I waited for him to pick a date, then made the decision myself.

"How about tomorrow? Noon?"

"We'll be there."

"Bye, Luca. Bye, Sadie. See you then," I let Lucy lead the way to the treat aisle and sniff the Milk Bone boxes.

"OK, we'll get some," I told her. "But not the jumbo box."

I felt pretty proud. A year before, I wouldn't have been so bold. But Luca seemed shy, and I wasn't going to stand in the store talking about our dogs for half an hour.

55

"So how was the puppy play date?" Eddie asked.

"His dog isn't a puppy," I said, adding the word *meaningful* to *mean* on the Scrabble board.

"Ah, so it was a people play date?"

"Stop. It wasn't a date at all. It was more of a mutual dog walk."

Eddie studied the Scrabble board. He was amazing at word games but most of the time let me lose without too much humiliation.

I was pretty proud to have played a word that was truly, ahem, meaningful.

"Are you going to give me any deets about this dog man?"

"His name is Luca. He's a roofer. Union. Pisces. Really cute in a boyish older man way."

"Hmm," Eddie nodded as if I had made sense. "Married?"

"Are you kidding me?" I flicked the letter W off his word *wry*.

"Yes. I am kidding you. So, divorced?"

"Divorced once yes. His second wife died. Cancer. Two years ago."

"Sad," Eddie said, reaching for his mandarin hard seltzer.

"Tragic, really. Her kids never came around. He had to take care of her for a year and a half as she died."

"That's a long death," Eddie said, rubbing his chin

thoughtfully.

"She went into remission several times, thanks to new drug trials. But the end was hideous." I shuddered thinking about it.

"Has he recovered?"

"Sadie helped a lot."

"Sadie?"

"His Corgi. The one he walked in the park."

"So, besides dogs, and sad endings to marriages, you two have anything else in common?"

"Well, he's kind of shy," I said, dredging a tortilla chip in salsa.

"Must be true that opposites attract, you being a loud-mouth and all."

"I'm not sure there is an attraction there," I said, ignoring his remark.

Luca had been sincere and sweet. He hesitated before he spoke, which was something I needed to learn since I tended to blurt things out. We had walked the dogs and looked at the daisies and fountains and statue of the city's founder.

He tended to look at his hands while he quietly spoke. They were deeply calloused, and one thumbnail was black from some work-related injury I didn't ask about.

"When I went for a quick hug good-bye, I think I saw him flinch," I told Eddie.

"Are you his first date since the wife?"

"No. He had lunch with a woman from work a few months ago. She told him there wasn't a love connection."

"Wow. Harsh."

"Yup. Anyway," I took a deep swig of my lime seltzer. "I

didn't exactly feel a spark either."

"For what it's worth, I've never felt that love at first sight crap. Things take time to develop. I say give it a few more tries before you give up."

56

AND SO I INVITED LUCA AND SADIE OVER TO MY HOUSE FOR dinner.

He arrived blushing because he was almost 40 minutes late.

"I am so sorry. I got terribly lost."

"Did you try Google Maps?" I suggested, holding the door open for him to come inside.

"I don't think I have that," he said, looking more worried.

"Well, the chicken is ready, so let's eat."

Luca politely waited for me to sit down before pulling in his chair.

I served up the roast chicken and garlic mashed potatoes and green beans.

"Wine?" I asked, already tilting the Moscato towards his glass.

"No," he said, holding up his hands. "I don't drink."

OK.

"I hope you don't mind if I have some?"

"Go right ahead, please. It just makes me sleepy."

"Gee, what kind of Italian are you, not liking wine?" I joked.

Luca turned visibly pink.

"This bread is delicious, did you make it?" he said, dipping it in olive oil and vinegar.

"Well, someone made it," I tried joking again.

There was an awkward silence. It seemed to happen every few minutes we spent together.

From the side of his chair, Sadie started to cry.

"Is she all right?" I asked, putting down my fork.

"She just misses me."

"But you're right here."

"She needs to be held most of the time; she gets lonely otherwise," Luca said, leaning down to stroke her back. "It's OK sweet girl. You're OK."

I had never seen a man with such affection for a dog.

"So, how was work?" I asked, wiping my mouth on the cloth napkin I dug out from the drawer in the china cabinet to have something fancy for dinner.

Luca cleared his throat. "It was good. Replaced a roof on a U-Haul business. Pretty hot actually. Some of the younger guys can't handle the heat like us old-timers. They take breaks and go sit in the parts of the roof that are shaded. We aren't allowed to climb down during the job."

It was the most Luca had ever said, and I wanted to encourage it.

"How about you? Did you get hot and move to the shade?"

"Ah, no," he said, looking down at his blackened thumb. "I don't take breaks. It's not how I was taught to work."

For a moment I thought he was going to share something about his father or a mentor, but Luca cleared his throat and was his old quiet self once again.

I brought out the chilled lemon meringue pie.

"How big a slice would you like?"

"I'm not much of a sweets eater," he said.

"Well then I guess you can watch me eat pie," I said, refusing to give up dessert for him or anyone else for that matter.

Luca also turned down coffee. Said it made him jittery.

"I guess I should hit the road," he said when I'd finished my pie. "I'm almost an hour away."

"Did it take that long?" I wondered how slowly he drove.

"Well, I have to drive with the window down so Sadie can stick her head out into the wind."

That was a cute image, Luca driving his truck and Sadie's little nose poking out.

We walked to the door.

"Thank you for dinner," he said, looking nervous again.

"You're very welcome."

He didn't say he had a nice time, and I didn't ask him to come over again soon.

"Drive safe."

I shut the door and looked at Lucy.

"Time for more pie."

57

"Good morning."

Luca's text came through as I was settling in at my desk.

The men were already knee-deep into a discussion about the town's water system that was about as boring as it could get.

"I tell ya, the source is the reservoir on East Lowell Street," Wes said, yawning.

"It's underground you dolt," Joe grouched.

"It doesn't matter where it comes from anyway," Paulie said patiently. "It still has hard minerals in it. Turns the laundry gray."

"That's only when they're flushing the hydrants," Joe argued. "You're not supposed to do any laundry or wash dishes or, for that matter, drink out of the faucet when they're flushing."

I tried to tune the men out. Would they ever, in history, talk about something that actually mattered?

I was surprised to get Luca's text. I hadn't expected to hear from him again after the no-wine, no-dessert, no-coffee dinner.

"How are you?" I texted back.

"Great. Big day ahead. Replacing a roof at Costco. It's a six-week project."

"That stinks, it's the middle of the summer! Don't get

too much sun out there."

"Too late. My skin's leather already."

Joe was looking at me pointedly. I shuffled papers around on my desk.

"Listen, I ended our date kind of suddenly last night. Didn't want to overstay my welcome."

"It's fine," I lied, although eating half a pie secretly by candlelight had salvaged the evening considerably.

"Let me make it up to you and cook dinner at my place. Your choice. Pick something Italian you like."

Honestly, I couldn't think of any Italian food I didn't like.

"Anything is good," I said.

"DO YOU WANT A SCONE JESS?" Paulie bellowed from across the room at the conference table.

I waved my hand at him to signal no. My skirt was tight and what's worse, it had an elastic waistband.

"Can I bring Lucy?"

"Of course. Sadie would be disappointed if she couldn't see her new best friend."

"I'm sorry, I have to go."

"Have a good day Jess."

58

Luca's house, just outside Meredia, was a small Cape Cod in a quiet cul-de-sac with less than a dozen houses. The hedges were carefully trimmed, and the lawn looked freshly mowed. As I went up to the front steps, I saw a lone string of Christmas lights still wrapped around the railing.

"I'm glad you could make it," he said, meeting me at the door.

The smell of lasagna wafted from the kitchen. I was starving.

Lucy and Sadie bounded to each other and trotted away to play.

"Come on down," he said, going down the stairs to the basement.

Downstairs was a small stove, washer and dryer, open shelves stocked with canned soup, cereal, and packages of pasta. There was also a rowing machine, stationary bike, and massive weight set. A comfy dog bed with a moose chew toy was on the floor by the exercise equipment.

"So you work out?"

"I do."

Luca took the lasagna out of the oven. It was a little burned along the edges.

"Damn, forgot to set the timer. Hope you don't mind well-done Italian food."

"It looks delicious."

I looked around for a dining table and chairs but there weren't any. Where exactly would we be eating?

He took out plain white dinner plates and served up two heaping helpings.

"Come on up," he said.

I followed him back up the short flight of stairs to the garage, then through another door leading to the main area of the house.

The kitchen was immaculate, as if it had never been used. There was no sign of a microwave, a toaster, coffee pot or any of the other things taking up space on my own countertops back home.

Luca put the plates down on a small table in the breakfast nook and we both sat down.

"This is nice," I said, looking at the yard out the window.

"Thanks. I built it. Used to be an exterior wall here. Tore it all down and put in windows."

"Wow. That's amazing."

"I put in those kitchen cabinets, the front picture windows, renovated the bathroom, put up the carport."

"You've been busy," I said, thinking about how he'd described his relentless work ethic.

I waited for Luca to pick up his fork so I could dig into my meal.

From over his shoulder, I could see a lamp with a red scarf draped over the shade. It cast a pink glow in the kitchen as the sun went down.

We ate in silence. I took a discreet look at the living room with its plain beige couch and chairs. Mine had too many pillows and fleece throws on them, but they were cozy. I could only describe Luca's house as "quiet."

"So you cook in the basement?" I kicked myself for using the word "basement." I could have just said "downstairs."

"Yes, it's an Italian thing," he said. "My grandmother used to let me sit on a step stool and watch her make meatballs and her secret sauce recipe."

Sadie padded in and gave a little whine.

Luca got up and took a can of the gourmet brand of dog food out of the cupboard.

"Can Lucy have some?" he asked.

"I don't want her stealing Sadie's dinner."

"She can have her own."

Luca set out two pink dog bowls of food. Lucy immediately charged at it and started gobbling it down, covering the hair on her chin with sauce. Sadie picked at hers daintily.

"Good girls," he said, stroking each of their backs.

"The lasagna is really good," I said, finishing up every bite.

"Thanks. I don't usually make fancy food, so it's nice to have a guest to cook for."

Luca got up and carried the dishes to the sink.

He opened the fridge and took out a pastry box. My heart sang!

Inside were four very chocolatey eclairs overstuffed with cream filling.

I had found his dessert-avoidance odd at my house, so it came as a nice surprise he did indulge from time to time.

"Let me get some more plates," Luca said, rushing back to the kitchen.

He brought back two small versions of the white dinner plates.

Phew. I was worried I would be having dessert alone. Not that it would have stopped me.

I was relieved when he cut himself a slice so I wouldn't be eating dessert alone. Not that it would have stopped me.

We ate the pastries in silence. When I was done, I scraped the remnants of cream off my plate before I put my fork down.

"Want another?"

"No, thanks," I lied. But I was full and pretty sure he wouldn't be eating more.

"I'll pack the rest up for you to take home then."

"No, you keep them."

"I don't have much of a sweet tooth actually, and I try not to overdo it because I want to keep my BMI low."

Well, good for him. I had no idea, and didn't want to know, what my BMI was at the moment. Or ever.

The dogs were passed out on the kitchen floor, both of their dog bowls completely empty.

"Do you want to go sit in the living room?"

"Sure."

I saw the fireplace mantle as soon as I sat down on the couch. There was a statue of Mary, a rosary, and several framed photos. Most were of a woman with dark curly hair and red lipstick. One was a man with sunglasses overlooking a coastal town near crystal clear turquoise water.

"Is that you?"

"Yes, that's me, before—" He stopped his sentence. "Before my wife got sick. I can't believe how young I looked, and it was only a few years ago."

He was right. In the photo, his face was tanned but unlined. Now he was deeply wrinkled.

"She's very pretty."

"I know I should take them down," he said without looking at the pictures.

I had no idea what to say, so I said nothing.

We sat down on the sofa. He had a bashful demeanor, so I was surprised when he slid towards me and put his arm over my shoulders.

We sat quietly for a few minutes.

"Can I kiss you?" he said, breaking the silence.

Could he? Would he?

"Sure," I said, wishing I'd at least rinsed my mouth out after dinner.

I nodded my head. Of course.

It was a pretty amazing kiss. Just the right amount of tongue.

Then he said something that startled me, being that he was a shy guy.

"I want to take off your clothes."

He wasn't blushing now. In fact, he looked confident and certain, which I really love.

Here? In the living room? Were we going to go at it on the couch with Sadie and Lucy sleeping on the floor? Were the curtains see-through?

Luca got up from the couch and held his hand out to me.

I stood in front of him, and he pulled off my T-shirt and unclasped my bra. Then he slid down my leggings, tangling up my panties with them. I kicked them off, losing my socks in the process.

We stood there kissing for what felt like a long time.

I was so glad I had shaved. I had debated about it, not

thinking there was a chance in hell anything would be happening that night.

Then Luca gently pushed me back down on the couch and just as I thought it was strange to be naked on his couch cushions, he pulled my hips forward and dipped his head down, placing my legs on his shoulders.

Well there you have it. So much for the shy man who hadn't had a single glass of wine to loosen up.

He looked very serious, but somehow it didn't feel awkward.

Luca traced his fingers inside my legs, spreading my lips so I was completely open and ready for whatever he had in mind.

I didn't have to wait long.

He pulled on the top of my slit, making my clit pop out from under its sheath.

That was something new and I loved it. I leaned back and closed my eyes.

Using just the very tip of his tongue, he flicked it, so lightly I wanted to buck my hips to get more. Then he used his whole tongue to press flat on me without any pressure. It was exquisite pleasure. I suppressed the need to pull his face closer between my legs.

He was taking his time with me. He covered my inner thighs with kisses tenderly and I knew then I was with a very sweet man.

He lowered his face at last and began to lick with abandon. My moans brought the dogs into the room, but after looking at us with bewilderment, they trotted back to the kitchen where Luca had left out kibble.

When I was starting to feel the first waves of orgasm,

Luca pressed his face into me harder and started using more pressure. Then he slid one or two fingers, I didn't know or care how many, inside me and started stroking.

I had brief orgasm anxiety, but it didn't last long. It was clear he wanted to put me over the edge.

My mind let go and my body leaped over the cliff into a full free-falling shattering orgasm. I was gasping and sputtering but I trusted him to enjoy watching my pleasure without making it weird.

When I opened my eyes at last, he was sitting back, wiping his chin, looking very proud.

He had a helluva lot to be proud of.

I immediately wanted to reciprocate but was utterly at a loss as to what I could do given the couch situation.

But Luca knew.

He stood up and unzipped his cargo pants, immediately releasing the bulge beneath black boxer briefs.

I didn't need an invitation. Within seconds, I yanked them down, almost knocking him over as they tangled around his ankles.

Would it be too much to ask where the bedroom was?

Luca kicked off his hiking boots and the pants, standing in front of me wearing just a T-shirt.

He was compact and muscular, and thankfully, also clean shaven. Thank goodness for manscaping.

"Wow, you really do work out," I said, stating the obvious.

"Yeah, pretty much every day. Just at home."

"I go to the gym," I said casually, praying the setting sun would create enough shadows through the window to filter out the shape of my thighs.

"Then you know how relaxing it can be."

"Right," I said, although I couldn't disagree more. Not unless self-inflicted pain was soothing.

But I had better things to think about at the moment.

I licked inside my right hand then settled it snugly over his erection, starting a rhythm as I moved it up and down. His groaning started right away.

Then I let go and sucked him into my mouth. He was both big and incredibly hard.

I had to be careful not to scrape him with my teeth.

Luca stood very still, and I tested to see how far back his penis would go without triggering my gag reflex. Pretty far!

I used my hand and lips to slide him in and out, thinking it would be an oral sex encounter, which was fine with me.

But he pulled away.

"Hold on," he said, leaving the room.

Pee break?

He came back in with a blue towel that he folded in half and laid on the couch. Then, he sat and opened his arms to bring me over.

Ah, so this position. Girl on top? It had been a while, OK, years, since I had settled myself down on a penis.

Gamely, I straddled him while sucking in my stomach, because it wasn't a flattering position for my belly where gravity was taking place and it was sagging downward.

But Luca was looking in my eyes and I forgot to be self-conscious.

I lowered myself down carefully. There was a lot to take in. He was long as well as wide, something I hadn't encountered recently, or maybe ever.

Gingerly, I used my knees to control how far I took him

in. He cupped my breasts and ran his hands over my nipples.

"Beautiful," he said.

It was very flattering he would say that, as gravity was also doing a number on them.

I started rocking up and down, taking most of him but leaving a little room so he didn't nudge my cervix.

I took a deep breath and cleared my mind.

Luca was mouthing my hard nipples in a kind of gentle-firm way that I loved. How did he know?

And then I forgot about his size and began to grind. When I sat all the way down on him, it put direct pressure on my clit, all swollen again despite the recent orgasm. It was almost the right amount of friction, almost, and then it wasn't enough, and my body backed away from the edge of the cliff.

But Luca had a plan. He reached down and wedged his fingers between my legs, and with the rocking motion of my body, it was the right place at the right time.

I had always aspired to a genuine, legit simultaneous orgasm. Some had been pretty close. A few had been faked when I had known I was just not gonna get there on time, if at all.

We were in sync with our rhythm and just as I began to shudder and see stars, I heard Luca groan loudly in pleasure and push into me for one final thrust.

Score! We had met the challenge of getting off together.

I dropped my face to his shoulder, not caring that my forehead was bathed in sweat. We caught our breath. Honestly, I was afraid to lift off him and drip sex juice all over.

Then I remembered the towel, and as I slid off, I pulled

the edge of the towel between us to mop up the wet spot.

"Well," I said, standing up and ignoring the pain in my thigh muscles from the strenuous activity. "That was something."

"It was amazing Jess."

It was only around 10 p.m. but I had a glorious after-glow that left me completely worn out.

Plus, it felt very out of place and quite chilly to be naked on his couch.

"I should get going," I said, trying not to let him get a clear view of my ass when I put my clothes back on.

"OK," he got up and pulled on his boxers and cargos, leaving the T-shirt on the floor. "Let me at least give you lasagna to take home. I can't eat it all."

"Sure," I said, certain I could lure Nadine over with the promise of homemade Italian food.

I looked around for Lucy and as if on cue, she came bounding into the living room, completely refreshed after her power nap. Maybe she would fall back asleep in the car ride home.

We trooped back down to the basement where the lasagna was still on the stove.

"Let me find a container," Luca said, rummaging in the cupboard.

I took a quick look around and for the first time noticed a twin bed—really, it was just a camping cot—in the corner and a corduroy dog bed next to it.

"You sleep down here?" I said, once again not thinking before speaking.

Luca was packing up the food and had his back to me.

It took so long for him to answer I began to wonder if

he'd heard me.

When he turned around, his face was pink again.

"I know it's weird, but Sadie and I sleep down here instead of upstairs," he said. "My wife was sick in our bedroom."

I wished I could pluck my question right out of the air like it never happened. Of course he didn't want to sleep in their bedroom. He had made a very organized life in the basement, and that was fine.

"It isn't weird. I completely understand."

Luca was visibly relieved.

The little dogs followed us to the door.

When we leaned in to kiss, Sadie began to whine.

"She's used to having me all to herself," he said, bending down to scoop her up.

59

"So, I want to hear all about what's going on with Hunter," I said to Nadine a few days later.

It was a Wednesday, and we were out for white cheese pizza.

Nadine smiled so widely her brown eyes looked like there was light shining behind them.

"He's good. Moving his stuff back in this weekend."

"That's so great!" I said, stirring the mint leaves at the bottom of my mojito.

"Yeah, so far so good. Tristan acts like he doesn't care either way, but I think he's glad to see us giving it another try."

"I'm happy for you," I said, reaching across the table to squeeze her hand.

"It's funny, it's only been six months, but I feel like it's all brand new with Hunter. Like we're out of the rut we dug ourselves into. Maybe we both grew up a little bit while we were separated."

"And missed each other."

"It's the small things I missed about him. Like how his favorite breakfast is PB&J on oat bread. Or how he folds his bath towel before hanging it up to dry. And looks sideways in the mirror to make sure his stomach isn't starting to sag."

"Is it?" I asked, laughing.

"Hell no," Nadine snorted. "He looks fantastic."

"I can't wait to spend more time with him."

"You will soon. Promise. We'll have a double date with you and Luca."

The server brought the pizza. I took the slice with the biggest globs of ricotta and took my time chewing.

"So how's it going with Luca?"

"Good, I guess. I don't really know."

"You don't know? He still too quiet?"

"Not in bed," I said. It was my turn to smile.

"Ah. Well, what more could you ask for?"

"I don't know," I said again. "I worry about him a little. He basically lives in his basement. I mean, there's nothing wrong with that; he said Italians always cook down there."

"And the problem is...?"

"His house, the upstairs, is a shrine to his wife that died. Her stuff is all over the bathroom, half-empty perfume bottles, hairbrushes. There are photos everywhere and scarves over the lampshades in a very romantic way."

"You have cheese on your chin," Nadine said. "Have you thought about asking him to put these things away?"

"I don't want to be bossy," I said, reaching for another slice even though I was already almost full. I would work it off at the gym. Ha!

"He has this routine he needs to stick to, like things would go haywire if he didn't follow it."

"Like what?" Nadine asked.

"He walks his dog, works out, eats lunch, does laundry, picks up groceries in the same exact order on weekends. I invited him out to lunch last weekend, and he said he was eating at home. I can forget about doing anything on weeknights because he has to get ready for work the next day."

"Some people like to follow a routine," Nadine pushed back her plate and wiped her mouth with a napkin.

"And he is never free to do anything on Sunday afternoons because he has to go home and go through the same schedule. He's the opposite of impulsive."

"He's not married, right?"

"He's a widower."

"Oh yes. He's just set in his ways. He's probably used to being alone by now."

Of course she was right. His routine was a structure for him. It was probably a way to keep moving on.

"I want to meet this guy and see for myself."

"Sounds like a plan."

The server brought the check. It was my turn to pay.

"Any new clients?" I asked Nadine.

She rolled her eyes.

"Can you believe it, another carpet installer. There's only so many creative slogans for carpets."

"Sounds like something is underfoot," I said.

"Hmm, that's cute but not quite right," Nadine said, standing up to put on her coat. "Keep thinking and text me if you're hit with inspiration."

60

THE NEXT NIGHT, THE BROWN RICE I WAS MAKING TO HAVE with our chicken dinner turned to mush while I waited for Luca.

Damn. Should have waited to cook it until he actually arrived.

Sighing, I got out the bag of jasmine rice.

Almost an hour later, after I had texted him twice to make sure he was OK, Luca showed up at my door.

"I am so sorry. Lost track of time."

He didn't lean down to kiss me, so I put my face up to reach his lips.

"It's fine. I cooked a new batch of rice. Are you ready to eat?"

"Can we talk for a minute?" he said.

My stomach clenched. Shit. I wasn't prepared for bad news in the kitchen. Again.

I sat down at the table and looked around for Lucy. Then I realized Luca hadn't brought Sadie, which was a terrible sign.

Luca clearly wasn't going to sit. In fact, he began to pace. When he started talking, he was facing my refrigerator.

"Jessica, look–"

Using my full name! Another sign of disaster ahead.

He turned to look at me, his face was deep red.

"You know I've enjoyed getting to know you."

I sat silently.

"It's just too much... I'm not ready..."

We'd had dinner and sex exactly three times. I had never asked for or expected more. Except maybe that he be more punctual.

"It's too soon–"

I held up my hand to stop him.

"I get it. You don't have to explain. I'm sure it's hard starting over."

"I'm just still in a funk," he said sadly. "I lose track of time; I can barely go upstairs at my house because it reminds me of my wife."

I stood up and went to the cabinet for Tupperware pack him chicken and rice to go.

When I turned and handed it to him, I realized how much I would miss him.

"Thank you," he said when I held out the food. "And again, I am so sorry."

We both hesitated at the door, but a kiss was clearly uncalled for, and a hug would have been too forced.

"Bye then," I said, opening the door.

"Bye Jess."

I got out a plate and served up the rest of the chicken and jasmine rice. Hearing silverware, Lucy trotted into the kitchen to investigate.

I sat at the table and fed her some bites of chicken. I wasn't hungry anymore.

My heart wasn't broken. But it was pretty banged up.

61

Ian rarely texted and that was hard on me.

I tried hard not to bombard him with texts, but every time something funny happened in the house, I wanted to share it with him.

"Lucy has started nosing through her food bowl, picking out the bits of kibble she likes, and spitting the other pieces out on the kitchen floor. Sometimes I even find them in the living room. I found one in my bedroom!"

I also wanted to tell him I was so glad he put in a new filter in the furnace. There was a sign at the firehouse reminding homeowners to check their filter, which I never would have remembered. Anyway, the one you put in last year was filthy! We must have been breathing in the dust."

I didn't text Ian to tell him I never went upstairs anymore. It had been his space, a place where I believed he was content. Now I basically pretended I lived in a ranch and didn't go up the stairs, because I knew I would end up at Ian's closed bedroom door. It was official. I'd become a female version of Luca.

I had thought Ian's life was on an orderly path: finish school, get a job, move into an apartment like his sister had done.

But he hadn't been happy upstairs in our house. He had the same sense of needing to be free that his father had.

They wanted to pull up the roots we'd set down as a family. I hadn't had a clue Ian was feeling restless and maybe even constrained.

How could I have missed the signs? Ian had spent more and more time in his room, but that was the life of a college kid. He had still come down to grab food, do his laundry, and play with Lucy. I had gotten used to his schedule of leaving early for school and coming home in the late afternoon. He had always told me about his day and asked about mine before going upstairs.

I almost always had a funny story about the Three Stooges or someone who had wandered into the town office with some random request like could we open a fire hydrant for their kids to play in, or did they have to bag their leaves or could they just rake them to the curb.

I thought I knew almost everything about my son. Then again, I'd had the same belief for much of my life about his father.

As it turned out, they both harbored the same wish to travel, which meant closing the chapter on their suburban life in one fell swoop, leaving me to handle the aftermath and miss them. My longing for Ian was a fresh wound, but seeing Adam again sifted the silt of complicated my emotions I believed I had long ago put to rest.

But I had survived Adam and Bryan leaving, and I knew if I dug down deep enough, I would find that strength again.

Ian moving out so suddenly was a different story entirely. All I could do was wake up every morning and put one foot in front of the other. That, and try to stay busy.

62

KEEPING BUSY MEANT MORE UBER HOURS AND GOING TO THE gym more frequently to sweat my ass off. Well, sweat anyway. My ass wasn't going anywhere anytime soon.

I'd long given up any semblance of fashionable workout gear. Instead, my exercise wardrobe consisted of one of Ian's old T-shirts that didn't cling to my waist and a pair of loose-fitting elastic waistband shorts.

Most of my fellow exercisers—in far better shape than I was—plugged into earbuds to blast music during their workouts. I liked to be more aware of my surroundings, to the whooshing sound made by the stationary bike, and even watching cooking shows on the TVs overhead.

There was a children's playroom on one side of the enormous room where parents could drop off their kids for babysitting while they exercised.

The moms would hold the doors open for their children, who were usually carrying sippy cups or juice boxes and a stuffed animal or security blanket. Some of the small children didn't want to be parted from their mother and made a fuss when they saw the playroom and realized mom would be disappearing.

I had kept Ian home until he was almost four years old, and Adam pushed me to get him into nursery school. I didn't see why, because I was able to spend all day with Ian, doing my freelance writing at night or when they napped. Neither of my kids were good nappers. Ian would stand up in his crib and throw all the blankets on the floor. Once he even pulled up the thin mattress and tried to toss that out. After that, I let him stay up with me during the day. We made dinosaurs with Play Doh, snuggled and read books, ran around the backyard, and baked cookies.

But Adam said Ian needed to socialize with children his own age, so I found a pre-school at a church close by and enrolled him for three mornings a week.

At first the allure of something new made Ian happily skip into the toy-laden classroom. But after the first couple weeks, he realized I wasn't sticking around for the three hours. The pre-school had an odd way to release the children to their moms for pick-up. The teachers would make the kids sit down and they had each mother go to the doorway one at a time. After a few times of this, the other moms and I went early to get in line and reunite with our kid. But sometimes I wasn't at the front of the line, and by the time I got to the doorway to the classroom, Ian was in tears thinking I wasn't coming.

I still picture Ian crying for me during the wait to get picked up. Now I was crying for him.

I knew he had no memory of that year before kindergarten, but I couldn't let it go. By the time he went to kindergarten, Ian had a neighborhood friend to sit with on the bus, and it was my turn to be lonely when he left.

I worked hard to keep these memories in a small compartment near my heart, so that they couldn't get out and bring me to my knees.

But when I saw the children coming in with their

mothers to go to the playroom in the gym, I thought about how very long it had been since I held a child's small hand.

63

ONE DAY IN THE END OF JULY, AFTER A PARTICULARLY INTENSE workout, I decided it was time to take the plunge. I was going to get on the scale in the women's locker room. It had been eight months since I signed up and was told I needed to "recapture my fitness."

Had I accomplished this? Or, the larger question, was I ever fit to begin with?

I set these doubts aside and waited until there was no one near the scale who could read the numbers and keel over in shock.

I stepped on carefully and held my breath, as if inhaling would increase my weight. Crap. It was a digital scale!

The number flashed in red. 148.8. In other words, just two ounces shy of 149.

I jumped off the scale and hurried to the back of the locker room.

Math was not my strong point, but even I could calculate that I had lost just seven pounds since I joined the gym. Less than a pound a month! I knew immediately it was the damn trips for pastries the men at the office made daily. For me, that meant chocolate chip scones. Or pumpkin scones. Or any kind of scone, actually.

Defiantly, I pulled on my mummy leggings and black T-shirt. Losing seven pounds, even over almost a year, was good enough. I wasn't going to give up baked goods to lose it faster.

Maybe I could try drinking more water at my desk instead of coffee. Doesn't water wash fat cells out? But take-out cups from Brew Coffee were so much better than tap water in a reusable bottle any day of the week.

I was also well-aware the frequent buckets of spaghetti weren't exactly helping shrink my waistline. Carbs, carbs, carbs, even if I let the kids or Eddie eat the meatballs.

I thought about the meatless burgers made with quinoa Eddie and I had learned to make in a cooking class and made a promise to myself to dig out the recipe.

As for the bakery goodies, those were here to stay.

64

In August, I realized I had been sweating it out at the gym for nearly a year, and all I wanted to do was find some recreational exercise I would actually enjoy.

I could set up the badminton net and ask Madison to come for a match. Ditto for frisbee in the park. Or a hike, if I could think of a place with a fairly flat trail because I wasn't really in shape for climbing anything close to a steep hill. But I had a bike in the shed I hadn't ridden in years.

Getting the bike out involved moving a lot of accumulated stuff in the front part of the shed. There were gardening tools, snow shovels, the snow blower itself, tennis racquets, a wicker love seat with a cushion long faded by the sun, a pair of rainboots I'd been looking for, the wooden crates I filled with hay for my autumn front porch decorating.

My bike was in rough shape. It was covered in filth and the tires were completely deflated. I spent another ten minutes looking for the manual bike pump and my bike helmet.

I dragged the bike and pump out onto the back lawn and found an old towel to clean off the dirt.

The tires made a hissing sound as I attached the nozzle to the pump and wrestled with the screw-on cap.

I had not remembered pumping up a small bike tire to require toned arm muscles and the ability to hunch over and not wrench your back.

Finally, I managed to semi-inflate both tires and wheel it out to the driveway. I snapped on my white helmet, now slightly yellowed with age, and swung my leg over the seat with a plan to glide gracefully onto the sidewalk.

Turns out, you can in fact forget how to ride a bicycle. After I sat down, I wobbled and had to put my feet on the ground just to stay up. When I coasted to the sidewalk, I cut the right turn too wide and ended up on my neighbor's lawn.

After a few more false starts, I managed to steer my way down the sidewalk and avoid the ruts. I headed towards the park downtown.

When I was around ten years old, I had a purple bike with a banana seat and pink streamers on the handlebars. My sister and I used to ride to school.

There was a walking path between us and our elementary school that made it easy to ride but it was not without its challenges. Near the path was a small muddy marsh filled with snarled weeds and water-soaked cattails and frogs. The boys on our street convinced my sister and me there was a swamp monster in there. They lived close to the pond and claimed to hear snarling noises at night and the cries of frogs as they were being eaten by the thing.

We pretended not to believe it but never rode our bikes down there after dark.

Around the twisty path was a thatch of woods the boys called Pirate's Island. It was a shortcut to school, but we risked being late rather than ride on the dirt path through the trees.

The boys said pirates were hung in the woods and once, on a dare, one of my sister's friends took twelve steps into

Pirate's Island and came running back shrieking that she had seen a noose hanging from one thick tree branch.

Fear made us ride faster and we were rarely late to school.

We were also allowed to ride our bikes home to put on our Halloween costumes then go back to school for the parties. We had a box of gowns and masks and brooms and wands to sift through and come up with costumes. In the end, after much deliberation, Kat was usually a princess, and I was a witch because I loved the hat with a dangling spider.

One year I decided to carry the witch's broom on my bike back to class, and disaster struck. The broom bristles got caught in my front tire, and I lost control of the handlebars and fell sideways onto the pavement. It was right near Pirate's Island, so I got up and rode furiously to school, not even bothering to check myself for injuries. When I got there and parked my bike, I realized the hat had fallen off my head. My hands were scraped from the fall but all I cared about was losing the witch's hat. My sister rode with me down the bike path after school but the witch hat was gone, taken by pirates no doubt.

I smiled at the memory.

Bike riding as a child had been effortless; as an adult I was embarrassingly shaky.

And then disaster struck. The bike lurched and suddenly my brakes didn't work, and I had to turn quickly and ride up a small hill just to stop. As I got off, the bike chain fell to the ground at my ankles.

I made a couple of feeble attempts to put the chain onto its cog, but ended up walking the damn thing back home, a process that took considerably longer than my ride downtown.

I was ready to put the bike back in the shed, but instead went inside and watched YouTube videos for how to fix bike chains.

I brought my phone out to the driveway and followed the steps. An incredible amount of cursing and two broken nails later, the chain was realigned.

The next time Lily came to visit, I asked her if she wanted to take a bike ride.

"You ride a bike?" she asked incredulously.

"Yes, missy, I ride. It's not just for kids you know."

"Meet you down at my house," she said, skipping down the sidewalk.

I smiled. Time with my little friend always cheered me up.

I steered my bike out of the shed and rode down to her house, waiting on the edge of the street.

Then I noticed Sawyer's car in their driveway at the side of Lily's house.

I seriously considered turning my bike around and riding away as speedily as possible. But as I was debating a mad rush home, Lily came out the door with Sawyer behind her holding her pink bike helmet.

He froze for a moment when he saw me.

I forced a smile and waved in what I hoped was a casual, friendly way.

Lily looked at me, then up at Sawyer.

"I can put it on," she said, taking her helmet and fastening it under her chin.

Then she disappeared around the corner to get her bike.

"How've you been?" I asked, determined to make the first move.

"Fine, good, you?"

Not for the first time, I realized how handsome he was, youthful really, except his eyes weren't crinkling now because he hadn't forced even a fake smile.

"Great, really good," I said, trying to convince myself I was.

Actually, I had been great before I'd run into Sawyer. I was getting some exercise and knew how to fix the chain if it fell off the bike. It was a beautiful day.

He stayed on the porch. We stood in awkward silence.

I silently wished I'd put on mascara or at least wasn't wearing my own helmet that mashed my hair down over my ears like shaggy sideburns.

Thankfully, Lily came back on her bike, cutting a sharp corner onto the lawn.

"Back in a while, crocodile," she said to Sawyer.

"Is your helmet on right?"

"Yes, Gramps, it's not loose at all."

"Have fun then," he said, not looking at me.

"We will!" My voice was unusually high-pitched and giddy.

I didn't even glance back when Lily and I rode away, but I knew for sure that he would not be standing on the porch watching us go.

65

It had been a long four hours of Uber driving one Saturday in July, and I'd stopped at two convenience stores to stretch, pee and stock up on coconut Cliff Bars and diet Mountain Dew.

I had a string of $4 fares taking riders about six blocks to the bank, hair salon, or grocery store. My daily total earnings were a whopping $22.

Just as I was ready to give up for the day and go home, my app flashed for a pick-up at the county fair. The fairgrounds were only a few miles outside Meredia, so I immediately hit the accept button.

It took less than ten minutes to get to the fairgrounds. The sun was going down, and lines of weary, dusty families were pushing strollers and dragging their feet back to the open field that served as the parking lot. Some carried along carnival prizes won by breaking balloons with darts or knocking down milk jugs. One father had a huge yellow teddy bear on his shoulders; another was carrying an enormous stuffed red chili pepper with a fiesta hat. The children's faces and T-shirts were stained with melted purple snow cones, blue cotton candy, and ketchup.

Madd, Ian, and I had spent a week every summer at the fair when they were kids. They loved to go through the animal barns and look at the chickens, long-eared rabbits, and backsides of milking cows. There was an annual summer horse show that made Madd beg for a horse every day for at least five years of her young life. The agriculture tents had prize-winning, wilting tomato and zucchini plants. There was a 4-H building with a beehive behind glass, and a bee-keeper all suited up handed out narrow tubes of honey. Ian had spent a lot of time trying to spot the queen bee in the buzzing hive.

We bought wristbands that gave the kids access to all the rides until dark. Ian waited three long years to be tall enough to get on the rides that turned them sideways and upside down. I stood in the shade nearby wondering what the procedure was for inspecting the many greasy gears and shifting arms of the enormous rides; surely some branch of state government looked them over? The tobacco-chew-ing, exhausted carnival workers that likely set the rides up looked like they didn't know or care if something was out of alignment.

When they reached their teens, Ian and Madd went to the fair with friends. Adam hadn't been interested in going, but a few mornings during the fair I would head up and get a corn dog or the Sunday morning waffle breakfast with real maple syrup. I'd wander the midway, where the rides had become more hazardous in my view. I had wondered if the kids would bring my grandchildren up to the fair, then shook the idea out of my mind, because that would be so far in the future, who knows, the whole county fair could be a thing of the past.

It had been at least 10 years since I'd been up to the fair-grounds, but I still knew my way around, and when I pulled up by the main gate, a heavyset woman with long red braids and a checked flannel vest waved me down.

"Phew, praise Jesus for air-conditioning," she flopped into the back seat and slammed the door, then pulled off the vest to reveal a lacy tank top showing tons of cleavage. I liked her immediately.

The app showed her destination was her home about 35 miles north. It would take me over an hour round trip to drop her off and get back to Meredia, but the fare would be close to $45.

"How're you doing honey?" she said from the back seat, rearranging the straps on her tank top.

I chuckled quietly. The woman was probably younger than me.

"Good. How was the fair today?"

"Excellent," she said emphatically. "I work there. If ya can call it work. It was a great day. Big crowd watching the show."

"What's the show?"

"Lady Lumberjanes," she said proudly. "My stage name is Paula Bunyan."

Ahh, well that explained the plaid flannel vest.

"Cool," I said, always ready to hear about a new fair attraction. "What's your show?"

"Me and the other Janes perform all the work done in the lumber industry, way back into hysterical times," Paula beamed.

I guessed she meant historical.

"We have a crosscut sawing competition to see who can cut through a 12-inch stump first. Lumberina, she's the new gal, usually wins. She's a pistol; her arms are bigger than my legs."

I was hooked.

"What else?"

"Well, then we do our log rolling; that's a crowd favorite. We stand on floating logs in our pool and try to push each other off. Keep in mind, this is all while our feet are dancing a mile a minute to keep that log spinning."

It sounded amazing.

"Course the highlight of the show is the hatchet-throwing," Paula said. "Everyone wants to see if we will be decapitated should the hatchet ricochet back at us. You know, like that girl in the viral Instagram video?"

I touched the brakes too hard, and we lurched forward in our seats.

"She lost her head?"

"Nah silly, the axe ricocheted right off the target, flew back at her with terrible speed, but she had the wherewithal to duck, just in time. Think it sheared off a bit of her hair," Paula said thoughtfully.

"How could that possibly be safe?" I said, picking up my water bottle.

"It isn't, not for amateurs, but for trained Lumberjanes like me, it's something we practice day in and day out. Ya gotta be smooth in every movement, can't get overly excited and throw the hatchet with too much force, or it could likely bounce back."

I was so entertained I hadn't noticed I had only another ten minutes left to hear more from Paula. What was her life like?

"So, you travel a lot?"

"Oh yeah," Paula said, pursing her lips and applying orange lipstick. "We're on the carnie circuit. On the road more than 320 days a year. It's tiring for sure, but that, as they say, is show business."

I smiled at her in the rearview mirror.

"I travel with the Janes and with my boyfriend Hal, the chainsaw sculptor."

"He sculpts chainsaws?"

Paula burst out laughing. "Na, silly, he uses a chainsaw to sculpt wood. His specialties are eagles and wolves. Their eyes look real and are said to burn right into your soul."

"How'd he learn to do that?" I was incredulous.

"Oh, ya know, he started small, with a pocketknife and a piece of tinder. Learned a lot of what he knows in Boy Scouts and online. Takes at least a day to get a full-sized wolf carved."

Paula pulled out a compact and started powdering her cheeks a bright shade of cherry.

"What does he do with them?" I checked my speed. As usual, I was five or six miles per hour over the limit, and the red warning light blipped on my phone.

"Sells `em, silly! They go for somewhere in the neighborhood of a thousand bucks a piece."

I tried to picture a lifelike wolf with burning eyes on my front porch. Lucy would probably attack it.

I was sorry when I pulled into Paula's driveway, because I wanted to hear more about her lumberjane life.

"Nice house," I said about the weather-worn bungalow.

"That there is what Airbnb will get ya," she said, fishing around in her leather tasseled purse. "Got it rented through the end of the week till we roll outta town."

She handed me some bills. "There ya go, sista. It was great talking to ya."

"My pleasure. Good luck with the show."

"Come on up and watch us one of these days! If ya sit in the front row of the bleachers, you get splashed by pool water during the log roll, so you can get nice and cooled off. People fight for those seats, so get there early."

Paula climbed out of the car.

Before she shut the door, she said, "Take care, sista!"

She was one of my most unique riders ever.

66

A FRAMED PHOTO ON MY NIGHTSTAND IS OF IAN AND MADD beneath a blue umbrella at the town pool squinting in the sun but both clearly saying "cheese" and showing all their teeth.

The pool had a splash zone for younger kids and twisty water slides that I went down with Madison on my lap when she was five or six, both of us shrieking with delight.

Ian had just learned to doggie-paddle, so we stayed in the shallow end with him. He would go down the stairs into the water and fling himself at his sister, who was always there to catch him.

Adam didn't like the sun as much as we did. His skin was lighter, and he was prone to sunburn. He usually sat in the shade at a picnic table in a wooded area near the pool. He would bring a book or newspaper, but I have to give him credit, he always looked up when Madd yelled for him to watch her jump off the diving board.

Some days we just brought snacks for the kids, but other times we made a little vacation of our trips to the pool. Adam would start the charcoal on the char-covered grills in the picnic area and soon the scent of sizzling hot dogs lured the kids out of the water. Madd wrapped herself in a towel with pink fish swimming in the ocean. Ian's had a sandcastle with a yellow flag on the top.

We shivered in the shade for a minute or two before we dried off. There was always plenty of kid-friendly food. Once, Ian ripped open a bag of pretzels and spilled them all over the ground. Small birds came out of nowhere to peck at them.

I made the kids wait 20 minutes after eating to go back in the water, even though I suspected that was an old wives' tale.

The summer trips to the pool felt like they had only been yesterday. Madison had progressed from little girl ruffled one-piece suits to a tie-dye tankini that made her feel very grown-up.

Some Saturdays we went later in the day and stayed until dusk, using the grill to toast marshmallows. It was never buggy when the sun went down like the swarms of mosquitoes that came out in our own back yard. We wondered if it was the smell of chlorine that permeated our skin and swimsuits.

The crickets would start chirping as we watched the fire burn down to embers.

The kids would be so worn out we had to carry them to the car.

We went to the park many years for the town's biggest fireworks show on the Fourth of July. We would put our favorite plaid camping blanket down in the field outside the picnic area to see better. Other families would gather and soon the grass was a patchwork quilt of blankets and beach towels.

When Ian was a toddler, he was scared by the loud sounds of the fireworks exploding in the sky, so I took him to the car, and we watched out the windows.

Madison always stayed out with her father. He would lift her up on his shoulders and she would raise her hands as if she could touch the glittering splashes of light.

I loved our family time with all my heart, foolishly believing it would last forever.

67

IT WAS THE END OF AUGUST, AND I WAS RATTLING AROUND AN empty house. With a little dog, who was also rattling. So, I put on a purple clay face mask and sat in bed.

I desperately needed a new something. New life? New haircut? New pair of leggings? None of the above. What I needed was a new hobby.

I leafed through the catalog of continuing ed classes at the Meredia High School until I found what seemed perfect: Dog yoga, aka doga.

The class blurb said doga involved stretching, meditation, massage and a little Reiki thrown in for good measure. The goal of doga was to achieve greater harmony with your dog.

I'd never done yoga before, although I had been known to get the kinks out of my back sometimes in the position known as the cat pose. Sure, I wasn't exactly graceful, but most of the poses were done sitting on a mat, weren't they?

Meditation seemed easy enough, and I loved to pet Lucy, so why not turn it into a massage?

"What do you think?" I asked Lucy, who was curled up in a perfect circle at the foot of the bed. "You're probably more flexible than I am by far."

The class started the following week at 6 p.m. I carried a squirming Lucy into the gym in case there were a lot of big dogs that might scare her. Aside from Luca's dog Sadie, she wasn't accustomed to socializing.

Most of the dogs were her size. But when I put her down, Lucy darted to the biggest dog, a collie, and introduced herself by sniffing his butt.

"Sorry," I told the dog's owner, an older man wearing white sneakers and sweatpants. Clearly, he was dressed to stretch.

"Not a problem," the man said, holding out his hand to shake. "I'm Earl, and this here is Bailey."

"Jess. And that's Lucy."

I tried to distract Lucy from Bailey's backside with no success.

The instructor blew a whistle like coaches did with sports teams in high school.

All the dogs and all the people stood at attention. One dog smaller than Lucy hid behind her owner's legs with alarm.

"Welcome to doga! I'm Trish, and I will be taking you and your pet on this journey."

Trish already seemed a bit new-age for me. Or maybe I was just envious of her sculpted arms, toned legs and flat stomach.

"Let's warm up. Pick your dog up then set him or her to the floor again. Remember, use your knees."

I had never thought of using Lucy as free weights before.

I looked at Earl. He shrugged and bent over. I hoped he wouldn't strain his back picking up Bailey, but the dog leapt into his owner's arms as if already trained.

I squatted and waited for Lucy to jump. She did not budge. So, I was forced to risk straining my own back by picking her up and down a couple times. She looked at me as if she knew how ridiculous the exercise was as a warm-up.

"OK, let's get down on our mats," Trish said.

Phew. That I could do. I settled on my brand-new purple yoga mat, relieved when Lucy lay down near my feet. Maybe yoga would involve only lying down and stretching. Throw in a little meditation and we could drift off.

It started off fine for Lucy and me.

We both lay on our bellies on the mat.

"Look deeply into each other's eyes to make a meaningful connection," Trish said.

Lucy was on her tummy grooming her paws. I had to make clucking noises with my tongue to get her attention, and we briefly made eye contact. Then she yawned and went back to her paws.

"Excellent," Trish said to the class, obviously not having seen Lucy ignore me. "Now let's do some *ohm*ing to center ourselves."

Earl *ohm*ed in a deep voice and I wondered briefly if he sang in a church choir. I sat cross-legged and made a quiet hum. Lucy climbed on my lap and tried to kiss me.

The first position was mountain pose, which meant lifting her high over my head while she looked down at me, utterly perplexed. The next position was the cat pose, which of course I found ironic in a class for dogs.

"Balance your pet on your back, then dip your belly towards the floor and feel the release in your spine," Trish said.

What?

I got on my hands and knees and tried without any confidence to get Lu to climb on my back. It was a ridiculous idea.

I looked at Earl, who had leaned his head down to the floor so Bailey could walk onto his back.

Show-off, I thought.

I ended up back on the mat on my stomach, trying to get Lucy to stay on my back. It was so outlandish I started to giggle at both of us.

Next up was the warrior pose, which thankfully did not include balancing Lucy on any of my limbs. We were allowed to hold our dogs in both arms as we lunged with our legs. Lucy snuggled into my neck and looked like she wanted to stay there.

Trish demonstrated the lotus pose, which was basically turning the body into something without a spine but with abs of steel.

"Lie on your stomach, and lift your feet and arms behind you," she said, nimbly bending herself into the pose. "Then let your dog lie on your back and feel the connection."

I managed to get my feet off the floor, but I needed my hands on the mat to hold them there. Forget about getting Lucy on my back. It hadn't worked the first time and it wasn't going to work now.

Earl turned out to have the flexibility of a male ballet dancer. He was downright graceful. Bailey was paying close attention and following his directions.

I lay back down and scratched under Lucy's chin. At least she hadn't peed on the mat.

Next, I attempted to hold my feet in the air and balance Lucy on my stomach. This made both of us nervous, so I kept my hands on her too. It was touch and go to balance her. Where was the relaxation they promised in the catalog?

"Pass your energy along to your dog," Trish said.

I had begun to sweat, and Lucy probably sensed my nervousness, which I hoped I didn't pass on to her.

Lucy rolled onto her back and showed me her tummy. I held my hands over her and started to feel the connection.

"I hope you feel Zenned out," Trish gushed.

I looked at Lucy, who was lying on her side on the yoga mat, half-asleep. She was definitely looking pretty Zen.

The last pose was, of course, Downward Facing Dog. Thankfully, all the dogs had to do was lie underneath us as we leaned over and lifted our asses toward the ceiling.

Lucy was fast asleep.

I was sweating by the end of the class from the stress of doing the movements while trying to coax Lucy to join in.

So much for doga calming the soul!

"See you next week," Earl said, hooking on Bailey's leash to lead her out of the gym.

"Practice a lot at home and it will become effortless," Trish called as we filed out.

Effortless? I was a doubter. But I wasn't a quitter.

Dutifully, Lucy and I lay down on the living room carpet just about every night and I attempted to put us into the ridiculously complicated poses.

After around 20 minutes of the session, I stopped trying to balance her above me and consulted the printout Trish had given us.

Lucy curled up into a little circle and fell asleep on the rug.

Apparently, Lu had found her Zen.

68

On a picture-perfect sunny day in August, I invited Eddie and Donny for a picnic in a park just north of Meredia.

It had walking paths around the edges of lush fields shaded by tall pine trees and a large fountain of a mermaid with water streaming from her crown. Why were mermaids always princesses?

I packed up ciabatta bread and Jarlsberg cheese, ripe pears and six bottles of Pure Leaf unsweetened iced teas.

The red checked picnic blanket was always in my trunk, should the need arise for a spontaneous meal in the grass.

"Come on Lou," I called to Lucy, who trotted to the door as soon as I took out her leash.

Eddie and Donny had staked out a prime spot in the park near the mermaid.

We settled down on the blanket and unpacked our feast. The men had brought chocolate frosted brownies. So much for the sugar-free tea!

"Dessert first?" Donny said, unwrapping the brownies and handing out napkins.

"You know me so well!" I laughed.

We ate in comfortable silence, licking frosting off our fingers, watching a group of college kids toss a Frisbee. The cloudy part of the day disappeared. Several couples languished on beach towels in the sun, certain to go home with sunburn. Two girls came to the fountain to take selfies and stopped to pet Lucy, who rolled over and showed them her tummy.

"How's the art class going?" I asked Eddie.

Eddie had jumped on the continuing-education bandwagon and was teaching a watercolor class, which had turned out to be very popular. He had 15 students of varying levels of experience and talent.

"It's a grand mixture of pleasure and pain," he sighed, finishing off his tea.

"That's called life, honey," Donny said, rubbing his husband's back.

"The pleasure is finding some of my students really unfolding as artists."

"And the pain?" I asked, helping myself to another brownie. Calories be damned. I'd burn it off in doga class, I convinced myself.

"The rest of the class not giving a shit. They slop the paint around, mix in too much water and saturate the drawing paper. Watercolor is meant to be done with grace and finesse. It's not like washing windows."

"How many more weeks to go?"

"Four," he sighed again. "Then I get to pick the good ones for the level 2 class."

Lucy had been scrounging the blanket for scraps of bread and cheese, but she gave up sniffing and suddenly bounded away.

I stood up to chase her. Then I saw Earl and his dog Bailey coming towards us across from the walking path. Bailey started running toward Lucy, pulling at the leash, making Earl run as well.

He was breathless when he reached our blanket.

"Hey missy," Earl said.

I introduced the men.

"This is my friend from doga."

"I've heard a lot of good things about that class," Eddie said. "Seems like Jess and Lucy find it pretty challenging."

I shot a dirty look at my friend.

"Secret is to do lots of practice," Earl said mildly. "Matter of fact, we're out today to do some doga."

"Here in the park?" I thought he must be kidding.

"Sure, why not?" Earl laughed. "It's a good way for Bailey to practice focusing on the poses and not getting distracted by other people."

With that, Earl got down on his hands and knees in the grass for the cat stretch. Bailey immediately climbed up on his back and stretched with him.

"Wow, it's like Bailey was made for doga," I said.

"How about you show us what you've got?" Eddie said to me.

"Are you serious? Here?"

"You said the other day you needed to get in more practice time. Well, here you are! So practice."

Earl had swung into the Lotus position, with Bailey in the small of his back. They looked like they'd been doing doga together all their lives.

I picked up Lucy and attempted to hold her over my head in the warrior pose. She was supposed to keep her body rigid, but she wriggled around and began licking my fingers, which probably tasted like cheese.

"Come on Lou, you can do this," Earl coached.

He held his hand under her legs and steadied her.

Miraculously, Lucy tightened her back and held herself straight like a little wooden plank.

We were actually doing proper doga! And outside no less!

Eddie and Donny broke out in applause.

Lucy wagged her tail in excitement.

"I knew you two could do it," Earl said, hooking on Bailey's leash. "You and your little girl there can do anything when you set your minds to it. You make a great team."

69

It was suddenly September. It seemed like overnight, the hot sun dissolved into calmer skies, you could draw in a deep breath free of humidity, there was a certain crispness to the air as if apples were already ripe and ready to be picked.

Lucy and I were on the front porch, rocking. Nadine and I were going out for dinner. We were craving pasta, of course.

Ian and his father came into town once or twice a month. I let Adam camp out in the backyard like the old times. What was once painful, now seemed to make sense, like we were some sort of family again.

Ian would sleep in his room and come downstairs wearing sweats and slippers for coffee with me in the morning. Madison would show up with some kind of fruit and we would sit at the kitchen table and laugh as if no time at all had passed. I loved my kids. They would always come first. But when Ian left to travel with Adam, it was a turning point. I didn't know how I was going to spend the next stage of my life now that my parenting days were over. I didn't know. But maybe not knowing was the best part.

The guys at the office had settled into their old routine of Brew Coffee, cinnamon buns most mornings, debating about the weather forecast and any other topic that struck them as important. They still left Sal's chair empty, but the deep gloom at his passing was dissipating. Jerky was starting to act like himself again, barking at traffic and pigeons trying to land on the ledge outside the window.

Linda, the trustee who hired me and checked in from time to time, finally caught on to the fact I was doing the bulk of the work while Joe kibbitzed with his cronies and moved papers around on his desk. She changed our job descriptions so he had to share the work, and best of all, Joe was now the official staff member to answer the phones. I was able to finish tasks without constant interruptions and Joe listening to everything I said and correcting me loudly. It was a blow to his pride, I knew, but after Sal died, some of the fun went out of the office and it became more of a place where work was actually done. But that didn't mean the trips for Danish and scones had been reduced. Heaven forbid.

Madison pulled up to the curb, then got out and opened the back car door for Rogue to bound out. Lucy jumped off my lap and raced to him.

"This is a nice surprise," I said.

"What are you up to, porch-sitting again?" Madd said frowning, "Haven't I broken you of this bad habit? You're not ninety, Mombo."

I watched our dogs tumble around in my now-perfect lawn, which had turned out to be the color of a lime green crayon.

"I'm waiting for Nadine. We're going out."

"Drinking?"

"Italian."

Madison sat down next to me on the porch, and we rocked in unison.

"So, I have news," she said.

"Good or bad?"

"Let me just show you," she said, pulling a piece of paper out of her backpack.

I drew in my breath when she handed me the fuzzy, black and white sonogram.

"NO! REALLY?" I shrieked, startling Lucy.

"Really," Madd's eyes had bursts of gold coming out of them. "I'm six weeks along."

I tipped over my chair in my hurry to throw my arms around her.

"How does Billy feel?"

"Cloud nine," Madison beamed. "Beyond cloud nine."

My heart was pounding wildly as I sat back down.

"Yep, Billy said you'd cry when I told you."

Of course I was crying.

And for the first time ever, I realized this was how it worked: I would never have baby Madison back to spend all those splendid years with. I would not have baby Madison. But I would be there for Madison's baby, and all the lullabies and milestones and tears and first days of school and lessons to be learned along the way. Madison's baby.

I couldn't wait to play Lego's with my grandbaby.

I wiped my eyes.

"Do you know—girl or boy?"

"Nope. We want to be surprised. But if it's a girl, we want to name her Penelope. Penny for short."

The breeze picked up, carrying a sweet scent of Penny's cherry tree, which had bloomed brilliantly. So much had changed in the year since she had been gone, but some things had remained the same: our intense love for each other, our belief that the best was still ahead, that we trusted the universe and were each on our own paths. Life was unfolding as it should. My family was deeply blessed, and I was grateful for every moment we'd had together, and for every second to come.

Apprentice House Press
Loyola University Maryland

Apprentice House is the country's only campus-based, student-staffed book publishing company. Directed by professors and industry professionals, it is a nonprofit activity of the Communication Department at Loyola University Maryland.

Using state-of-the-art technology and an experiential learning model of education, Apprentice House publishes books in untraditional ways. This dual responsibility as publishers and educators creates an unprecedented collaborative environment among faculty and students, while teaching tomorrow's editors, designers, and marketers.

Outside of class, progress on book projects is carried forth by the AH Book Publishing Club, a co-curricular campus organization supported by Loyola University Maryland's Office of Student Activities.

Eclectic and provocative, Apprentice House titles intend to entertain as well as spark dialogue on a variety of topics. Financial contributions to sustain the press's work are welcomed. Contributions are tax deductible to the fullest extent allowed by the IRS.

To learn more about Apprentice House books or to obtain submission guidelines, please visit www.apprenticehouse.com.

Apprentice House
Communication Department
Loyola University Maryland
4501 N. Charles Street
Baltimore, MD 21210
410-617-5265
info@apprenticehouse.com
www.apprenticehouse.com

CPSIA information can be obtained
at www.ICGtesting.com
Printed in the USA
LVHW081254291022
731834LV00013B/317